A RIVER RUNS THROUGH IT

A RIVER RUNS THROUGH IT

and Other Stories

Norman Maclean

THE UNIVERSITY OF CHICAGO PRESS

Chicago and London

NORMAN MACLEAN was William Rainey Harper Professor of English at the University of Chicago until his retirement in 1973.

The author and publisher wish to thank R. Williams for the book illustrations. Thanks are due as well to Region One of the United States Forest Service, and to the Montana Fish and Game Commission, for providing photographs on which some of the illustrations are based.

The University of Chicago Press, Chicago 60637
The University of Chicago Press, Ltd., London
© 1976 by The University of Chicago
All rights reserved. Published 1976
Printed in the United States of America
80 79 78   987654

Library of Congress Cataloging in Publication Data
Maclean, Norman F
A river runs through it, and other stories.

CONTENTS: A river runs through it.—Logging and Pimping and "Your pal, Jim."—USFS 1919.
I. Title.
PZ4.M16345Ri   [PS3563.A317993]   823'.9'12   75-20895
ISBN 0-226-50055-1

For Jean and John
to whom I have long told stories

CONTENTS

Acknowledgments

Although it's a little book, it took a lot of help to become a book at all. When one doesn't start out to be an author until he has reached his biblical allotment of three score years and ten, he needs more than his own power. Then, to add further to their literary handicaps, these stories turned out to be Western stories—as one publisher said in returning them, "These stories have trees in them."

It was my children, Jean and John, who started me off. They wanted me to put down in writing some of the stories I had told them when they were young. I don't want, though, to put the blame on my children for what resulted. As is known to any teller of stories who eventually tries to put a few of them down in writing, the act of writing changes them greatly, so none of these stories closely resembles any story I ever told my children. For one thing, writing makes everything bigger and longer; all these stories are much longer than is needed to achieve one of the primary ends of telling children stories—namely, that of putting children to sleep. However, the stories do give evidence of retaining another of those purposes—that of letting children know what kind of people their parents are or think they are or hope they are.

Another problem soon arises after one gets help enough to start writing upon retirement. It arises from the fact that one can get started writing then only by not letting anyone know he has. He is so secret about it that even his own children don't know he has taken their advice. But being covert makes him suspicious of his own actions, and so he soon stands in need of some sort of public sanction. It was at this point that I accumulated my second round of debts.

I had just finished my first story and was wondering what it was like and whether I should be allowed to go on when the secretary of a scholarly club I belong to telephoned to tell me it was my turn to give the paper at the next monthly meeting. The club calls itself the Stochastics (the Thinkers), and originally they were all biologists who, however, in keeping with recent cultural changes have taken in a certain number of humanists and social scientists. On the whole, the experiment has proved successful, since no distinction can be observed among these different social classes in the amount they drink before and during dinner and during the scientific and scholarly speeches that follow.

Suddenly, I saw my chance to escape from creative claustrophobia. I said to the secretary, "I have just finished a paper I would be glad to read." The first story I wrote was the short one based on a couple of summers I spent in logging camps. The secretary replied, "That's fine. Do you happen yet to have a title for it? You know I have to send out the title along with the speaker on the postcard announcing the meeting."

In the process of creating this story, then, I have had at least one inspired moment, because in a flash I answered, "On the postcard where it says 'Title' put down 'Logging and Pimping' and where it says 'Speaker' put down 'Norman Maclean, noted authority.'"

Finally I could hear breathing over the telephone, so, to aid in the process of resuscitation, I added, "It's a scholarly work—as scholars say, a genuine contribution to knowledge."

Afterwards, the secretary told me the attendance at the meeting was the largest in the records of the society. However, I was left in some doubt whether this scholarly reception was for the story or the title.

Nevertheless, I was invited back for a repeat performance the following autumn when the Stochastics have what they call their "heterosexual meeting" and the wives are invited. By this time I had almost finished the story "USFS 1919." In the spirit of the occasion I read them the section that has a woman in it, even though she happens to be a whore. She and I were so well received by the faculty wives that I didn't need any more moral support until I was nearly finished with the book.

In retirement the realization comes late that getting a book published—all the way published—is a major step in the act of creation. Unless one has friends left at the end of life, this realization may come too late. To make a very long story short, I will connect it back to the Stochastics, only in this case to individual members who had written enough books when they were young to realize that I shouldn't be left wandering around unprotected and alone at this moment of life. I wish to thank especially David Bevington, Wayne Booth, John Cawelti, Dr. Jarl Dyrud, Gwin Kolb, Kenneth Northcott, and Edward Rosenheim. I am sure that, without them, what I would have now would be some handwritten children's stories too long to tell children.

The University of Chicago Press is proud of its tradition of never allowing its authors to thank any of its staff by name. I respect this tradition, but some members of the Press had to be sufficiently interested in these stories to seek and obtain permission to publish a work of original fiction for the first time in its long history. I would be emotionally numb if I did not appreciate such an honor. Perhaps I can find other ways of letting them know, if I may use an old Western phrase, that I am forever grateful to them.

I accumulated still another set of debts soon after the University Press and its Board agreed to publish its first book of fiction. It's primarily fiction all right, but most children's stories have a fairly obvious secondary intention of instruction and these stories are no exception. Children, much more than adults, like to know how things were before they were born, especially in parts of the world that now seem strange or have even disappeared but were once lived in by their parents, so I acquired the habit long ago of slipping in pictures of how men and horses did things in Western parts of the world where often the main thoroughfares were game trails. Moreover, it was always important to me to lead my children into real woods, not the woods of Little Red Riding Hood—to me, the constant wonder has been how strange reality has been. So a time came in creation when my thinking took a classical critical turn, and I remembered that Socrates said if you paint a picture of a table you have to call in expert carpenters to know whether you have done well. The following are the chief experts I consulted to find out how well I had painted the land I love and fly fishing and the logging camps and Forest Service I had worked in when I was young.

For their sensitive and expert reading of "A River Runs through It," I am indebted to Jean and John Baucus, owners of the great Sieben sheep ranch, which runs from the Helena valley to Wolf Creek to the Big Blackfoot River, a triangle of the earth that contains a great deal of my life and several of my stories. For expert opinion on my story about the Bitterroots and my early years in the Forest Service, I turned to W. R. (Bud) Moore, Chief of Fire Management and Air Operations in the United States Forest Service. As a woodsman, he is a legend in our mountain land and is made of such stuff as honorary doctoral degrees although he never went beyond grade school. When he was in his early teens, he spent his winters running a trapline across the Bitterroot Divide, where I started working for the Forest Service. In the winters, now that he is retired from the Service, he spends two days of a week that's crowded with writing, teaching, and research in running a trapline from Rock Creek across the Sapphire mountains to the Bitterroot Valley. I advise none of my young readers to try to follow him on snowshoes across this desperate stretch of country.

I am also indebted to three expert women of the Forest Service for giving me a helping hand while I was writing these stories—Beverly Ayers, archivist of photographs, and Sara

Heath and Joyce Hayley, cartographic technicians. They are absolutely first rate and have the added gift of always knowing what it is I am looking for, even when I don't.

I turned the story about my brother and fly fishing over to George Croonenberghs, who tied flies for my brother and me over forty years ago, and David Roberts, who has lived a long life fishing and hunting and writing about them three or four times a week. They are the two finest fly fishermen I know.

They also bring to mind an indebtedness of another time and order. They and I are indebted to my father for our love of fly fishing—George Croonenberghs received his first lessons in fly tying from him, and David Roberts still writes an occasional column about him. As for me, all my stories can be thought of as partial acknowledgments of my indebtedness to him.

Perhaps it is a question to you why I needed the great expert on the Cheyenne Indians, Father Peter Powell, to read my stories when only one Cheyenne Indian appears in them and she is not a full blood. I needed this great and good man in his most pristine calling—to assure me there are still moments in my memories that are touched with the life of the spirit.

Finally, I have published practically nothing that has not profited from the criticisms (which she calls "suggestions") of Marie Borroff, first woman full professor in English at Yale. If you think I am wasting a lady's time in asking her to read stories about logging camps and the Forest Service as they were half a century ago, then I probably will have to tell you the kind of thing she tells me. Before I give you an example, though, perhaps I should add that she is also a poet. Of my first story (the one about logging) she said (among other things) I was concentrating so on telling a story that I didn't take time to be a poet and express a little of the love I have of the earth as it goes by. Compare now the two long stories I wrote after she told me this with my first story, which is short, and you should get some notion of how carefully I listen to the lady from Yale.

This, then, in summary, is a collection of Western stories with trees in them for children, experts, scholars, wives of scholars, and scholars who are poets. I hope there are others also who don't mind trees.

A River Runs through It

In our family, there was no clear line between religion and fly fishing. We lived at the junction of great trout rivers in western Montana, and our father was a Presbyterian minister and a fly fisherman who tied his own flies and taught others. He told us about Christ's disciples being fishermen, and we were left to assume, as my brother and I did, that all first-class fishermen on the Sea of Galilee were fly fishermen and that John, the favorite, was a dry-fly fisherman.

It is true that one day a week was given over wholly to religion. On Sunday mornings my brother, Paul, and I went to Sunday school and then to "morning services" to hear our father preach and in the evenings to Christian Endeavor and afterwards to "evening services" to hear our father preach again. In between on Sunday afternoons we had to study *The Westminster Shorter Catechism* for an hour and then recite before we could walk the hills with him while he unwound between services. But he never asked us more than the first question in the catechism, "What is the chief end of man?" And we answered together so one of us could carry on if the other forgot, "Man's chief end is to glorify God, and to enjoy Him forever." This always seemed to satisfy him, as indeed such a beautiful answer should have, and besides he was anxious to be on the hills where he could restore his soul and be filled again to overflowing for the evening sermon. His chief way of recharging himself was to recite to us from the sermon

1

that was coming, enriched here and there with selections from the most successful passages of his morning sermon.

Even so, in a typical week of our childhood Paul and I probably received as many hours of instruction in fly fishing as we did in all other spiritual matters.

After my brother and I became good fishermen, we realized that our father was not a great fly caster, but he was accurate and stylish and wore a glove on his casting hand. As he buttoned his glove in preparation to giving us a lesson, he would say, "It is an art that is performed on a four-count rhythm between ten and two o'clock."

As a Scot and a Presbyterian, my father believed that man by nature was a mess and had fallen from an original state of grace. Somehow, I early developed the notion that he had done this by falling from a tree. As for my father, I never knew whether he believed God was a mathematician but he certainly believed God could count and that only by picking up God's rhythms were we able to regain power and beauty. Unlike many Presbyterians, he often used the word "beautiful."

After he buttoned his glove, he would hold his rod straight out in front of him, where it trembled with the beating of his heart. Although it was eight and a half feet long, it weighed only four and a half ounces. It was made of split bamboo cane from the far-off Bay of Tonkin. It was wrapped with red and blue silk thread, and the wrappings were carefully spaced to make the delicate rod powerful but not so stiff it could not tremble.

Always it was to be called a rod. If someone called it a pole, my father looked at him as a sergeant in the United States Marines would look at a recruit who had just called a rifle a gun.

My brother and I would have preferred to start learning how to fish by going out and catching a few, omitting entirely anything difficult or technical in the way of preparation that would take away from the fun. But it wasn't by way of fun that we were introduced to our father's art. If our father had had his say, nobody who did not know how to fish would be allowed to disgrace a fish by catching him. So you too will have to approach the art Marine- and Presbyterian-style, and, if you have never picked up a fly rod before, you will soon find it factually and theologically true that man by nature is a damn mess. The four-and-a-half-ounce thing in silk wrappings that trembles with the underskin motions of the flesh becomes a stick without brains, refusing anything simple that is wanted of it. All that a rod has to do is lift the line, the leader, and the fly off the water, give them a good toss over the head, and then shoot them forward so they will land in the water without a splash in the following order: fly, transparent leader, and then the line—otherwise the fish will see the fly is a fake and be gone. Of course, there are special casts that anyone could predict would be difficult, and they require artistry—casts where the line can't go over the fisherman's head because cliffs or trees are immediately behind, sideways casts to get the fly under overhanging willows, and so on. But what's remarkable about just a straight cast—just picking up a rod with line on it and tossing the line across the river?

Well, until man is redeemed he will always take a fly rod too far back, just as natural man always overswings with an ax or golf club and loses all his power somewhere in the air; only with a rod it's worse, because the fly often comes so far back it gets caught behind in a bush or rock. When my father said it was an art that ended at two o'clock, he often added, "closer to twelve than to two," meaning that the rod should be taken back only slightly farther than overhead (straight overhead being twelve o'clock).

Then, since it is natural for man to try to attain power without recovering grace, he whips the line back and forth making it whistle each way, and sometimes even snapping off the fly from the leader, but the power that was going to transport the little fly across the river somehow gets diverted into building a bird's nest of line, leader, and fly that falls out of the air into the water about ten feet in front of the fisherman. If, though, he pictures the round trip of the line, transparent leader, and fly from the time they leave the water until their return, they are easier to cast. They naturally come off the water heavy line first and in front, and light transparent leader and fly trailing behind. But, as they pass overhead, they have to have a little beat of time so the light, transparent leader and fly can catch up to the heavy line now starting forward and again fall behind it; otherwise, the line starting on its return trip will collide with the leader and fly still on their way up, and the mess will be the bird's nest that splashes into the water ten feet in front of the fisherman.

Almost the moment, however, that the forward order of line, leader, and fly is reestablished, it has to be reversed, because the fly and transparent leader must be ahead of the heavy line when they settle on the water. If what the fish sees is highly visible line, what the fisherman will see are departing black darts, and he might as well start for the next hole. High overhead, then, on the forward cast (at about ten o'clock) the fisherman checks again.

The four-count rhythm, of course, is functional. The one count takes the line, leader, and fly off the water; the two count tosses them seemingly straight into the sky; the three count was my father's way of saying that at the top the leader and fly have to be given a little beat of time to get behind the line as it is starting forward; the four count means put on the power and throw the line into the rod until you reach ten o'clock—then check-cast, let the fly and leader get ahead of the line, and coast to a soft and perfect landing. Power comes not from power everywhere, but from knowing where to put it on. "Remember," as my father kept saying, "it is an art that is performed on a four-count rhythm between ten and two o'clock."

My father was very sure about certain matters pertaining to the universe. To him, all good things—trout as well as eternal salvation—come by grace and grace comes by art and art does not come easy.

So my brother and I learned to cast Presbyterian-style, on a metronome. It was mother's metronome, which father had taken from the top of the piano in town. She would occasionally peer down to the dock from the front porch of the cabin, wondering nervously whether her metronome could float if it had to. When she became so overwrought that she thumped down the dock to reclaim it, my father would clap out the four-count rhythm with his cupped hands.

Eventually, he introduced us to literature on the subject. He tried always to say something stylish as he buttoned the glove on his casting hand. "Izaak Walton," he told us when my brother was thirteen or fourteen, "is not a respectable writer. He was an Episcopalian and a bait fisherman." Although Paul was three years younger than I was, he was already far ahead of me in anything relating to fishing and it was he who first found a copy of *The Compleat Angler* and reported back to me, "The bastard doesn't even know how to spell 'complete.' Besides, he has songs to sing to dairymaids." I borrowed his copy, and reported back to him, "Some of those songs are pretty good." He said, "Whoever saw a dairymaid on the Big Blackfoot River?

"I would like," he said, "to get him for a day's fishing on the Big Blackfoot—with a bet on the side."

The boy was very angry, and there has never been a doubt in my mind that the boy would have taken the Episcopalian money.

When you are in your teens—maybe throughout your life—being three years older than your brother often makes you feel he is a boy. However, I knew already that he was going to be a master with a rod. He had those extra things besides fine training—genius, luck, and plenty of self-confidence. Even at this age he liked to bet on himself against anybody who would fish with him, including me, his older brother. It was sometimes funny and sometimes not so funny, to see a boy always wanting to bet on himself and almost sure to win. Although I was three years older, I did not yet feel old enough to bet. Betting, I assumed, was for men who wore straw hats on the backs of their heads. So I was confused and embarrassed the first couple of times he asked me if I didn't want "a small bet on the side just to make things interesting." The third time he asked me must have made me angry because he never again spoke to me about money, not even about borrowing a few dollars when he was having real money problems.

We had to be very careful in dealing with each other. I often thought of him as a boy, but I never could treat him that way. He was never "my kid brother." He was a master of an art. He did not want any big brother advice or money or help, and, in the end, I could not help him.

Since one of the earliest things brothers try to find out is how they differ from each other, one of the things I remember longest about Paul is this business about his liking to bet. He would go to county fairs to pretend that he was betting on the horses, like the men, except that no betting booths would take his bets because they were too small and he was too young. When his bets were refused, he would say, as he said of Izaak Walton and any other he took as a rival, "I'd like to get that bastard on the Blackfoot for a day, with a bet on the side."

By the time he was in his early twenties he was in the big stud poker games.

Circumstances, too, helped to widen our differences. The draft of World War I immediately left the woods short of men, so at fifteen I started working for the United States Forest Service, and for many summers afterwards I worked in the woods, either with the Forest Service or in logging camps. I liked the woods and I liked work, but for a good many summers I didn't do much fishing. Paul was too young to swing an ax or pull a saw all day, and besides he had decided this early he had two major purposes in life: to fish and not to work, at least not allow work to interfere with fishing. In his teens, then, he got a summer job as a lifeguard at the municipal swimming pool, so in the early evenings he could go fishing and during the days he could look over girls in bathing suits and date them up for the late evenings.

When it came to choosing a profession, he became a

reporter. On a Montana paper. Early, then, he had come close to realizing life's purposes, which did not conflict in his mind from those given in answer to the first question in *The Westminster Catechism.*

Undoubtedly, our differences would not have seemed so great if we had not been such a close family. Painted on one side of our Sunday school wall were the words, God Is Love. We always assumed that these three words were spoken directly to the four of us in our family and had no reference to the world outside, which my brother and I soon discovered was full of bastards, the number increasing rapidly the farther one gets from Missoula, Montana.

We also held in common the knowledge that we were tough. This knowledge increased with age, at least until we were well into our twenties and probably longer, possibly much longer. But our differences showed even in our toughness. I was tough by being the product of tough establishments—the United States Forest Service and logging camps. Paul was tough by thinking he was tougher than any establishment. My mother and I watched horrified morning after morning while the Scottish minister tried to make his small child eat oatmeal. My father was also horrified—at first because a child of his own bowels would not eat God's oats, and, as the days went by, because his wee child proved tougher than he was. As the minister raged, the child bowed his head over the food and folded his hands as if his father were saying grace. The child gave only one sign of his own great anger. His lips became swollen. The hotter my father got, the colder the porridge, until finally my father burned out.

Each of us, then, not only thought he was tough, he knew the other one had the same opinion of himself. Paul knew that I had already been foreman of forest-fire crews and that, if he worked for me and drank on the job, as he did when he was reporting, I would tell him to go to camp, get his time slip, and keep on down the trail. I knew that there was about as much chance of his fighting fire as of his eating oatmeal.

We held in common one major theory about street fighting—if it looks like a fight is coming, get in the first punch. We both thought that most bastards aren't so tough as they talk—even bastards who look as well as talk tough. If suddenly they feel a few teeth loose, they will rub their mouths, look at the blood on their hands, and offer to buy a drink for the house. "But even if they still feel like fighting," as my brother said, "you are one big punch ahead when the fight starts."

There is just one trouble with this theory—it is only statistically true. Every once in a while you run into some guy who likes to fight as much as you do and is better at it. If you start off by loosening a few of his teeth he may try to kill you.

I suppose it was inevitable that my brother and I would get into one big fight which also would be the last one. When it came, given our theories about street fighting, it was like the Battle Hymn, terrible and swift. There are parts of it I did not see. I did not see our mother walk between us to try to stop us. She was short and wore glasses and, even with them on, did not have good vision. She had never seen a fight before or had any notion of how bad you can get hurt by becoming mixed up in one. Evidently, she just walked between her sons. The first I saw of her was the gray top of her head, the hair tied in a big knot with a big comb in it; but what was most noticeable was that her head was so close to Paul I couldn't get a good punch at him. Then I didn't see her anymore.

The fight seemed suddenly to stop itself. She was lying on the floor between us. Then we both began to cry and fight in a rage, each one shouting, "You son of a bitch, you knocked my mother down."

She got off the floor, and, blind without her glasses, staggered in circles between us, saying without recognizing which one she was addressing, "No, it wasn't you. I just slipped and fell."

So this was the only time we ever fought.

Perhaps we always wondered which of us was tougher, but, if boyhood questions aren't answered before a certain point in time, they can't ever be raised again. So we returned to being

gracious to each other, as the wall suggested that we should
be. We also felt that the woods and rivers were gracious to us
when we walked together beside them.

It is true that we didn't often fish together anymore. We
were both in our early thirties now, and "now" from here on is
the summer of 1937. My father had retired and he and
mother were living in Missoula, our old home town, and Paul
was a reporter in Helena, the state capital. I had "gone off
and got married," to use my brother's description of this
event in my life. At the moment, I was living with my wife's
family in the little town of Wolf Creek, but, since Wolf Creek
is only forty miles from Helena, we still saw each other from
time to time, which meant, of course, fishing now and then
together. In fact, the reason I had come to Helena now was to
see him about fishing.

The fact also is that my mother-in-law had asked me to. I
wasn't happy, but I was fairly sure my brother would finally
say yes. He had never said plain no to me, and he loved my
mother-in-law and my wife, whom he included in the sign on
the wall, even though he could never understand "what had
come over me" that would explain why marriage had ever
crossed my mind.

I ran into him in front of the Montana Club, which was
built by rich gold miners supposedly on the spot where gold
was discovered in Last Chance Gulch. Although it was only
ten o'clock in the morning, I had a hunch he was about to buy a
drink. I had news to give him before I could ask the question.

After I gave him the news, my brother said, "He'll be just as
welcome as a dose of clap."

I said to my brother, "Go easy on him. He's my brother-
in-law."

My brother said, "I won't fish with him. He comes from the
West Coast and he fishes with worms."

I said, "Cut it out. You know he was born and brought up in
Montana. He just works on the West Coast. And now he's
coming back for a vacation and writes his mother he wants to
fish with us. With you especially."

My brother said, "Practically everybody on the West Coast

was born in the Rocky Mountains where they failed as fly
fishermen, so they migrated to the West Coast and became
lawyers, certified public accountants, presidents of airplane
companies, gamblers, or Mormon missionaries."

I wasn't sure he was about to buy a drink, but he had
already had one.

We stood looking at each other, not liking anything that
was happening but watching that we didn't go too far in
disagreeing. Actually, though, we weren't very far apart about
my brother-in-law. In some ways, I liked him even less than
Paul did, and it's no pleasure to see your wife's face on
somebody you don't like.

"Besides," my brother said, "he's a bait fisherman. All those
Montana boys on the West Coast sit around the bars at night
and lie to each other about their frontier childhood when they
were hunters, trappers, and fly fishermen. But when they
come back home they don't even kiss their mothers on the
front porch before they're in the back garden with a red Hills
Bros. coffee can digging for angleworms."

My brother and his editor wrote most of the Helena paper.
The editor was one of the last small-town editors in the classic
school of personal invective. He started drinking early in the
morning so he wouldn't feel sorry for anyone during the day,
and he and my brother admired each other greatly. The rest
of the town feared them, especially because they wrote well,
and in a hostile world both of them needed to be loved by
their families and were.

I could tell by now that I was keeping my brother from
buying a drink, and, sure enough, he said, "Let's go in and
hoist one."

I made the mistake of sounding as if I were afraid to come
out and criticize his morals. I said, "I'm sorry, Paul, but it's too
early in the morning for me to start drinking."

Having to say something else quick, I didn't improve my
morals, at least not in my own eyes, by adding, "Florence
asked me to ask you."

I hated to pass the buck to my mother-in-law. One reason

Paul and I loved her was that she looked like our father. Both of them were Scots by way of Canada, both of them had blue eyes and sandy hair which was red when they were younger, and both of them pronounced "about" the way Canadians do, who, if they were poets, would rhyme it with "snoot."

I couldn't feel too sorry, though, because it really was she who had put me up to asking, and she had begun confusing me by mixing a certain amount of truth with her flattery. "Although I know nothing about fishing," she said, "I know Paul is the best fisherman anywhere." This was a complicated statement. She knew how to clean fish when the men forgot to, and she knew how to cook them, and, most important, she knew always to peer into the fisherman's basket and exclaim "My, my!" so she knew all that any woman of her time knew about fishing, although it is also true that she knew absolutely nothing about fishing.

"I would like very much to think of Neal with him and you," she concluded, no doubt hoping that we would improve his morals even more than his casting. In our town, Paul and I were known as "the preacher's kids," and most mothers refrained from pointing us out to their children, but to this Scottish woman we were "the pastor's sons," and besides as fly fishermen we would be waist deep in cold water all day, where immorality is faced with some real but, as it turned out, not insurmountable problems.

"Poor boy," she said, adding as many Scottish *r*'s as she could to "poor." More than most mothers, Scottish mothers have had to accustom themselves to migration and sin, and to them all sons are prodigal and welcome home. Scotsmen, however, are much more reserved about welcoming returning male relatives, and do so largely under the powerful influence of their women.

"Sure I will," Paul said, "if Florence wants me to." And I knew that, having been given his word, I would never get another kick from him.

"Let's have a drink," I said, and at 10:15 A.M. I paid for it.

Just before 10:15 I told him Neal was coming to Wolf Creek

day after tomorrow and that the day following we were to go
fishing on the Elkhorn. "It's to be a family picnic," I told him.

"That's fine," he said. The Elkhorn is a small stream
running into the Missouri and Paul and I were big-fish
fishermen, looking with contempt upon the husbands of
wives who have to say, "We like the little ones—they make the
best eating." But the Elkhorn has many special features,
including some giant Brown Trout that work their way up
from the Missouri.

Although the Elkhorn was our favorite small stream, Paul
said, after paying for our second drink, "I don't have to be on
the beat tomorrow until evening, so what about just you and
me taking the day off and fishing the big river before we have
to go on the picnic?"

Paul and I fished a good many big rivers, but when one of
us referred to "the big river" the other knew it was the Big
Blackfoot. It isn't the biggest river we fished, but it is the most
powerful, and per pound, so are its fish. It runs straight and
hard—on a map or from an airplane it is almost a straight line
running due west from its headwaters at Rogers Pass on the
Continental Divide to Bonner, Montana, where it empties
into the South Fork of the Clark Fork of the Columbia. It
runs hard all the way.

Near its headwaters on the Continental Divide there is a
mine with a thermometer that stopped at 69.7 degrees below
zero, the lowest temperature ever officially recorded in the
United States (Alaska omitted). From its headwaters to its
mouth it was manufactured by glaciers. The first sixty-
five miles of it are smashed against the southern wall of its
valley by glaciers that moved in from the north, scarifying the
earth; its lower twenty-five miles were made overnight when
the great glacial lake covering northwestern Montana and
northern Idaho broke its ice dam and spread the remains of
Montana and Idaho mountains over hundreds of miles of the
plains of eastern Washington. It was the biggest flood in the
world for which there is geological evidence; it was so vast a
geological event that the mind of man could only conceive of

it but could not prove it until photographs could be taken from earth satellites.

The straight line on the map also suggests its glacial origins; it has no meandering valley, and its few farms are mostly on its southern tributaries which were not ripped up by glaciers; instead of opening into a wide flood plain near its mouth, the valley, which was cut overnight by a disappearing lake when the great ice dam melted, gets narrower and narrower until the only way a river, an old logging railroad, and an automobile road can fit into it is for two of them to take to the mountainsides.

It is a tough place for a trout to live—the river roars and the water is too fast to let algae grow on the rocks for feed, so there is no fat on the fish, which must hold most trout records for high jumping.

Besides, it is the river we knew best. My brother and I had fished the Big Blackfoot since nearly the beginning of the century—my father before then. We regarded it as a family river, as a part of us, and I surrender it now only with great reluctance to dude ranches, the unselected inhabitants of Great Falls, and the Moorish invaders from California.

Early next morning Paul picked me up in Wolf Creek, and we drove across Rogers Pass where the thermometer is that stuck at three-tenths of a degree short of seventy below. As usual, especially if it were early in the morning, we sat silently respectful until we passed the big Divide, but started talking the moment we thought we were draining into another ocean. Paul nearly always had a story to tell in which he was the leading character but not the hero.

He told his Continental Divide stories in a seemingly light-hearted, slightly poetical mood such as reporters often use in writing "human-interest" stories, but, if the mood were removed, his stories would appear as something about him that would not meet the approval of his family and that I would probably find out about in time anyway. He also must have felt honor-bound to tell me that he lived other lives, even if he presented them to me as puzzles in the form of funny stories. Often I did not know what I had been told about him as we crossed the divide between our two worlds.

"You know," he began, "it's been a couple of weeks since I fished the Blackfoot." At the beginning, his stories sounded like factual reporting. He had fished alone and the fishing had not been much good, so he had to fish until evening to get his limit. Since he was returning directly to Helena he was driving up Nevada Creek along an old dirt road that followed section lines and turned at right angles at section corners. It was moonlight, he was tired and feeling in need of a friend to keep him awake, when suddenly a jackrabbit jumped on to the road and started running with the headlights. "I didn't push him too hard," he said, "because I didn't want to lose a friend." He drove, he said, with his head outside the window so he could feel close to the rabbit. With his head in the moonlight, his account took on poetic touches. The vague world of moonlight was pierced by the intense white triangle from the headlights. In the center of the penetrating isosceles was the jackrabbit, which, except for the length of his jumps, had become a snowshoe rabbit. The phosphorescent jack-rabbit was doing his best to keep in the center of the isosceles but was afraid he was losing ground and, when he looked back to check, his eyes shone with whites and blues gathered up from the universe. My brother said, "I don't know how to explain what happened next, but there was a right-angle turn in this section-line road, and the rabbit saw it, and I didn't."

Later, he happened to mention that it cost him $175.00 to have his car fixed, and in 1937 you could almost get a car rebuilt for $175.00. Of course, he never mentioned that, although he did not drink when he fished, he always started drinking when he finished.

I rode part of the way down the Blackfoot wondering whether I had been told a little human-interest story with hard luck turned into humor or whether I had been told he had taken too many drinks and smashed hell out of the front end of his car.

Since it was no great thing either way, I finally decided to forget it, and, as you see, I didn't. I did, though, start thinking about the canyon where we were going to fish.

The canyon above the old Clearwater bridge is where the Blackfoot roars loudest. The backbone of a mountain would not break, so the mountain compresses the already powerful river into sound and spray before letting it pass. Here, of course, the road leaves the river; there was no place in the canyon for an Indian trail; even in 1806 when Lewis left Clark to come up the Blackfoot, he skirted the canyon by a safe margin. It is no place for small fish or small fishermen. Even the roar adds power to the fish or at least intimidates the fisherman.

When we fished the canyon we fished on the same side of it for the simple reason that there is no place in the canyon to wade across. I could hear Paul start to pass me to get to the hole above, and, when I realized I didn't hear him anymore, I knew he had stopped to watch me. Although I have never pretended to be a great fisherman, it was always important to me that I was a fisherman and looked like one, especially when fishing with my brother. Even before the silence continued, I knew that I wasn't looking like much of anything.

Although I have a warm personal feeling for the canyon, it is not an ideal place for me to fish. It puts a premium upon being able to cast for distance, and yet most of the time there are cliffs or trees right behind the fisherman so he has to keep all his line in front of him. It's like a baseball pitcher being deprived of his windup, and it forces the fly fisherman into what is called a "roll cast," a hard cast that I have never mastered. The fisherman has to work enough line into his cast to get distance without throwing any line behind him, and then he has to develop enough power from a short arc to shoot it out across the water.

He starts accumulating the extra amount of line for the long cast by retrieving his last cast so slowly that an unusual amount of line stays in the water and what is out of it forms a slack semiloop. The loop is enlarged by raising the casting arm straight up and cocking the wrist until it points to 1:30. There, then, is a lot of line in front of the fisherman, but it takes about everything he has to get it high in the air and out over the water so that the fly and leader settle ahead of the line—the arm is a piston, the wrist is a revolver that uncocks, and even the body gets behind the punch. Important, too, is the fact that the extra amount of line remaining in the water until the last moment gives a semisolid bottom to the cast. It is a little like a rattlesnake striking, with a good piece of his tail on the ground as something to strike from. All this is easy for a rattlesnake, but has always been hard for me.

Paul knew how I felt about my fishing and was careful not to seem superior by offering advice, but he had watched so long that he couldn't leave now without saying something. Finally he said, "The fish are out farther." Probably fearing he had put a strain on family relations, he quickly added, "Just a little farther."

I reeled in my line slowly, not looking behind so as not to see him. Maybe he was sorry he had spoken, but, having said what he said, he had to say something more. "Instead of retrieving the line straight toward you, bring it in on a diagonal from the downstream side. The diagonal will give you a more resistant base to your loop so you can put more power into your forward cast and get a little more distance."

Then he acted as if he hadn't said anything and I acted as if I hadn't heard it, but as soon as he left, which was immediately, I started retrieving my line on a diagonal, and it helped. The moment I felt I was getting a little more distance I ran for a fresh hole to make a fresh start in life.

It was a beautiful stretch of water, either to a fisherman or a photographer, although each would have focused his equipment on a different point. It was a barely submerged waterfall. The reef of rock was about two feet under the water, so the whole river rose into one wave, shook itself into spray, then fell back on itself and turned blue. After it recovered from the shock, it came back to see how it had fallen.

No fish could live out there where the river exploded into the colors and curves that would attract photographers. The fish were in that slow backwash, right in the dirty foam, with the dirt being one of the chief attractions. Part of the speckles would be pollen from pine trees, but most of the dirt was edible insect life that had not survived the waterfall.

I studied the situation. Although maybe I had just added three feet to my roll cast, I still had to do a lot of thinking before casting to compensate for some of my other shortcomings. But I felt I had already made the right beginning—I had already figured out where the big fish would be and why.

Then an odd thing happened. I saw him. A black back rose and sank in the foam. In fact, I imagined I saw spines on his dorsal fin until I said to myself, "God, he couldn't be so big you could see his fins." I even added, "You wouldn't even have seen the fish in all that foam if you hadn't first thought he would be there." But I couldn't shake the conviction that I had seen the black back of a big fish, because, as someone often forced to think, I know that often I would not see a thing unless I thought of it first.

Seeing the fish that I first thought would be there led me to wondering which way he would be pointing in the river. "Remember, when you make the first cast," I thought, "that you saw him in the backwash where the water is circling upstream, so he will be looking downstream, not upstream, as he would be if he were in the main current."

I was led by association to the question of what fly I would cast, and to the conclusion that it had better be a large fly, a number four or six, if I was going after the big hump in the foam.

From the fly, I went to the other end of the cast, and asked myself where the hell I was going to cast from. There were only gigantic rocks at this waterfall, so I picked one of the

biggest, saw how I could crawl up it, and knew from that
added height I would get added distance, but then I had to
ask myself, "How the hell am I going to land the fish if I hook
him while I'm standing up there?" So I had to pick a smaller
rock, which would shorten my distance but would let me slide
down it with a rod in my hand and a big fish on.

I was gradually approaching the question all river fishermen should ask before they make the first cast, "If I hook
a big one, where the hell can I land him?"

One great thing about fly fishing is that after a while
nothing exists of the world but thoughts about fly fishing. It is
also interesting that thoughts about fishing are often carried
on in dialogue form where Hope and Fear—or, many times,
two Fears—try to outweigh each other.

One Fear looked down the shoreline and said to me (a third
person distinct from the two fears), "There is nothing but
rocks for thirty yards, but don't get scared and try to land him
before you get all the way down to the first sandbar."

The Second Fear said, "It's forty, not thirty, yards to the
first sandbar and the weather has been warm and the fish's
mouth will be soft and he will work off the hook if you try to
fight him forty yards downriver. It's not good but it will be
best to try to land him on a rock that is closer."

The First Fear said, "There is a big rock in the river that
you will have to take him past before you land him, but, if you
hold the line tight enough on him to keep him this side of the
rock, you will probably lose him."

The Second Fear said, "But if you let him get on the far side
of the rock, the line will get caught under it, and you will be
sure to lose him."

That's how you know when you have thought too much—
when you become a dialogue between *You'll probably lose* and
You're sure to lose. But I didn't entirely quit thinking, although
I did switch subjects. It is not in the book, yet it is human
enough to spend a moment before casting in trying to imagine what the fish is thinking, even if one of its eggs is as
big as its brain and even if, when you swim underwater, it is

hard to imagine that a fish has anything to think about. Still, I could never be talked into believing that all a fish knows is hunger and fear. I have tried to feel nothing but hunger and fear and don't see how a fish could ever grow to six inches if that were all he ever felt. In fact, I go so far sometimes as to imagine that a fish thinks pretty thoughts. Before I made the cast, I imagined the fish with the black back lying cool in the carbonated water full of bubbles from the waterfalls. He was looking downriver and watching the foam with food in it backing upstream like a floating cafeteria coming to wait on its customers. And he probably was imagining that the speckled foam was eggnog with nutmeg sprinkled on it, and, when the whites of eggs separated and he saw what was on shore, he probably said to himself, "What a lucky son of a bitch I am that this guy and not his brother is about to fish this hole."

I thought all these thoughts and some besides that proved of no value, and then I cast and I caught him.

I kept cool until I tried to take the hook out of his mouth. He was lying covered with sand on the little bar where I had landed him. His gills opened with his penultimate sighs. Then suddenly he stood up on his head in the sand and hit me with his tail and the sand flew. Slowly at first my hands began to shake, and, although I thought they made a miserable sight, I couldn't stop them. Finally, I managed to open the large blade to my knife which several times slid off his skull before it went through his brain.

Even when I bent him he was way too long for my basket, so his tail stuck out.

There were black spots on him that looked like crustaceans. He seemed oceanic, including barnacles. When I passed my brother at the next hole, I saw him study the tail and slowly remove his hat, and not out of respect to my prowess as a fisherman.

I had a fish, so I sat down to watch a fisherman.

He took his cigarettes and matches from his shirt pocket and put them in his hat and pulled his hat down tight so it wouldn't leak. Then he unstrapped his fish basket and hung it on the edge of his shoulder where he could get rid of it quick should the water get too big for him. If he studied the situation he didn't take any separate time to do it. He jumped off a rock into the swirl and swam for a chunk of cliff that had dropped into the river and parted it. He swam in his clothes with only his left arm—in his right hand, he held his rod high and sometimes all I could see was the basket and rod, and when the basket filled with water sometimes all I could see was the rod.

The current smashed him into the chunk of cliff and it must have hurt, but he had enough strength remaining in his left fingers to hang to a crevice or he would have been swept into the blue below. Then he still had to climb to the top of the rock with his left fingers and his right elbow which he used like a prospector's pick. When he finally stood on top, his clothes looked hydraulic, as if they were running off him.

Once he quit wobbling, he shook himself duck-dog fashion, with his feet spread apart, his body lowered and his head flopping. Then he steadied himself and began to cast and the whole world turned to water.

Below him was the multitudinous river, and, where the rock had parted it around him, big-grained vapor rose. The mini-molecules of water left in the wake of his line made momentary loops of gossamer, disappearing so rapidly in the rising big-grained vapor that they had to be retained in memory to be visualized as loops. The spray emanating from him was finer-grained still and enclosed him in a halo of himself. The halo of himself was always there and always disappearing, as if he were candlelight flickering about three inches from himself. The images of himself and his line kept disappearing into the rising vapors of the river, which continually circled to the tops of the cliffs where, after becoming a wreath in the wind, they became rays of the sun.

The river above and below his rock was all big Rainbow water, and he would cast hard and low upstream, skimming the water with his fly but never letting it touch. Then he would pivot, reverse his line in a great oval above his head, and drive his line low and hard downstream, again skimming the water with his fly. He would complete this grand circle four or five times, creating an immensity of motion which culminated in nothing if you did not know, even if you could not see, that now somewhere out there a small fly was washing itself on a wave. Shockingly, immensity would return as the Big Blackfoot and the air above it became iridescent with the arched sides of a great Rainbow.

He called this "shadow casting," and frankly I don't know whether to believe the theory behind it—that the fish are alerted by the shadows of flies passing over the water by the first casts, so hit the fly the moment it touches the water. It is more or less the "working up an appetite" theory, almost too fancy to be true, but then every fine fisherman has a few fancy stunts that work for him and for almost no one else. Shadow casting never worked for me, but maybe I never had the strength of arm and wrist to keep line circling over the water until fish imagined a hatch of flies was out.

My brother's wet clothes made it easy to see his strength. Most great casters I have known were big men over six feet, the added height certainly making it easier to get more line in the air in a bigger arc. My brother was only five feet ten, but he had fished so many years his body had become partly shaped by his casting. He was thirty-two now, at the height of his power, and he could put all his body and soul into a four-and-a-half-ounce magic totem pole. Long ago, he had gone far beyond my father's wrist casting, although his right wrist was always so important that it had become larger than his left. His right arm, which our father had kept tied to the side to emphasize the wrist, shot out of his shirt as if it were engineered, and it, too, was larger than his left arm. His wet shirt bulged and came unbuttoned with his pivoting shoulders and hips. It was also not hard to see why he was a street fighter, especially since he was committed to getting in the first punch with his right hand.

Rhythm was just as important as color and just as

complicated. It was one rhythm superimposed upon another, our father's four-count rhythm of the line and wrist being still the base rhythm. But superimposed upon it was the piston two count of his arm and the long overriding four count of the completed figure eight of his reversed loop.

The canyon was glorified by rhythms and colors.

I heard voices behind me, and a man and his wife came down the trail, each carrying a rod, but probably they weren't going to do much fishing. Probably they intended nothing much more than to enjoy being out of doors with each other and, on the side, to pick enough huckleberries for a pie. In those days there was little in the way of rugged sports clothes for women, and she was a big, rugged woman and wore regular men's bib overalls, and her motherly breasts bulged out of the bib. She was the first to see my brother pivoting on the top of his cliff. To her, he must have looked something like a trick rope artist at a rodeo, doing everything except jumping in and out of his loops.

She kept watching while groping behind her to smooth out some pine needles to sit on. "My, my!" she said.

Her husband stopped and stood and said, "Jesus." Every now and then he said, "Jesus." Each time his wife nodded. She was one of America's mothers who never dream of using profanity themselves but enjoy their husbands', and later come to need it, like cigar smoke.

I started to make for the next hole. "Oh, no," she said, "you're going to wait, aren't you, until he comes to shore so you can see his big fish?"

"No," I answered, "I'd rather remember the molecules."

She obviously thought I was crazy, so I added, "I'll see his fish later." And to make any sense for her I had to add, "He's my brother."

As I kept going, the middle of my back told me that I was being viewed from the rear both as quite a guy, because I was his brother, and also as a little bit nutty, because I was molecular.

Since our fish were big enough to deserve a few drinks and

quite a bit of talk afterwards, we were late in getting back to Helena. On the way, Paul asked, "Why not stay overnight with me and go down to Wolf Creek in the morning?" He added that he himself had "to be out for the evening," but would be back soon after midnight. I learned later it must have been around two o'clock in the morning when I heard the thing that was ringing, and I ascended through river mists and molecules until I awoke catching the telephone. The telephone had a voice in it, which asked, "Are you Paul's brother?" I asked, "What's wrong?" The voice said, "I want you to see him." Thinking we had poor connections, I banged the phone. "Who are you?" I asked. He said, "I am the desk sergeant who wants you to see your brother."

The checkbook was still in my hand when I reached the jail. The desk sergeant frowned and said, "No, you don't have to post bond for him. He covers the police beat and has friends here. All you have to do is look at him and take him home."

Then he added, "But he'll have to come back. A guy is going to sue him. Maybe two guys are."

Not wanting to see him without a notion of what I might see, I kept repeating, "What's wrong?" When the desk sergeant thought it was time, he told me, "He hit a guy and the guy is missing a couple of teeth and is all cut up." I asked, "What's the second guy suing him for?" "For breaking dishes. Also a table," the sergeant said. "The second guy owns the restaurant. The guy who got hit lit on one of the tables."

By now I was ready to see my brother, but it was becoming clear that the sergeant had called me to the station to have a talk. He said, "We're picking him up too much lately. He's drinking too much." I had already heard more than I wanted. Maybe one of our ultimate troubles was that I never wanted to hear too much about my brother.

The sergeant finished what he had to say by finally telling me what he really wanted to say, "Besides he's behind in the big stud poker game at Hot Springs. It's not healthy to be behind in the big game at Hot Springs.

"You and your brother think you're tough because you're

street fighters. At Hot Springs they don't play any child games
like fist fighting. At Hot Springs it's the big stud poker game
and all that goes with it."

I was confused from trying to rise suddenly from molecules
of sleep to an understanding of what I did not want to
understand. I said, "Let's begin again. Why is he here and is
he hurt?"

The sergeant said, "He's not hurt, just sick. He drinks too
much. At Hot Springs, they don't drink too much." I said to
the sergeant, "Let's go on. Why is he here?"

According to the sergeant's report to me, Paul and his girl
had gone into Weiss's restaurant for a midnight sandwich—a
popular place at midnight since it had booths in the rear
where you and your girl could sit and draw the curtains. "The
girl," the sergeant said, "was that half-breed Indian girl he
goes with. You know the one," he added, as if to implicate me.

Paul and his girl were evidently looking for an empty booth
when a guy in a booth they had passed stuck his head out of
the curtain and yelled, "Wahoo." Paul hit the head, separating
the head from two teeth and knocking the body back on the
table, which overturned, cutting the guy and his girl with
broken dishes. The sergeant said, "The guy said to me, 'Jesus,
all I meant is that it's funny to go out with an Indian. It was
just a joke.'"

I said to the sergeant, "It's not very funny," and the
sergeant said, "No, not very funny, but it's going to cost your
brother a lot of money and time to get out of it. What really
isn't funny is that he's behind in the game at Hot Springs.
Can't you help him straighten out?"

"I don't know what to do," I confessed to the sergeant.

"I know what you mean," the sergeant confessed to me.
Desk sergeants at this time were still Irish. "I have a young
brother," he said, "who is a wonderful kid, but he's always in
trouble. He's what we call 'Black Irish.'"

"What do you do to help him?" I asked. After a long pause,
he said, "I take him fishing."

"And when that doesn't work?" I asked.

"You better go and see your own brother," he answered.

Wanting to see him in perspective when I saw him, I stood still until I could again see the woman in bib overalls marveling at his shadow casting. Then I opened the door to the room where they toss the drunks until they can walk a crack in the floor. "His girl is with him," the sergeant said.

He was standing in front of a window, but he could not have been looking out of it, because there was a heavy screen between the bars, and he could not have seen me because his enlarged casting hand was over his face. Were it not for the lasting compassion I felt for his hand, I might have doubted afterwards that I had seen him.

His girl was sitting on the floor at his feet. When her black hair glistened, she was one of my favorite women. Her mother was a Northern Cheyenne, so when her black hair glistened she was handsome, more Algonkian and Romanlike than Mongolian in profile, and very warlike, especially after a few drinks. At least one of her great grandmothers had been with the Northern Cheyennes when they and the Sioux destroyed General Custer and the Seventh Cavalry, and, since it was the Cheyennes who were camped on the Little Bighorn just opposite to the hill they were about to immortalize, the Cheyenne squaws were among the first to work the field over after the battle. At least one of her ancestors, then, had spent a late afternoon happily cutting off the testicles of the Seventh Cavalry, the cutting often occurring before death.

This paleface who had stuck his head out of the booth in Weiss's café and yelled "Wahoo" was lucky to be missing only two teeth.

Even I couldn't walk down the street beside her without her getting me into trouble. She liked to hold Paul with one arm and me with the other and walk down Last Chance Gulch on Saturday night, forcing people into the gutter to get around us, and when they wouldn't give up the sidewalk she would shove Paul or me into them. You didn't have to go very far down Last Chance Gulch on Saturday night shoving people into the gutter before you were into a hell of a big fight, but she always felt that she had a disappointing evening and had not been appreciated if the guy who took her out didn't get into a big fight over her.

When her hair glistened, though, she was worth it. She was one of the most beautiful dancers I have ever seen. She made her partner feel as if he were about to be left behind, or already had been.

It is a strange and wonderful and somewhat embarrassing feeling to hold someone in your arms who is trying to detach you from the earth and you aren't good enough to follow her.

I called her Mo-nah-se-tah, the name of the beautiful daughter of the Cheyenne chief, Little Rock. At first, she didn't particularly care for the name, which means, "the young grass that shoots in the spring," but after I explained to her that Mo-nah-se-tah was supposed to have had an illegitimate son by General George Armstrong Custer she took to the name like a duck to water.

Looking down on her now I could see only the spread of her hair on her shoulders and the spread of her legs on the floor. Her hair did not glisten and I had never seen her legs when they were just things lying on a floor. Knowing that I was looking down on her, she struggled to get to her feet, but her long legs buckled and her stockings slipped down on her legs and she spread out on the floor again until the tops of her stockings and her garters showed.

The two of them smelled worse than the jail. They smelled just like what they were—a couple of drunks whose stomachs had been injected with whatever it is the body makes when it feels cold and full of booze and knows something bad has happened and doesn't want tomorrow to come.

Neither one ever looked at me, and he never spoke. She said, "Take me home." I said, "That's why I'm here." She said, "Take him, too."

She was as beautiful a dancer as he was a fly caster. I carried her with her toes dragging behind her. Paul turned and, without seeing or speaking, followed. His overdeveloped right wrist held his right hand over his eyes so that in some

drunken way he thought I could not see him and he may also
have thought that he could not see himself.

As we went by the desk, the sergeant said, "Why don't you
all go fishing?"

I did not take Paul's girl to her home. In those days, Indians
who did not live on reservations had to live out by the city
limits and generally they pitched camp near either the
slaughterhouse or the city dump. I took them back to Paul's
apartment. I put him in his bed, and I put her in the bed
where I had been sleeping, but not until I had changed it so
that the fresh sheets would feel smooth to her legs.

As I covered her, she said, "He should have killed the
bastard."

I said, "Maybe he did," whereupon she rolled over and
went to sleep, believing, as she always did, anything I told
her, especially if it involved heavy casualties.

By then, dawn was coming out of a mountain across the
Missouri, so I drove to Wolf Creek.

In those days it took about an hour to drive the forty miles
of rough road from Helena to Wolf Creek. While the sun
came out of the Big Belt Mountains and the Missouri and left
them behind in light, I tried to find something I already knew
about life that might help me reach out and touch my brother
and get him to look at me and himself. For a while, I even
thought what the desk sergeant first told me was useful. As a
desk sergeant, he had to know a lot about life and he had told
me Paul was the Scottish equivalent of "Black Irish." Without
doubt, in my father's family there were "Black Scots" oc-
cupying various outposts all the way from the original family home on the Isle of Mull in the southern Hebrides to
Fairbanks, Alaska, 110 or 115 miles south of the Arctic Circle,
which was about as far as a Scot could go then to get out of
range of sheriffs with warrants and husbands with shotguns. I
had learned about them from my aunts, not my uncles, who
were all Masons and believed in secret societies for males. My
aunts, though, talked gaily about them and told me they were
all big men and funny and had been wonderful to them when

they were little girls. From my uncles' letters, it was clear that they still thought of my aunts as little girls. Every Christmas until they died in distant lands these hastily departed brothers sent their once-little sisters loving Christmas cards scrawled with assurances that they would soon "return to the States and help them hang stockings on Christmas eve."

Seeing that I was relying on women to explain to myself what I didn't understand about men, I remembered a couple of girls I had dated who had uncles with some resemblances to my brother. The uncles were fairly expert at some art that was really a hobby—one uncle was a watercolorist and the other the club champion golfer—and each had selected a profession that would allow him to spend most of his time at his hobby. Both were charming, but you didn't quite know what if anything you knew when you had finished talking to them. Since they did not earn enough money from business to make life a hobby, their families had to meet from time to time with the county attorney to keep things quiet.

Sunrise is the time to feel that you will be able to find out how to help somebody close to you who you think needs help even if he doesn't think so. At sunrise everything is luminous but not clear.

Then about twelve miles before Wolf Creek the road drops into the Little Prickly Pear Canyon, where dawn is long in coming. In the suddenly returning semidarkness, I watched the road carefully, saying to myself, hell, my brother is not like anybody else. He's not my gal's uncle or a brother of my aunts. He is my brother and an artist and when a four-and-a-half-ounce rod is in his hand he is a major artist. He doesn't piddle around with a paint brush or take lessons to improve his short game and he won't take money even when he must need it and he won't run anywhere from anyone, least of all to the Arctic Circle. It is a shame I do not understand him.

Yet even in the loneliness of the canyon I knew there were others like me who had brothers they did not understand but wanted to help. We are probably those referred to as "our brothers' keepers," possessed of one of the oldest and possibly one of the most futile and certainly one of the most haunting of instincts. It will not let us go.

When I drove out of the canyon, it was ordinary daylight. I went to bed and had no trouble not going to sleep until my wife called me. "Don't forget," Jessie said, "you're going with Florence and me to meet Neal at the train." The truth was I had forgotten, but when I thought about him I felt relieved. It was good to remember that there was someone in my wife's family they worried about, and it was even better to remember that to me he was a little bit funny. I was in need of relief, and comic relief seemed about as good as any.

My wife kept standing at the door, waiting for me to roll over and try to go to sleep again. To her surprise, I jumped out of bed and started dressing. "It will be a pleasure," I told her. Jessie said to me, "You're funny," and I asked, "What's funny about me?" And Jessie said, "I know you don't like him." I said, "I do not like him," saying "do not" instead of "don't" in case my voice was blurred in waking up. Jessie said, "You're funny," and closed the door, then opened a crack of it and said, "You are not funny," and my wife's "not" was also distinct.

He was last off the train, and he came down the platform trying to remember what he thought an international-cup tennis player looked like. He undoubtedly was the first and last passenger ever to step off a Great Northern coach car at Wolf Creek, Montana, wearing white flannels and two sweaters. All this was in the days when the fancy Dans wore red-white-and-blue tennis sweaters, and he had a red-white-and-blue V-neck sweater over a red-white-and-blue turtle-neck sweater. When he recognized us as relatives and realized that he couldn't be Bill Tilden or F. Scott Fitzgerald, he put down his suitcase and said, "Oh," except when he saw me he said nothing. Then he turned his profile, and waited to be kissed. While the women took turns, I had a good look at his suitcase. It rested next to his elegant black-and-white shoes, and its straw sides had started to break open and one of

its locks did not lock. Between its handles were the initials
F. M., his mother's initials before she had married. When his
mother saw the suitcase, she cried.

So he came home with about what he had when he left
Montana, because he still had his mother's suitcase and his
own conception of himself as a Davis Cup player, which had
first come to the surface in Wolf Creek where you couldn't
jump over a net without landing in cactus.

It was not until eight-thirty or nine that night that he tried
to reduce himself in size so he could squeeze out of the door
without being seen, but Florence and Jessie were waiting for
him. My wife was barren of double-talk, so, to avoid being
told, I got up and accompanied him to Black Jack's Bar,
sometimes although rarely called a tavern.

Black Jack's was a freight car taken off its wheels and set on
gravel at the other end of the bridge crossing the Little Prickly
Pear. On the side of the box car was the sign of the Great
Northern Railroad, a mountain goat gazing through a white
beard on a world painted red. This is the only goat that ever
saw the bottom of his world constantly occupied by a bottle of
bar whiskey labeled "3-7-77," the number the Vigilantes
pinned on the road agents they hanged in order to represent
probably the dimensions of a grave. (The numbers are
thought to mean three feet wide, seven feet long, and
seventy-seven inches deep.) The bar was a log split in two by
someone who wasn't much good with an ax, maybe Black Jack·
himself, but his customers had done a much better job in
greasing it with their elbows. Black Jack was short, trembled,
and never got far from a revolver and a blackjack that lay
behind the greased log. His teeth were bad, probably the
result of drinking his own whiskey, which was made
somewhere up Sheep Gulch.

The stools in front of the bar were reconstructed grocery
crates. When Neal and I walked in, two of the crates were
occupied, both by characters long familiar to the Great
Northern goat. On the first was a bar character called Long
Bow, because in this once Indian country anyone making an

art of telling big lies about his hunting and shooting was said
"to pull the long bow."

Having seen him shoot once, though, I myself never acted
on the assumption that he lied about what he could do with
firearms. I had seen a friend of his throw five aspirin tablets in
the air which bloomed into five small white flowers immediately following five shots that sounded like one.

I was just as sure he could challenge the champion sheepherder of the Sieben ranch at his own game. The Sieben
ranch is one of the finest in western Montana, spreading all
the way from the Helena valley to Lincoln and beyond. Its
owners, Jean and John Baucus, tell about a favorite
sheepherder they once had to take to the hospital where his
condition rapidly changed for the worse. They couldn't get
his underwear off—it had been on him so long his hair had
grown through it. Finally, they had to pluck him like a
chicken, and when his underwear finally came off, pieces of
skin came with it. At the opening of Long Bow's shirt, which
wasn't buttoned for quite a way down, you could see hair
sprouting out of his underwear.

On the crate at the other end of the bar was a female
character known as Old Rawhide to the goats up and down
the Great Northern line. About ten years before, at a Fourth
of July celebration she had been elected beauty queen of Wolf
Creek. She had ridden bareback standing up through the 111
inhabitants, mostly male, who had lined one of Wolf Creek's
two streets. Her skirts flew high, and she won the contest. But,
since she didn't quite have what it takes to become a
professional rider, she did the next best thing. However, she
still wore the divided skirts of a western horsewoman of the
day, although they must have been a handicap in her new
profession.

For a small town, Wolf Creek loomed large upon the map.
It had two almost national celebrities, one a steer wrestler and
the other a fancy roper. These two local artists spent their
summers at county fairs and were good enough to come out
five or six hundred dollars ahead for the season, less, of

course, their hospital expenses. Old Rawhide did not intend to spend the rest of her life as a disappointed athlete, so she would shack up one winter with the fancy roper and the next winter with the steer wrestler. Occasionally, in late autumn when it looked as if it were going to be an especially hard winter, she would marry one of them, but marriage wasn't Old Rawhide's natural state of bliss, and before spring she would be shacked up with the other one. Shacking up brought out Old Rawhide's most enduring and durable qualities, and, unlike marriage, could be counted on to last all winter.

In the summers, while her artists were living off hot dogs at county fairs and rupturing their intestines while twisting the necks of steers, Old Rawhide inhabited Black Jack's Bar, reduced to picking up stray fishermen, most of them bait and hardware fishermen from Great Falls, so for her, as for the rest of the world, life had its ups and downs. However, she didn't show much the effects of life's gravitational pulls. Like many fancy riders, she was rather small and very tough and very strong, especially in the legs. She had weathered enough to deserve her name, but she didn't look much older than her thirty years spent mostly with horses and horsemen and the sporting element of Great Falls.

Even when she and Long Bow were at the bar, they sat at opposite ends so that itinerant fishermen had to sit between them and buy the drinks.

That's where Neal and I sat when we came in.

"Hi, Long Bow," Neal said, and overshook his hand. Long Bow did not like to be called Long Bow, although he knew he was called Long Bow behind his back , but to Neal he was just plain old Long Bow, and after a couple of shots of 3-7-77 Neal was outshooting, outhunting, and outtrapping the govern-ment trapper.

There was something deep in Neal that compelled him to lie to experts, even though they knew best that he was lying. He was one of those who need to be caught telling a lie while he is telling it.

As for Old Rawhide, Neal hadn't looked at her yet. I was already wise to the fact that Neal's opening ploy with women was to ignore them, and indeed was beginning to recognize what a good opening it is.

The mirror behind the bar looked like a polished Precambrian mudstone with ripples on it. Neal watched it constantly, evidently fascinated by the dark distorted image of himself living automatically—buying all the drinks and doing all the talking and none of the listening. I tried to break the monopoly by talking to Old Rawhide who was sitting next to me, but she was aware only of being ignored so she ignored me.

Finally, I listened, since no one would listen to me, although I didn't go so far as to buy the drinks. Neal had trailed an otter and her pups up to Rogers Pass, where the thermometer officially recorded 69.7 degrees below zero. While he trailed this otter, I tried to trace its lineage from his description of it. "I had a hard time following it," he said, "because it had turned white in the winter," so it must have been part ermine. After he treed her, he said, "She stretched out on the lower branch ready to pounce on the first deer that came along," so she had to have a strain of mountain lion in her. She also must have been part otter, because she was jokey and smiled at him. But mostly she was 3-7-77, because she was the only animal in western Montana besides man that had pups in the winter. "They snuggled up right in my shirt," he said, showing us a shirt under his two red-white-and-blue sweaters.

Long Bow gently tapped the thick bottom of his empty glass on the bar, without saying a word for fear of appearing inattentive. But Old Rawhide couldn't stand the silent treatment any longer, no matter what. She leaned in front of me and said to the side of Neal's face, "Hey, Buster, what are otters doing on the top of the Continental Divide? I thought otters swam in creeks and played on mud slides?"

Neal stopped in the middle of a sentence and stared at the mirror, trying to pick out the distortion other than his own which had spoken. "Let's have another drink," he said to all the distortions. Then for the first time he formally recognized that a woman was present by looking not at the image but at the reality of Black Jack behind the bar, and saying, "Give her one, too."

Old Rawhide closed her hand when a drink was put in it, but kept on staring at Neal's profile. In the ranch town of Wolf Creek, she and the Great Northern goat had probably seen only a couple of other men who were pale and had sunken eyes.

As I pushed myself out of my crate to keep my promise to go home early, Long Bow said, "Thanks." Since I hadn't bought a drink all evening, I knew he must be thanking me for leaving them my brother-in-law. The moment I rose from my crate, Old Rawhide moved into it to be closer to Neal. She peered into his profile, and romance stirred under her epidermis.

On the way out, I said to Neal over my shoulder, "Don't forget, you're going fishing tomorrow morning," and he looked over her shoulder and said, "What?"

Paul was in Wolf Creek early next morning, just as he said he would be. Although he and I had acquired freedoms as we grew up, we never violated our early religious training of always being on time for church, work, and fishing.

Florence met him at the door and said nervously, "I'm sorry, Paul, but Neal isn't up yet. He got home late."

Paul said, "I didn't even go to bed last night. Get him up,. Florence."

She said, "He isn't very well."

He said, "Neither am I, but I am going fishing in a few minutes."

They stared at each other. No Scottish mother likes to be caught with a lazy son in bed, and no Scot going fishing likes to stand around waiting for a male relative with a hangover. Although the Scots invented whiskey, they try not to acknowledge the existence of hangovers, especially within the family circle. Normally, it would have been no better than a standoff between my brother and my mother-in-law, but in this rare case a Scottish lady couldn't think of a thing to say in her son's defense, so she had to wake him up, although as little as possible.

We slowly loaded the half-ton truck that belonged to Kenny, my one brother-in-law who had remained in Wolf Creek. The three women had already covered the shady end of the box with an old mattress, and then they covered the mattress with their relative from the West Coast. After space had been found for the potato salad, the grill and our fishing tackle, six of us tried to be comfortable without in any way disturbing the mattress.

All but the first three miles of the road to the Elkhorn parallels the Missouri as it emerges from the gigantic opening that Lewis and Clark called the Gateway to the Mountains. Although the water remains clear for a few miles farther down, the earth itself turns tawny almost the moment the river pours out of the mountains. It is just below the dark opening where the Elkhorn empties into the Missouri that the road ends. Like most dirt roads paralleling the Missouri, it is mostly gray dust and chuckholes. The chuckholes did not improve Neal's health, and the gray dust would turn to gumbo if it rained.

Kenny, as the one of Jessie's brothers who stayed in Wolf Creek, was like most who live in towns with two streets—he could do nearly anything with his hands. Among other things, he could drive a half-ton truck over country where it would be hard to take a pack mule, and he had married Dorothy, a registered nurse. She was short and powerful and had been trained as a surgical nurse. Ranchers holding their intestines in their hands would ride in from the back country looking for the "the RN" to sew them together again. Florence and Jessie were also medical in varying degrees, and the three of them were thought of as the medical center of Wolf Creek. Now, the three women bent over an old mattress, constituting, as it were, the intensive-care unit.

Ken was friendly with all 111 inhabitants of Wolf Creek and most of the ranchers in the surrounding country, especially

with the ranchers from Scotland, who had come to the West
early, knowing ahead of time how to raise cattle in mountains
and snow. That's how we got permission to fish in the
Elkhorn. Jim McGregor owned it to its headwaters, and every
fence was posted, reading from top to bottom, "No Hunting,"
"No Fishing," and finally, as an afterthought, "No Trespass-
ing." As a result, he furnished pasture for about as many
elk as cows, but he figured this was cheaper than opening his
range to hunters from Great Falls who have difficulty telling
an elk from a cow.

One thing about a ranch road—there is less and less of it
the closer it gets to the cows. It became just two ruts that made
switchbacks to the top of a ridge, and then it repeated roughly
the same number down to the Elkhorn, which is just a curve
of willows and water winding through high grass until
suddenly a mountain opens and the willows disappear. At the
top of the ridge the ruts were still made of gray dust, and
black clouds rested upon the black mountains ahead.

Paul was out of the truck as soon as it stopped at the creek
bottom. He had his rod up and his leader and flies on before I
could free myself from the vise in which I had been sitting
between Dorothy and Jessie, who had been holding me tight
by the soft part of the arm and muttering, "Don't you run off
and leave my brother." Besides, I had to hop around for a
minute or so, because a leg had gone to sleep in the vise.

By that time, Paul was saying behind his back, "I'll walk
three fishing distances down and then fish upstream. You
spread out and fish downstream until we meet." Then he was
gone.

One reason Paul caught more fish than anyone else was that
he had his flies in the water more than anyone else. "Brother,"
he would say, "there are no flying fish in Montana. Out here,
you can't catch fish with your flies in the air." His outfit was
set up ready to go the moment he stepped out of the car; he
walked fast; he seldom wasted time changing flies but instead
changed the depth he was fishing them or the motion with
which he retrieved them; if he did change flies, he tied knots

with the speed of a seamstress; and so on. His flies were in the
water at least twenty percent more of the time than mine.

I guessed there was also another reason why today he was
separating himself from me as fast and as far as possible—he
did not want me to talk to him about the other night.

Ken said he would go upstream to fish the beaver dams. He
liked beaver dams and he knew how to fish them. So off he
went happily to wade in ooze and to get throttled by brush
and to fall through loose piles of sticks called beaver dams and
to end up with a wreath of seaweed round his neck and a
basketful of fish.

Jessie gave me another pinch on the arm and shortened her
warning to, "Don't leave my brother." Rubbing my arm, I
made him go first so he couldn't escape immediately. We went
down the trail around the first bend where the creek comes
out of osiers and crosses a meadow. Then his steps faltered
and became intentionally pitiful. "I'm still not well," he said;
"I think I'll stop here and fish the meadow." Because of the
bend in the creek, he couldn't be seen, and yet, if he walked
back, he would have only a couple of hundred yards to go.

"Why not?" I asked, already knowing a foolish question
when I asked one.

Even though Paul must have had three or four fish by now,
I took my time walking down the trail, trying with each step to
leave the world behind. Something within fishermen tries to
make fishing into a world perfect and apart—I don't know
what it is or where, because sometimes it is in my arms and
sometimes in my throat and sometimes nowhere in particular
except somewhere deep. Many of us probably would be better
fishermen if we did not spend so much time watching and
waiting for the world to become perfect.

The hardest thing usually to leave behind, as was the case
now, can loosely be called the conscience.

Should or shouldn't I speak to my brother about what
happened the other night? I referred to it vaguely as "what
happened the other night" so as not to visualize it, especially
not the casting hand. Shouldn't I at least offer to help him

with money, if he has to pay damages? I thought about these old questions in new forms now framed by long dancing legs spread on a jail floor until finally the questions of conscience disappeared, again as usual, without any answers to them. I still didn't know whether I had resolved to talk to my brother today.

However, I still kept worrying about something, whatever it was, until I turned around in the trail and went back to the meadow so I could say that I had.

Across the meadow was a dam and above it a big blue hole where Neal sat nodding on a rock, the red Hills Bros. coffee can beside him. His neck was bowed, pale, exposed to the sun and soon to match the coffee can.

"What are you doing?" I asked.

It took him some time to arrange an answer. "I have been fishing," he said finally. Then he tried over again for greater accuracy. "I have been fishing and not feeling well," he said.

"This dead water isn't much of a place to fish, is it?" I asked.

"Why," he said, "look at all those fish at the bottom of the hole."

"Those are squaw fish and suckers," I told him, without looking.

"What's a sucker?" he asked, and so became the first native of Montana ever to sit on a rock and ask what a sucker was.

In the deep water below him was a little botch of pink that was sure to be angleworms with one hook running through all their guts. On the leader, just above the worms, were two red beads, strung there no doubt for cosmetic purposes. The botch of angleworms and the two beads hung within six inches of the nearest sucker. Not a fish stirred, and neither did the fisherman, although both were in plain view of each other.

"Would you like to go fly fishing sometime with Paul and me?" I asked.

"Thanks," he said, "but not just now."

"Well, then," I said, "take care of yourself and have a good time."

"I am," he said.

I walked down the trail again under the mistaken notion I might have done myself some good by going back to see my brother-in-law. However, that big cloud coming out of the entrance to the Rocky Mountains kept telling me that, much as I was looking for moments of perfection, I wasn't going to find any today. And also that I wasn't going to catch many fish unless I quit fooling around.

I turned off the trail at the next meadow, and could have caught my limit in two or three holes. Because Jim McGregor allowed only a few fishermen a year on this small creek, it was overpopulated with fish that would probably never grow longer than ten or eleven inches.

I had only one problem in catching them and it lasted for only the first few fish. I was too fast in setting the hook. There is a barb on the end of the hook, and unless the hook gets imbedded in the fish's mouth or jaw deep enough to "set" the barb in it, the fish spits or tears the hook out. So, as the fish strikes, the line has to be given a little jerk, either directly with the left hand or with the rod in the right hand. The timing and the pressure have to be perfect—too soon or too late or too little or too much and the fish may have a sore mouth for a few days but will probably live longer for his experience.

I was setting the fly so fast I was taking it away from the fish before they could get hold of it. Every different kind of trout is on a different speedometer, and the correct timing will vary also with the stream and even the weather and time of day. I had been fishing too long in the fast water of the Big Blackfoot where big Rainbows charge out from behind the fortresses of big rocks. Some early rancher had planted the Elkhorn with Eastern Brook Trout, and, as the name suggests, they are a more meditative type.

Once I got my timing slowed down, I lost interest in them. They are beautiful to see—black backs, yellow and orange spots on their sides, red bellies ending in under-fins fringed with white. They are compositions in colors, and were often painted on platters. But they are only fairly good fighters and they feel like eels because their scales are so small. Besides, their name is against them in western Montana where the word "brook" is not a socially acceptable substitute for "creek."

All of a sudden I wondered what my brother was doing because I knew he certainly wasn't wasting time catching his limit of ten-inch Eastern Brook Trout. If I wanted to stay in shooting distance of him, I had better start trying to catch some of those Brown monsters that work their way up from the Missouri.

Fishing is a world created apart from all others, and inside it are special worlds of their own—one is fishing for big fish in small water where there is not enough world and water to accommodate a fish and a fisherman, and the willows on the side of the creek are all against the fisherman.

I stopped, cleaned my Eastern Brook Trout, and arranged them in my basket between layers of wild hay and mint where they were more beautiful than those painted on platters. Then, in preparation for big game, I changed to an eight-pound test leader and to a number six fly.

I waxed the first thirty feet of my line in case it had become water-soaked and would not float, took one final look at my ten-inch Eastern Brook Trout lying in mint, and then closed my basket on the world of small fish.

A huge shadow met me coming across the meadow, with one big cloud behind it. The Elkhorn Canyon is so deep and narrow that a black cloud or a cloud and a half can constitute the sky. The black cloud and a half can pass on to sunshine or it can make room for blacker clouds. From the bottom of the canyon, there is no way of seeing what is coming, but I had a feeling it wasn't sunshine.

Suddenly, so many fish began to jump that it looked as if the first extra-large raindrops had arrived. When fish start jumping like this, something is happening to the weather.

At that moment, the world was totally composed of the Elkhorn, a mythological Brown Trout, the weather and me, and all that existed of me were thoughts about the Elkhorn, the weather, and a mythological fish that may have been a fingerling of my imagination.

The Elkhorn looks just like what it is—a crack in the earth

to mark where the Rocky Mountains end and the Great Plains begin. The giant mountains are black-backed with nearly the last of mountain pines. Their eastern sides turn brown and yellow as the tall prairie grasses begin, but there are occasional black spots where the pines scatter themselves out to get a last look back. The mythological Brown Trout and the canyon harmonized in my thoughts. The trout that might be real and close at hand was massive, black on the back, yellow and brown on the sides, had black spots and a final fringe of white. The Elkhorn and the Brown Trout are also alike in being beautiful by being partly ugly.

I walked past 150 or 200 yards of water where little "Brookies" were still bouncing like rain and came finally to a beautiful stretch with not a fish jumping in it. At the head of the hole the water parted on a big rock, swirled backwards, deepened, deposited, and finally lost depth and motion by drifting under osiers. I thought, it can't be that no fish jumps in such beautiful water because no fish is in it. It must be one fish is there so big he is like a bull elk with "a royal head" that in rutting season runs all male contenders out of the herd.

Since it is generally better to fish creeks upstream so the water to be fished next is not dirtied, I stepped back on shore where the fish couldn't see me and walked to the lower end of the hole before making my first cast. By then, I had lost faith in my theory about the one bull elk in the hole, but I did expect to pick up a Brookie or two in the shallow water. When I didn't create a stir, I moved upstream to deeper water where the osiers began and bugs dropped off them.

Not even a glitter in the water from the side of a trout that started for the fly and suddenly decided that something looked wrong. I began to wonder if somebody had thrown a stick of dynamite into the hole and had blown all the fish belly up, along with my one bull-elk theory. If there was one fish in all this water, there was only one place left for him to be—if he wasn't in the open water and if he wasn't around the edges of the osiers, then he had to be under the osiers, and I wasn't happy about the prospect of casting into willow bushes.

Years ago at the end of a summer that I had worked in the

Forest Service I was fishing with Paul, and, being out of practice, I was especially careful to keep in open water. Paul watched me fish a hole that went under willows until he couldn't bear the sight any longer.

"Brother," he said, "you can't catch trout in a bathtub.

"You like to fish in sunny, open water because you are a Scot and afraid to lose a fly if you cast into the bushes.

"But the fish are not taking sunbaths. They are under the bushes where it is cool and safe from fishermen like you."

I only supported his charges in defending myself. "I lose flies when I get mixed up in the bushes," I complained.

"What the hell do you care?" he asked. "We don't pay for flies. George is always glad to tie more for us. Nobody," he said, "has put in a good day's fishing unless he leaves a couple of flies hanging on the bushes. You can't catch fish if you don't dare go where they are.

"Let me have your rod," he said. I suppose he took my rod so I wouldn't think that the cast into the bushes could be done only by his rod. It was in this way that I came to know that my rod can be made to cast into bushes, but the truth is I have never mastered the cast, probably because I still flinch from the prospect of losing flies that I don't have to pay for.

I had no choice now but to cast into the willows if I wanted to know why fish were jumping in the water all around me except in this hole, and I still wanted to know, because it is not fly fishing if you are not looking for answers to questions.

Since I hadn't used this cast for some time, I decided to practice up a bit, so I dropped downstream to make a few casts into the bushes. Then I walked cautiously upstream to where the osiers were thickest, watching my feet and not rattling any rocks.

The cast was high and soft when it went by my head, the opposite of what it would have been if it was being driven into the wind. I was excited, but kept my arm cool and under my control. Instead of putting on power as the line started forward, I let it float on until the vertical periscope in my eye or brain or arm or wherever it is told me my fly was over the edge of the nearest osiers. Then I put a check cast into the line, and it began to drop almost straight down. Ten or fifteen feet before the fly lights, you can tell whether a cast like this is going to be perfect, and, if necessary, still make slight corrections. The cast is so soft and slow that it can be followed like an ash settling from a fireplace chimney. One of life's quiet excitements is to stand somewhat apart from yourself and watch yourself softly becoming the author of something beautiful, even if it is only a floating ash.

The leader settled on the lowest branch of the bush and the fly swung on its little pendulum three or four inches from the water, or maybe it was five or six. To complete the cast, I was supposed next to shake the line with my rod, so, if the line wasn't caught in the bush, the fly would drop into the water underneath. I may have done this, or maybe the fish blew out of the water and took my fly as it soared up the bush. It is the only time I have ever fought a fish in a tree.

Indians used to make baskets out of the red branches of osiers, so there was no chance the branches would break. It was fish or fisherman.

Something odd, detached, and even slightly humorous happens to a big-fish fisherman a moment after a big fish strikes. In the arm, shoulder, or brain of a big-fish fisherman is a scale, and the moment the big fish goes in the air the big-fish fisherman, no matter what his blood pressure is, places the scale under the fish and coolly weighs him. He doesn't have hands and arms enough to do all the other things he should be doing at the same time, but he tries to be fairly exact about the weight of the fish so he won't be disappointed when he catches him. I said to myself, "This son of a bitch weighs seven or eight pounds," and I tried to allow for the fact that I might be weighing part of the bush.

The air was filled with dead leaves and green berries from the osiers, but their branches held. As the big Brown went up the bush, he tied a different knot on every branch he passed. He wove that bush into a basket with square knots, bowlines, and double half hitches.

The body and spirit suffer no more sudden visitation than that of losing a big fish, since, after all, there must be some slight transition between life and death. But, with a big fish, one moment the world is nuclear and the next it has disappeared. That's all. It has gone. The fish has gone and you are extinct, except for four and a half ounces of stick to which is tied some line and a semitransparent thread of catgut to which is tied a little curved piece of Swedish steel to which is tied a part of a feather from a chicken's neck.

I don't even know which way he went. As far as I know, he may have gone right on up the bush and disappeared into thin air.

I waded out to the bush to see if any signs of reality had been left behind. There was some fishing tackle strung around, but my hands trembled so I couldn't untie the complicated knots that wove it into the branches.

Even Moses could not have trembled more when his bush blew up on him. Finally, I untied my line from the leader and left the rest of the mess in the willows.

Poets talk about "spots of time," but it is really fishermen who experience eternity compressed into a moment. No one can tell what a spot of time is until suddenly the whole world is a fish and the fish is gone. I shall remember that son of a bitch forever.

A voice said, "He was a big one." It could have been my brother, or it could have been the fish circling back in the air and bragging about himself behind my back.

I turned and said to my brother, "I missed him." He had seen it all, so if I had known of something else I would have mentioned it. Instead, I repeated, "I missed him." I looked down at my hands, and the palms were turned up, as if in supplication.

"There wasn't anything you could have done about it," he said. "You can't catch a big fish in the brush. In fact, I never saw anyone try it before."

I figured he was just trying to sprinkle me with comfort, especially when I couldn't help seeing a couple of gigantic brown tails with gigantic black spots sticking out of his basket. "How did you catch yours?" I asked. I was very excited, and asked whatever I wanted to know.

He said, "I got them in shallow, open water where there weren't any bushes."

I asked, "Big ones like that in shallow, open water?"

He said, "Yes, big Brown Trout. You are used to fishing for big Rainbow in big water. But big Browns often feed along the edges of a bank in a meadow where grasshoppers and even mice fall in. You walk along the shallow water until you can see black backs sticking out of it and mud swirling."

This left me even more dismayed. I thought that I had fished the hole perfectly and just the way my brother had taught me, except he hadn't told me what to do when a fish goes up a tree. That's one trouble with hanging around a master—you pick up some of his stuff, like how to cast into a bush, but you use it just when the master is doing the opposite.

I was still excited. There was still some great hollow inside me to be filled and needed the answer to another question. Until I asked it, I had no idea what it would be. "Can I help you with money or anything?" I asked.

Alarmed by hearing myself, I tried to calm down quickly. Instead, having made a mistake, I made it worse. "I thought you might need some help because of the other night," I said.

Probably he took my reference to the other night as a reference to his Indian girl, so, to change the subject, I said, "I thought maybe it cost you a lot to fix the front end of your car the night you chased the rabbit." Now I had made three mistakes.

He acted as if his father had offered to help him to a bowl of oatmeal. He bowed his head in silence until he was sure I wouldn't say anything more. Then he said, "It's going to rain."

I glanced at the sky which I had forgotten about since the world had become no higher than a bush. There was a sky above all right, but it was all one black cloud that must have been a great weight for the canyon to bear.

My brother asked, "Where's Neal?"

The question caught me by surprise, and I had to think until I found him. "I left him at the first bend," I said finally.

"You'll get hell for that," my brother told me.

That remark enlarged my world until it included a half-ton truck and several Scottish women. "I know," I replied, and started taking my rod down. "I'm through for the day," I said, nodding at my rod.

Paul asked, "Do you have your limit?" I said, "No," even though I knew he was asking if I wasn't already in enough trouble without quitting short of my limit. To women who do not fish, men who come home without their limit are failures in life.

My brother also felt much the same way. "It would take you only a few minutes to finish up your limit with Brookies," he said, "they are still jumping all over. I'll smoke a cigarette while you catch six more."

I said, "Thanks, but I'm through for the day," although I knew he couldn't understand why six more little Eastern Brook Trout would make no difference in my view of life. Clearly by now it was one of those days when the world out-side wasn't going to let me do what I really wanted to do—catch a big Brown Trout and talk to my brother in some helpful way. Instead there was an empty bush and it was about to rain.

Paul said, "Come on, let's go and find Neal." Then he added, "You shouldn't have left him behind."

"What?" I asked.

"You should try to help him," he replied.

I could find words but not sentences they could fit. "I didn't leave him. He doesn't like me. He doesn't like Montana. He left me to go bait fishing. He can't even bait-fish. Me, I don't like anything about him."

I could feel all the excitement of losing the big fish going through the transformer and coming out as anger at my brother-in-law. I could also feel that I was repeating myself without quite saying the same thing. Even so, I asked, "Do you think you should help him?"

"Yes," he said, "I thought we were going to."

"How?" I asked.

"By taking him fishing with us."

"I've just told you," I said, "he doesn't like to fish."

"Maybe so," my brother replied. "But maybe what he likes is somebody trying to help him."

I still do not understand my brother. He himself always turned aside any offer of help, but in some complicated way he was surely talking about himself when he was talking about Neal needing help. "Come on," he said, "let's find him before he gets lost in the storm." He tried to put his arm around my shoulders but his fish basket with big tails sticking out of it came between us and made it difficult. We both looked clumsy—I in trying to offer him help, and he in trying to thank me for it.

"Let's get a move on," I said. We hit the trail and started upstream. The black cloud was taking over the canyon completely. The dimensions of the world were compressed to about 900′ × 900′ × 900′. It must have been something like this in 1949 when the giant fire from Mann Gulch, the next gulch up the Missouri, swept over the divide into the Elkhorn. Mann Gulch was where the Forest Service dropped sixteen of its crack smoke jumpers, thirteen of whom had to be identified later by their dental work. That's the way the storm came down the Elkhorn—about to obliterate it.

As if a signal had been given, not a fish jumped. Then the wind came. The water left the creek and went up in the bushes, like my fish. The air along the creek was filled with osier leaves and green berries. Then the air disappeared from view. It was present only as cones and branches that struck my face and kept going.

The storm came on a wild horse and rode over us.

We started across the meadow at the bend to look for Neal but soon we weren't even sure where we were. My lips ran with wet water. "The bastard isn't here," I said, although

neither of us knew exactly where "here" was. "No," my
brother said, "he's there." Then he added, "And dry." So we
both knew where "there" was.

By the time we got back to the truck the rain had become
steady, controlled now by gravity. Paul and I had put our
cigarettes and matches inside our hats to keep them dry, but I
could feel the water running around the roots of my hair.

The truck emerged out of the storm as if out of the pioneer
past, looking like a covered wagon besieged by circling rain.
Ken must have hurried back from the beaver dams in time to
get out a couple of old tarpaulins, cut some poles and then
stretch the tarps over the box of the truck. It was up to me
and not my brother to be the first to poke my head through
the canvas and be the "African dodger" in the sideshow at the
old circus who stuck his head through a canvas drop and let
anyone throw a baseball at it for a dime. With my head in the
hole, however, I froze, powerless to duck anything that might
be thrown or even to determine the order in which things
appeared. The actual order turned out not to be of my
choosing.

First it was the women who appeared and then the old
mattress, the women appearing first because two of them held
carving knives and the other, my wife, held a long fork, all of
which glittered in the semidarkness under the tarps. The
women squatted on the floor of the box, and had been
making sandwiches until they saw my head appear like a
target on canvas. Then they pointed their cutlery at me.

In the middle of the box there was a leak where the tarps
sagged and did not quite come together. Behind in the far
end of the box was the old mattress, but, because of the
cutlery, I couldn't see it in detail.

My wife said, pointing the long fork at me, "You went off
and left him."

My mother-in-law, stroking her knife on steel, said, "Poor
boy, he's not well. He was exposed to the sun too long."

With the only words I was able to utter while my throat was
in this exposed position, I asked, "Is that what he told you?"

"Yes, poor boy," she said, and wiggled to the rear of the box and stroked his head with one hand while keeping a firm hold on the carving knife with the other. Being short a hand, she left the steel behind.

The cracks between the tarps let in a lot of water but not much light, so it took some time for my eyes to get adjusted to my brother-in-law lying on the mattress. The light first picked up his brow, which was serene but pale, as mine would have been if my mother had spent her life in making me sandwiches and protecting me from reality.

My brother stuck his head through the tarps and stood beside me. It made me feel better having a representative of my family present. I thought, "Some day I hope I can help him as much."

The women made my brother a sandwich. As for me, my head and shoulders were under cover, but the rest of me might as well have been under a rain spout. Paul was in the same shape, and no one made a move to push closer together and make room for us inside. The bastard had the whole upper end of the box to himself. Instead of lying all over the mattress, all he had to do was sit up.

Outside, the water came down my back on a wide front, crowded into a narrow channel across my rear end, and then divided into two branches and emptied into my socks.

When the women weren't using their hardware to make sandwiches for Neal they were pointing it at me. I could smell all the sandwiches they weren't making for me and I could smell water leaking through canvas and turning to vapor from the warmth of crowded bodies and I could also smell the vapor of last night's booze rising from the old mattress. You probably know that Indians build their sweat baths on the banks of rivers. After they become drenched with sweat they immediately jump into the cold water outside, and, it may be added, sometimes they immediately die. I felt that at the same time I was both halves of myself and a sweat bath and a cold river and about to die.

I entertained a series of final thoughts. "How could the

bastard suffer from too much sun? The bastard hasn't seen more than a couple of hours of sunlight since he left Montana to go to the West Coast." I had a special thought for my wife. To keep things straight with her, I thought, "I did not leave your brother. Your brother, who is a bastard, left me." All this, of course, was internal. For my mother-in-law I tried to think of the time she must have committed adultery. For both my wife and her mother, I thought, "The only thing the matter with the bastard is that all the antifreeze he poured into his radiator last night at Black Jack's has drained out."

It rained all the way back to Wolf Creek, and we were stuck in the gumbo all the way from the Elkhorn to Jim McGregor's ranch house, where the road turned to gravel. Of course, Ken drove the truck and Paul and I pushed. I pushed on an empty stomach. Just before I felt the sides of my stomach collapse, I went around to the driver's side of the cab, and asked, "Ken, how about getting your brother off his mattress to help us push?"

Ken said to me, "You know more about a truck than that. You know I have to have ballast in the rear end, or the rear wheels will just spin and not pull us out of the mud."

I went back to the rear end, and Paul and I pushed the ballast to the ranch house. It was just as hard pushing downhill as uphill. We might as well have been in eastern Montana pushing a half-ton truck plus ballast up the Powder River, where they invented gumbo.

When we reached Wolf Creek, Paul stayed to help me unload the truck, which was overweight with mud and water. We unloaded the mattress last. Then I started for bed, being all in, or maybe being just weak from hunger, and Paul left for Helena. On my way to my room I saw Neal and his mother at the front door. The ballast had put on two red-white-and-blue Davis Cup sweaters. He was lying to his mother who had caught him before he got all the way out. He was in the pink of condition. I knew of two grocery crates who would be glad to see him.

I went to bed and fought off sleep until I collected enough

of my wits to come to a fairly obvious conclusion and to consolidate it into one sentence. "If I don't get out of my wife's home for a few days I am not going to have any wife left." So I telephoned my brother the next morning from the grocery store where no one at the house could hear. I asked him if he didn't have a little time coming yet from his summer vacation, because I needed to be at Seeley Lake for a while.

Seeley Lake is where we have our summer cabin. It is only seventeen miles from the Blackfoot Canyon and not much farther from the Swan, a river beautiful as its name as it floats by the Mission Glaciers. I think my brother still felt yesterday's rain running down his back, when no one moved to let us crawl under the tarp, so he understood what was on my mind. Anyway, he said, "I'll ask the boss."

That night I asked my wife a question—in dealing with her I had a better chance to dominate the situation by asking a question than by making a series of declarative sentences. So I asked my wife, "Don't you think it would be a good idea for Paul and me to spend a few days at Seeley Lake?" She looked right through me and said, "Yes."

I survived the next day and the day following, when Paul and I crossed the Continental Divide and left the world behind, so I thought. But the moment we started flowing into the Pacific, Paul began to tell me about a new girl he had picked up. I listened on my toes, ready to jump in any direction.

I was in the same old box. Maybe he was telling me something I wouldn't like but would dislike less if I heard it first as literature—or maybe I was wasting my time in being suspicious—maybe he was just my brother and a reporter passing on news items to me that were too personal or poetical to be published.

"She's kind of funny," he said, when it was clear we were coasting down the western slope of our continent. "Yes," he said, as though I had commented, "she's kind of funny. The only place she'll let you screw her is in the boys' locker room in the high school gymnasium."

What he said next sounded as if it also were in answer to something I had said, and maybe it was. "Oh, she's got that all figured out. She knows a window in the boys' toilet that's always unlocked and I push her up and then she reaches down and gives me a hand."

The next he said on his own. "She makes you screw her on the rubbing table."

I spent the rest of the way to Seeley Lake trying to figure out whether he was telling me he was in trouble with some dame or whether he was seeing to it that I kept enlarging my mental life even though I had gone off and married. I went on thinking until I noticed that I could smell witch hazel, rubbing alcohol, hot radiators with sweat clothes drying on them, and the insides of boys' lockers that wouldn't be cleaned out until the end of the football season.

I also thought, "It's damn hot right here now. The fishing isn't going to be much good. The fish will all be lying on the bottom." Then I tried to imagine a fish lying on its back on a rubbing table. It was hard to keep things fluid and not to fix on the picture of the fish helping the fisherman through the window in the toilet of the boys' locker room. About then we drove into the big tamaracks where our cabin is. There suddenly it was cool. The tamaracks are from eight to twelve hundred years old, their age and height keeping the heat out. We went swimming even before we unloaded the car.

After we had dressed but before we had combed our hair · we carried out our swimming trunks and were hanging them on a clothes line that runs between two balsams. The line had been put up high where deer couldn't catch their horns in it, so I was standing on my toes trying to get a clothespin to stay when I heard a car turn off the Forest Service road into our lane.

My brother said, "Don't look around."

The car drove right up behind my back and stopped. Its engine panted in the heat. Even though it was panting in the curve of my back I didn't look around. Then somebody fell out of its front door.

When I looked, clothespin still in hand, I saw I had been in error in thinking somebody had fallen out of the front door of the car, because the car had no front door. It had floorboards, though, in the front, and on the floorboards sat a Hills Bros. coffee can, a bottle of 3-7-77, and an open bottle of strawberry pop. In Montana, we don't care whether the whiskey is much good if we can get strawberry pop for a chaser.

Just as if the scene had been taken for a Western film, it was high noon. My brother-in-law nodded in the driver's seat, as he probably had all the way from Wolf Creek.

Old Rawhide picked herself up out of the tamarack needles where she had fallen, took a look around to get reoriented, and then started walking straight for me. She would have walked through my brother if he hadn't reluctantly moved out of the way.

"Glad to meet you," she said to me, reaching out toward my hand that held the clothespin. Mechanically, I shifted the clothespin to the other hand, so she could shake the hand she was reaching for.

Sometimes a thing in front of you is so big you don't know whether to comprehend it by first getting a dim sense of the whole and then fitting in the pieces or by adding up the pieces until something calls out what it is. I put only a few pieces together before my voice called to me, "You'll never make your brother believe you didn't sucker him into this."

"How are you, anyway?" she asked. "I've brought Buster to go fishing with you."

She always called Neal "Buster." She had slept with so many men that the problem of remembering their names boggled her mind. By now all men besides Black Jack, Long Bow, and her two rodeo artists she called Buster, except me—me she just called "you." She could remember me but she could never remember that she had met me.

"Buster hasn't any money anymore," she said. "He needs your help."

Paul said to me, "Help him."

I asked, "How much money does he need?"

"We don't want your money," she said, "We want to go fishing with you."

She was drinking pink whiskey out of a pink paper cup. I went over to the car and asked the window next to the driver's seat, "Do you want to go fishing?"

Clearly, he had memorized a line in case he could not hear. He said, "I would like to go fishing with you and Paul."

I told him, "It's too hot to go fishing now." The dust was still drifting through the woods from the gravel turnoff to our lane.

He repeated, "I would like to go fishing with you and Paul."

Paul said, "Let's go."

I said to Paul, "Let's all get in our car, and I'll drive."

Paul said, "I'll drive," and I said, "OK."

Old Rawhide and Neal didn't like the idea of all of us going in our car. I think they wanted to be alone but they had become frightened or tired of being alone and wanted us somewhere around, though not in the front seat. Paul and I didn't argue. He got in the driver's seat and I sat next to him, and they mumbled to themselves. Finally, she started moving their stuff to our back seat—first the pink pop and then the red Hills Bros. coffee can.

I thought I noticed for the first time that they didn't have a fishing rod with them. If it had been anybody but Paul I would have asked him to hold it a minute while I checked to see if their rods had been left in their car, but for Paul the world of mercy did not include fishermen who left their tackle behind. He was tender to me and quick to offer them help, and would never kick about having to take them fishing at high noon while all the fish were lying at the bottom, but it would be just too damn bad for them if they didn't think enough about fishing to be able to fish when they got there.

They leaned on each other and slept. I was glad I did not have to drive—I had too many things to feel about. For instance, I felt about why women are such a bunch of suckers and how they all want to help some bastard like him—and not me. I felt an especially long time about why, when I tried to help somebody, I ended up offering him money or taking him fishing.

One steep grade and we were out of the pines and the cool chain of lakes and into the glare of Blanchard Flats. Paul asked, "Which way do you want to turn when we get to the junction with the Blackfoot road?" "Up," I said. "The canyon is too rough water for them to fish. Let's turn up to the head of the canyon where there are some fine holes before the river goes into the cliffs." So we left the main road at the head of the flats and bumped over glacial remains until we came to a big fork in the river with Ponderosa pines beside it where we could park our car in the shade.

In the middle of the river where it had forked was a long sand bar. If you could wade out there, you had a perfect fishing spot. Big fish on either side of you, and no sunken logs or big roots or rocks to foul you up when you were landing them—just sand to skid them over so that they scarcely noticed they lay on land until they gasped for water.

Although I had fished this hole many times, I went to take another look at it before I put up my rod. I approached it step by step like an animal that has been shot at before. Once I had rushed down rod in hand to demolish a fish on the first cast and actually had made the first cast when part of the mountain on the other side started falling into the river. I had never seen the bear and he evidently had never seen me until he heard me swear when I was slow in reacting to the first strike. I didn't even know what the bear had been doing—fishing, swimming, drinking. All I know is that he led a landslide up the mountain.

If you have never seen a bear go over the mountain, you have never seen the job reduced to its essentials. Of course, deer are faster, but not going straight uphill. Not even elk have the power in their hindquarters. Deer and elk zigzag and switchback and stop and pose while really catching their breath. The bear leaves the earth like a bolt of lightning retrieving itself and making its thunder backwards.

Paul had his rod up when I got back to the car. He asked me, "Are Neal and his friend coming?" I looked in the back of

the car where they were still asleep, except that they stirred
when I merely looked so maybe they weren't. I said, "Neal,
wake up and tell us what you want to do." Much against his
will, he made fitful efforts to wake up. Finally, he shed Old
Rawhide off his shoulder and got out of the car stiffly,
already an old man. Looking over the bank, he asked, "What
about that hole?" I told him, "It's a good one. In fact, so are
the next four or five."

"Can you wade out to the sand bar?" he asked, and I told
him not usually but it had been so hot lately the river had
dropped a foot or more and he shouldn't have any trouble.

"That's what I'll do, I'll stay here and fish," Neal said. He
never once referred to her. Besides being devoted to the art
of ignoring women, he also knew that Paul and I didn't think
she should be here, so he may have thought if he didn't
mention her we wouldn't notice her.

Old Rawhide woke up and handed Paul the bottle of
3-7-77. "Have a snort," she said. Paul took her hand and
moved it around to where she was offering the drink to Neal.
As I said, for several reasons, including our father, Paul and I
did not drink when we fished. Afterwards, yes, in fact, as soon
as our wet clothes were off and we could stand on them
instead of the pine needles one of us would reach for the
glove compartment in the car where we always carried a
bottle.

If you think what I am about to tell you next is a
contradiction to this, then you will have to realize that in
Montana drinking beer does not count as drinking.

Paul opened the trunk of our car and counted out eight
bottles of beer. He said to Neal, "Four for you and four for us.
We'll sink two of them in each of the next two holes for you.
They'll make you forget the heat." He told them where we
would bury the bottles and then he should have thought
before he told them he would hide our beer in the two
following holes where we would finish fishing on our way
back from the cliffs.

What a beautiful world it was once. At least a river of it was.
And it was almost mine and my family's and just a few others'

who wouldn't steal beer. You could leave beer to cool in the
river, and it would be so cold when you got back it wouldn't
foam much. It would be a beer made in the next town if the
town were ten thousand or over. So it was either Kessler Beer
made in Helena or Highlander Beer made in Missoula that
we left to cool in the Blackfoot River. What a wonderful world
it was once when all the beer was not made in Milwaukee,
Minneapolis, or St. Louis.

We covered the beer with rocks so it wouldn't wash away.
Then we started walking downstream a fishing distance. It
was so hot even Paul was in no great rush. Suddenly he
interrupted the lethargy. "Some day," he said, "Neal is going
to find out about himself and he won't come back to Montana.
He doesn't like Montana."

My only preparation for this remark was that I had seen
him studying Neal's face when he was waking up. I said, "I
know he doesn't like to fish. He just likes to tell women he
likes to fish. It does something for him and the women. And
for the fish, too," I added. "It makes them all feel better."

It was so hot we stopped and sat on a log. When we were
silent we could hear the needles falling like dry leaves.
Suddenly the needles stopped. "I should leave Montana," he
said. "I should go to the West Coast."

I had thought that, too, but I asked, "Why?"

"Here," he said, "I cover local sports and personal items
and the police blotter. I don't have anything to do. Here I will
never have anything to do."

"Except fish and hunt," I told him.

"And get into trouble," he added.

I told him again, "I've told you before I think I could be of
some help if you want to work for a big paper. Then maybe
you could do your own stuff—special features, even some day
your own column."

It was so hot that the mirages on the river melted into each
other. It was hard to know whether the utterances I had
heard were delphic. He said, "Jesus, it's hot. Let's hit the river
and cool off."

He stood and picked up his rod, and his beautiful

silk-wrapped rod shimmered like the air around it. "I'll never leave Montana," he said. "Let's go fishing."

As we separated he said, "And I like the trouble that goes with it." So we were back to where we had started, and it was so hot the fishing just couldn't be any good.

And it wasn't. In the middle of a heat spell death comes to running water at high noon. You cast and cast on top of it, and nothing comes up out of it. Not even frogs jump. You begin to think you are the only moving thing in it. Maybe in the evolutionary process all life migrated from water to dry land, all except you and you are on the way with the part of you not in the water parching in the unaccustomed air. With the sun bouncing back at you from the water and hitting under your eyebrows, even your hat doesn't do any good.

I knew it was going to be tough before I started, so I tried to be extra sharp. I fished in front and back of big rocks where the fish çould be in the shade and the water would bring them food without their having to work for it. I concentrated, too, on the water that slid under bushes where the fish could lie in the shade and wait for insects to hatch in the limbs and drop before them. There was nothing in the shade but shadows.

On the assumption that if an idea doesn't produce anything at all, then the opposite might work, I gave up shade entirely and walked into the open meadow that was crackling with grasshoppers. To one familiar with a subject, there is no trouble to find reasons for the opposite idea. I said to myself, "It is summer and the grasshoppers are out in the sun and the fish will be, too." I put on a cork-bellied fly that looked like one of those big, juicy, yellow hoppers. I fished close to shore where even big fish wait for grasshoppers to make one mistake. After fishing with the floating cork grasshopper, I put on a big fly with a yellow wool body that would absorb water and sink like a dead grasshopper. Still, not even a frog jumped.

The brain gives up a lot less easily than the body, so fly fishermen have developed what they call the "curiosity theory," which is about what it says it is. It is the theory that fish, like men, will sometimes strike at things just to find out what they are and not because they look good to eat. With most fly fishermen, it is the "last resort theory," but it sometimes almost works. I put on a fly that George Croonenberghs had tied for me when he was a kid and several decades before he became one of the finest fly tyers of the West. This fly, tied in a moment of juvenile enthusiasm, had about everything on it from deer hair to fool-hen feathers.

Once when I was fishing on the upper Blackfoot I saw a strange thing with a neck and head being washed downstream while trying to swim straight across. I couldn't figure out what it was until it landed and shook itself. Then I recognized that it was a bobcat, and, in case you don't know what a wet bobcat looks like, it looks like a little wet cat. While this one was wet, it was a skinny, meek little thing, but after it got dry and fluffy again and felt sure that it was a cat once more, it turned around, took a look at me, and hissed.

I hope my old fishing pal, George Croonenberghs, doesn't mind my saying that this juvenile creation of his struggling in the water looked something like the bobcat. Anyway, it looked like something interesting to a fish.

Out of the lifeless and hopeless depths, life appeared. He came so slowly it seemed as if he and history were being made on the way. After a while he got to be ten inches long. He came closer and closer, but beyond a certain point he never got any bigger, so I guess that's how big he was. At what seemed a safe distance, the ten-incher began to circle George's Bobcat Special. I have never seen such large disbelieving eyes in such a little fish. He kept his eyes always on the fly and seemed to let the water circle him around it. Then he turned himself over to gravity and slowly sank. When he got to be about a six-incher he reversed himself and became a ten-incher again to give George's fly a final inspection. Halfway round the circle he took his eye off the fly and saw me and darted out of sight. This undoubtedly is the only time that a fish ever seriously studied George's juvenile creation, although I still carry it with me for sentimental reasons.

I abandoned the curiosity theory, got down on my belly and had a drink of water and was thirstier when I finished. I began to think of that beer, and of quitting this waste of time. In fact, I would have quit and sat in the shade, except that I didn't want to be sitting in the shade when my brother asked, "How many did you get?" and I had to answer, "I went for the horse collar." So I said to myself prayerfully, "I'll try one more hole."

I don't like to pray and not have my prayers come true, so I walked a long way on the bank looking for this last prayerful hole. When I saw it, actually I wasn't looking hard because it was an ordinary piece of water, but when I took a sudden second look I could see that fish were jumping all over it. Almost at the same moment I smelled something, and it smelled bad. In fact, on a hot day it smelled very bad. I didn't want to 'get any closer, but hitherto nonexistent fish were jumping right in front of me. I circled the dead beaver halfway down the bank and made for the water. I knew I was set.

When I saw the dead beaver I knew why the fish were jumping. Even a weekend fisherman would know that the dead beaver had drawn a swarm of bees that were flying low over the ground and water. Being my kind of fisherman, I knew I had the right fly to match them, and I did not think that my brother would. He didn't carry many flies—they were all in his hat band, twenty or twenty-five at the most, but really only four or five kinds, since each one was in several sizes. They were what fishermen call "generals," each a fly with which a skillful fisherman can imitate a good many insects and in different stages from larval to winged. My brother felt about flies much the way my father, who was a fine carpenter, felt about tools—he maintained anybody could make a showing as a carpenter if he had enough tools. But I wasn't a good enough fisherman to be disdainful of tools. I carried a boxful of flies, the "generals" and also what fishermen call the

"specials"—flies that imitate a very specific hatch, such as
flying ants, mayflies, stone flies, spruce bugs. And bees.

I took a fly out of my box that George Croonenberghs had
tied to imitate a bee. It didn't look much like a bee. If you are
starting to be a fly fisherman you better be careful not to
confuse yourself with the fish and buy "counter flies"—flies
that in a drugstore counter look to you like the insect they are
named after. George had a glass tank in his backyard which
he filled with water. Then he would lie under it and study the
insect he was going to imitate floating on top where it doesn't
look like an insect anywhere else. I put on George's Bee that
did not look like a bee, and caught three just like that. They
were nice-sized but not big—fourteen inches or so. Still, I was
grateful to get the horse collar off my neck.

Somehow it's hard to quit with an odd number of fish, so I
wanted one more for four, but I had to work hard to get him.
When I finally did, he was small and I knew that he was the
last and that the rest had got wise to George's Bee. The
increasing heat of the afternoon had the opposite effect on
the dead beaver and he gathered strength, so I climbed the
bank and walked into the wind to the next bend where I could
sit and look downstream for Paul. Now he could ask me, and I
wouldn't be ashamed to be caught sitting in the shade.

I sat there in the hot afternoon trying to forget the beaver
and trying to think of the beer. Trying to forget the beaver, I
also tried to forget my brother-in-law and Old Rawhide. I
knew I was going to have a long time to sit here and forget,
because my brother would never quit with three or four fish,
as I had, and even he was going to have a hard time getting
more. I sat there and forgot and forgot, until what remained
was the river that went by and I who watched. On the river
the heat mirages danced with each other and then they
danced through each other and then they joined hands and
danced around each other. Eventually the watcher joined the
river, and there was only one of us. I believe it was the river.

Even the anatomy of a river was laid bare. Not far downstream was a dry channel where the river had run once,

and part of the way to come to know a thing is through its
death. But years ago I had known the river when it flowed
through this now dry channel, so I could enliven its stony
remains with the waters of memory.

In death it had its pattern, and we can only hope for as
much. Its overall pattern was the favorite serpentine curve of
the artist sketched on the valley from my hill to the last hill I
could see on the other side. But internally it was made of
sharp angles. It ran seemingly straight for a while, turned
abruptly, then ran smoothly again, then met another obstacle,
again was turned sharply and again ran smoothly. Straight
lines that couldn't be exactly straight and angles that couldn't
have been exactly right angles became the artist's most
beautiful curve and swept from here across the valley to
where it could be no longer seen.

I also became the river by knowing how it was made. The
Big Blackfoot is a new glacial river that runs and drops fast.
The river is a straight rapids until it strikes big rocks or big
trees with big roots. This is the turn that is not exactly at right
angles. Then it swirls and deepens among big rocks and
circles back through them where big fish live under the foam.
As it slows, the sand and small rocks it picked up in the fast
rapids above begin to settle out and are deposited, and the
water becomes shallow and quiet. After the deposit is
completed, it starts running again.

On a hot afternoon the mind can also create fish and arrange them according to the way it has just made the river. It will have the fish spend most of their time in the "big blue" at the turn, where they can lie protected by big rocks and take it easy and have food washed to them by big waters. From there, they can move into the fast rapids above when they are really hungry or it is September and cool, but it is hard work living in such fast water all the time. The mind that arranges can also direct the fish into the quiet water in the evening when gnats and small moths come out. Here the fisherman should be told to use his small dry flies and to wax them so they will float. He should also be informed that in quiet evening water everything must be perfect because, with the glare from the sun gone, the fish can see everything, so even a few hairs too many in the tail of the fly can make all the difference. The mind can make all these arrangements, but of course the fish do not always observe them.

Fishermen also think of the river as having been made with them partly in mind, and they talk of it as if it had been. They speak of the three parts as a unity and call it "a hole," and the fast rapids they call "the head of the hole" and the big turn they call "the deep blue" or "pool" and the quiet, shallow water below they call "the tail of the hole," which they think is shallow and quiet so that they can have a place to wade across and "try the other side."

As the heat mirages on the river in front of me danced with and through each other, I could feel patterns from my own life joining with them. It was here, while waiting for my brother, that I started this story, although, of course, at the time I did not know that stories of life are often more like rivers than books. But I knew a story had begun, perhaps long ago near the sound of water. And I sensed that ahead I would meet something that would never erode so there would be a sharp turn, deep circles, a deposit, and quietness.

The fisherman even has a phrase to describe what he does when he studies the patterns of a river. He says he is "reading the water," and perhaps to tell his stories he has to do much the same thing. Then one of his biggest problems is to guess where and at what time of day life lies ready to be taken as a joke. And to guess whether it is going to be a little or a big joke.

For all of us, though, it is much easier to read the waters of tragedy.

"Did you do any good?" The voice and the question suggested that if I woke up and looked around I would see my brother. The suggestion became a certainty when the voice asked, "What the hell are you doing here?"

"Oh, just thinking," I answered, as we all answer when we don't know what we have been doing.

He said it was too hot to fish but he had fished until he caught "a fairly good mess," which meant ten or twelve and just fair-sized. "Let's go and get that beer," he said. When he said "beer," everything else came back to me—the beer, the beaver, the brother-in-law, and his fishing companion.

"God, let's get that beer," I said.

Paul kept spinning a bottle opener around his little finger. We were so dry that we could feel in our ears that we were trying to swallow. For talk, we only repeated the lyric refrain of the summer fisherman, "A bottle of beer would sure taste good."

A game trail cut from the bank to the river where we had left the beer for ourselves, and we went down it stiff-legged. Paul was ahead, and when he got near the bottom he loosened his knees and made for the river. We had buried the beer in moving water to keep it cool but not where the water was so fast it would wash the beer downstream.

"I can't see it," he said, feeling with his feet. "Oh," I said, "you just haven't found the right place. It has to be there." And I waded out to find it for him, already having doubts that I could.

He said, "There's no use looking around. That's where we buried it." He pointed to holes in the clay of the bottom where we had pulled out rocks to cover the bottles. I felt in one of the holes with the toe of my wading boot as if a bottle of beer

might have escaped my attention in a hole the size of a small
rock. He was doing the same thing. There were no bottles of
beer hiding in holes too small for a bottle to get into.

We had been saving our thirst for a long time. Now knee-
deep by the holes in the clay bottom, we cupped our hands
and started drinking out of the river. Between us and the
car there were still three more holes where we had buried
the beer, but we had about quit hoping for beer.

Paul said, "All told, we buried eight bottles of beer in four
holes. Do you think they could have drunk eight bottles of
beer, besides the rest of that 3-7-77?"

He was being gentle, for my sake and for the sake of my
wife and my mother-in-law. But I couldn't argue against
anything he was thinking. Although we had walked back on
the trail, we were always in sight of the river and neither of us
had seen a fisherman. Who else could have taken it?

I said, "Paul, I'm sorry. I wish I knew how I could have
stayed away from this guy."

"You couldn't," he said.

Suddenly we did something that for a time seemed strange
to me, given the fact that we knew without hurrying to look
that all the beer was gone and that we also knew without
evidence who had taken it. Suddenly we turned and came out
of that water with a roar, like two animals as they finish
fording a river, making jumps when the water gets shallower
and bringing waves to shore long after they get there. Later, I
could see easily that our being gentle was for each other and
the roar and the jumps to the shore were for those who had
taken our beer.

The rocks rattled and leaped out of our way as we walked
along the shore. In each of the next three holes we enacted
the rite of staring at the emptiness of stones that have been
rolled aside.

We came then to where in the distance we could see our car
on the bank and where below the river forked with a sandbar
in between.

Nobody had moved the car to keep it in the shade. I could feel how hot it would be if we rubbed against a fender while shedding our wet clothes.

I said, "I don't see them." "I don't either," Paul said.

"They can't be in the car," I said. He added, "Today a dog would die in a car if he were left in it."

Walking fast and watching for them, I wasn't watching where I was going and stumbled over a rock and lit on my elbow which I had stuck out to avoid falling on my rod. I was picking the grit out of my cut when Paul said, "What's on the sandbar?" Still trying to pick the blue-black specks out of my bruise, I said, "Maybe it's the bear."

"What bear?" he asked.

"The bear that went over the mountain," I told him. "That's where he comes down the mountain to drink."

"That's no bear," he said.

I studied the sandbar. "Maybe it's two bears," I suggested.

"It's two, all right," he said, "but it's not bears."

"Why do you keep saying 'it' when it's two?" I asked him.

"It's not bears," he said. "It's red."

"Wait until you see it go up the mountain," I told him. "Then you'll see it's bears. Bears go straight up a mountain."

We were walking very slowly now, as if ready to jump sideways if it moved suddenly.

"It's red," he said, "and it's whatever drank our beer."

I told him, "It isn't even human. It's red as you say."

By now, we had come to an uneasy stop, like animals approaching a waterhole and seeing something in the water where they were going to drink. We didn't snort or paw, but we could feel what it would be like to snort and paw. We had no choice but to go ahead.

We kept going until we knew, but couldn't believe it. "Bear, hell, " Paul said. "It's a bare ass."

"Two bare asses," I said.

"That's what I meant," he said. "It's two bare asses. Both are red."

We kept not believing after we knew. "I'll be a son of a bitch," Paul said. "Me, too," I said to confirm it.

You have never really seen an ass until you have seen two sunburned asses on a sandbar in the middle of a river. Nearly all the rest of the body seems to have evaporated. The body is a large red ass about to blister, with hair on one end of it for a head and feet attached to the other end for legs. By tonight, it will run a fever.

That's the way it looked then, but, when I view it now through the sentimentality of memory, it belongs to a pastoral world where you could take off your clothes, screw a dame in the middle of the river, then roll over on your belly and go to sleep for a couple of hours.

If you tried something like that on the Blackfoot River these days, half the city of Great Falls would be standing on the shore waiting to steal your clothes when you went to sleep. Maybe sooner.

"Hey," Paul yelled with a hand on each side of his mouth. Then he blasted a whistle with a finger from each hand.

"Do you think they are all right?" he asked me. "You used to work every summer in the sun in the Forest Service."

"Well," I told him, "I never knew anybody who died of sunburn, but they sure as hell aren't going to wear any wool underwear for a couple of weeks."

"Let's get them to the car," he said. We took off our baskets and leaned our rods against a log so they could be seen and nobody would step on them.

We had waded almost to the sandbar when Paul stopped and barred me with his arm. "Just a minute," he said. "I want to take another look so I'll always remember."

We stood there for a minute and made an engraving on what little was left of the blank tablets of our minds. It was an engraving in color. In the foreground of the engraving was a red Hills Bros. coffee can, then red tenderized soles of feet pointing downward, two red asses sizzling under the solar system, and in the background a pile of clothes with her red panties on top. To the side were the remains of the 3-7-77, red hot when touched. There was no fishing rod or basket in sight.

Paul said, "May he get three doses of clap, and may he recover from all but the first."

I never again threw a line in this hole, which I came to regard as a kind of wild game sanctuary.

We waded the rest of the way to the sandbar without splashing, fearful of waking them. I think we thought, "When they wake up they will start peeling." I know what I thought. I had worked several summers in rattlesnake country in late August, and I thought when they wake up and find out how hot it is they will shed their skins and be blind for a while and strike at anything they hear. I can remember I kept thinking, they will be very dangerous when they wake up, so I walked around them warily, staying beyond striking distance.

When we got close to them, they developed anatomical parts that couldn't be seen from shore. They developed legs between their asses and their feet, and they sprouted backs and necks, especially necks, between their asses and their hair. It was red into their hair, which was curly. It was hard to know whether their hair was naturally curly or whether it had frizzled in the sun. Each hair was distinct and could have been made with a hot curling iron.

Paul had gone over to see what was left in the bottle of 3-7-77, but I stayed to study the anatomy. Each hair was sore at its root, but that's not what I backed off to tell Paul. I was so studious I backed off until I bumped into him.

"She's got a tattoo on her ass," I told him.

"No kidding," he said.

He circled her as if to get on the downwind side of big game before trying to approach it. Then he backed off and completed the circle back to me.

"What are the initials of her cowboys?" he asked. "B. I. and B. L.," I told him.

He said, "Are you sure?"

I said, "Sure, I'm sure."

"Well," he said, "they don't fit, because she has LO tattooed on one cheek of her ass and VE on the other."

I told him, "LOVE spells love, with a hash-mark between."

"I'll be damned," he said, and backed away, circled around and started to study the situation all over again.

She jumped straight up like a barber pole. She was red, white, and blue. She was white where she had been lying on her belly in the sand, and her back completed the patriotic color scheme, red into her hair except for the blue-black tattoo. Somebody should have spun her around and played "The Stars and Stripes Forever."

She looked wildly about her to get oriented, and then streaked for the clothes pile and pulled on her red panties. When she was sure you couldn't look without paying at the part that made her living, she relaxed. She didn't put on any more clothes, but came sauntering back, took one look at me, and said, "Oh, it's you."

Then she looked at both of us, and said, "Well, what's on your mind, boys?" She was ready to entertain company.

I said, "We came out to get Neal."

She was disappointed. "Oh," she said, "you mean Buster."

I said, "I mean him," and when I pointed at him he groaned. I think he did not want to wake up and find out about his sunburn and hangover. He groaned again and sank even deeper into the sand. Her white belly was covered with sand, and had creases in it where her skin had folded over when she was lying on it. Sand ran out of her navel.

Paul said, "Get your clothes on and help us with him." She looked indignant. She said, "I can take care of him." Paul said, "You already have."

She said, "He's my man. I can take care of him. The sun doesn't bother me." And I suppose she was right—it's under the sun where a fisherman's whore makes her money.

Paul said, "Get your clothes on or I'll kick you in the ass." Both she and I knew he meant it.

Paul went over to the clothes pile and started separating out Neal's clothes from hers. They were in the order in which they had come off. That's why her red pants were on top of the pile, and her belt on the bottom.

I said to Paul, "That's a good thing to do, but we can't put any clothes on him. I don't think he can stand their touch."

"We'll take him home naked, then," Paul said.

When Neal heard the word "home" he sat up so suddenly that the sand ran off him in streams.

"I don't want to go home," he said.

"Where do you want to go, Neal?" I asked. "I don't know," he said, "but I don't want to go home."

I told him, "There are three women there who know how to take care of you."

"I don't want to see three women," he said, and more sand ran off him.

Old Rawhide held her clothes under one arm. I reached down, picked up Neal's clothes, and put them under his arm. "Here," I said, taking his other arm, "I'll help you wade back to shore."

He jumped away in pain. "Don't touch me," he said. To Old Rawhide he said, "You carry my clothes. They hurt when I hold them."

"You take them," she said to me, and I did, and she took Neal by the arm he had pulled away from me and led him to the edge of the water. Part way out, she turned around and said to me, "He's my man." She was a strong woman and very tough. The Blackfoot is a big river and hard to wade. The man couldn't have made it without the strength in her legs.

Part way across Paul turned around and went back for what was left of the bottle of 3-7-77. After Old Rawhide got Neal all the way across she left him feeling his way through the rocks with his tenderized feet, and waded back to the sandbar. Her feet were tenderized, too, but she waded back to the sandbar to get the Hills Bros. coffee can.

I met her on the shore when she returned.

"What's good about the coffee can?" I asked her.

"I don't know," she said. "But Buster always likes to have it with him."

There was a light blanket on the back seat of the car that we used to spread on the ground when we were going to have a picnic. Fir needles had stuck on it. We put Neal and Old Rawhide in the back seat and threw the light blanket over them—probably for several reasons. Probably to keep them from getting further burned, especially by the wind, and probably also so the state police wouldn't arrest us for indecent exposure. But the moment the blanket touched their shoulders, they writhed until it fell off. So we drove to Wolf Creek, completely exposed to the elements and the police.

Neal never sat up straight, but he murmured from time to time, "I don't want to see three women." Each time he murmured this, Old Rawhide would sit up straight and say, "Don't worry. I'm your woman. I'll take care of you." I was driving. Each time he murmured this, I took a firm grip on the wheel. I didn't want to see three women either.

For most of the trip Paul and I didn't speak to each other or to them. We just let one murmur through his armpit and the other jump up straight and then recede into the clothes pile. But as we neared Wolf Creek I could feel Paul getting ready to change the format. Slowly his body shifted until he could reach to the back seat. A murmur came again, "I don't want to go home." Paul reached and grabbed the arm that belonged to the armpit, and pulled him up. The arm turned white, even when it was sunburned. "You're almost home," Paul said. "There's no other place you can go." There were no more murmurs. Paul kept holding the arm.

The whore was still tough, and she and Paul got into a big argument. Paul was used to talking to tough women and she was used to tough talk. The argument was over whether we were going to dump her as soon as we got to town or whether she was going to stay and take care of Buster. Mostly what was said was, "God damn you, I am," and "God damn you, you're not." He said to me, as part of the argument, "When you get to town, stop at the log dance hall."

The log dance hall was the first building at the edge of town. It was a good place to have fights, and there had been plenty of them there, especially on Saturday nights—every time some home-town drunk from Wolf Creek tried to dance

with the girl of some drunk who had come from the Dearborn
country.

You couldn't tell by the profanity who was winning the
argument, but as we got closer to town she would reach into
the clothes pile and put some of it on her. There is a bend in
the creek and the road just before you get to the log dance
hall. When she saw the bend, she realized she wouldn't have
all her clothes on by the time we reached the dance hall, so she
scurried through the pile grabbing the rest that belonged to
her.

Just as I stopped the car, she made one wild grab into the
pile, opened the door of the car and jumped out. She was on
the opposite side of the car from Paul, and must have figured
that would give her a big enough head start. She left the back
door swinging and took a good hold on the clothes in her
arms. At the top of the clothes in her arms was Neal's
underwear, which she had taken either by accident or for a
keepsake. She made one more grunt as she tightened her
hold on her belongings, like a packer throwing a double
diamond hitch just to be sure the whole load will stick
together on the rough trip ahead.

Then she said to my brother, "You stinking bastard."

Paul came out of that car as if the body of it had fallen off,
and took after her.

I think I knew how he felt. Much as he hated her, he really
had no strong feeling about her. It was the bastard in the back
seat without any underwear that he hated. The bastard who
had ruined most of our summer fishing. The bait-fishing
bastard. The bait-fishing bastard who had violated everything
that our father had taught us about fishing by bringing a
whore and a coffee can of worms but not a rod. The
bait-fishing bastard who had screwed his whore in the middle
of our family river. And after drinking our beer. The bastard
right in the back of the car who was untouchable because of
three Scotch women.

She was running barefoot and trying to hang on to the rest
of her clothes and his underwear, so Paul caught up to her in

about ten jumps. On the run he kicked her, I think, right where the "LO" and the "VE" came together. For several seconds both of her feet trailed behind her in the air. It was to become a frozen moment of memory.

When I could move, I took two quick looks at my brother-in-law, and counted to four. The four was for those four women in the street ready to protect him—one in the middle of the street and three in a house part way down it.

Suddenly, I developed a passion to kick a woman in the ass. I was never aware of such a passion before, but now it overcame me. I jumped out of the car, and caught up to her, but she had been kicked in the ass before and by experts, so I missed her completely. Still, I felt better for the effort.

Paul and I stood together and watched her high-tail it down the road through town. She had no choice. She lived on the other side of a town which is in a narrow gulch. After she got near home, she stopped several times to look back, and Paul and I didn't like what we couldn't hear she was saying. Each of these times we pretended that we were going to start after her again, and she edged closer to her shack. Finally, she and her clothes pile disappeared, and we were left with the back seat. "Now we haven't anything left to do but take him home," my brother said. As we walked back to the car, he added, "You're in trouble." "I know, I know," I said. But I didn't really know. I still didn't know what Scottish women look like when they struggle to keep their pride and haven't much reason left to keep it. In case you have any doubts, they keep it.

Even Neal tried to pull himself together. He tried to put on some clothes before the women saw him. He piled his clothes outside the car, and, when he couldn't find his underwear, he started trying to get into his pants, but he stumbled and kept stumbling. He held his pants out in front of him and tried to catch up to them. He was stumbling so fast he was running after them, but he never got any closer to them than an arm's length.

He was breathless when we caught him and he gasped when we put on his pants. His feet were too swollen for shoes.

We put his shirt over his shoulders with its tails hanging out. When we brought him into the house, he looked like something shipwrecked we had found on an island.

Florence came out of the kitchen and when she saw what Paul and I had, she began drying her hands on her dish towel.

"What have you done to my boy?" she asked the brothers who were holding him up.

Jessie then followed from the kitchen when she heard her mother. She was tall and red-headed anyway, and I was shrunken before her from trying to hold up her brother.

"You bastard," she said to me. The bastard I was holding weighed a ton.

"No," Paul said.

"Get out of the way," I told her. "We have to put him to bed."

"He's badly sunburned," Paul said.

The women I was brought up with never stood around trying on different life styles when there was something to be done, especially something medical. Most people have an immediate chemical reaction to shrink from pain or disfigurement, but the women I was brought up with were magnetized by the medical.

"Let's get him undressed," Florence said, backing to the bedroom door and holding it open.

"I'll find Dotty," Jessie said. Dotty was the registered nurse.

Neal didn't want his mother to undress him and his mother thought we were clumsy and kept pushing us away. Before a situation could develop, Jessie was in the bedroom with Dorothy. I didn't know how a nurse could get into a uniform so fast, but I could hear the swish of starch as she came through the door. When Neal heard the starch, he stopped wriggling away from us. Dorothy was short and powerful and Jessie and her mother were tall and skinny, but strong. Paul and I stood by the bed wondering why we hadn't been able to get off a pair of pants and a shirt. In an instant he was a red carcass on a white sheet.

In almost the same instant Paul and I, who held the world

in our hands when we held a four-and-a-half-ounce fishing rod, were not even orderlies. We were left to one side as if we couldn't warm water or find a bandage or bring it in if we found it.

The first time Jessie passed me she made a point of saying, "Get out of the way." I knew she hadn't liked it when I had said it to her.

By chemical reaction, Paul and I backed for the bedroom door, but he beat me to it and was on his way to Black Jack's for a drink, which I needed, too. I didn't get the bedroom door closed, though, before I was to be visited by three women.

As soon as Florence saw her boy in red she came close to knowing what the score was. With Scottish women, the medical barely precedes the moral. She took another look to make sure that Dorothy had taken charge, and then she called to me.

She stood in front of me as rigid as if she were posing for the nineteenth-century Scottish photographer David Octavius Hill. Her head might have been held for the slow exposure by an unseen rod behind her neck. "Tell me," she said, "how does it happen that he is burned from head to foot?"

I wasn't going to tell her, and I wasn't going to lie if for no reason other than that I knew I couldn't get away with it. I had long ago learned, sometimes to my sorrow, that Scottish piety is accompanied by a complete foreknowledge of sin. That's what we mean by original sin—we don't have to do it to know about it.

I told her, "He didn't feel like going fishing with us, and when we got back he was lying asleep in the sand."

She knew I wasn't going to go beyond that. Finally the nineteenth-century photographer released her neck from the brace. "I love you," she said, and I knew she couldn't think of anything else to say. I also knew she meant it. "Why don't you get out of here?" she added.

"Wait," Dorothy said to me, and turned her job over to Florence. Dorothy and I were the ones who had married into the family and often had the feeling that if we didn't hang together we would be strung up separately. "Don't worry about him," she said. "Second-degree burn. Blisters. Peeling. Fever. A couple of weeks. Don't worry about him. Don't worry about us. We women can handle it.

"In fact," she said, "why don't you and Paul get out of here? We have Ken and he can do anything and Neal is his brother.

"Besides," she said, "I think you aren't even wanted here. All you can do is stand around and watch, and right now nobody in the family wants to be watched."

Although she was short, she had big hands. She took one of mine in one of hers, and put on the pressure. I thought that was her good-bye and turned to go, but she pulled me back and gave me a fast kiss and was on the job again.

It seemed as if the women had agreed on some kind of a shuttle system whereby two were always working on Neal and one on me. "Wait," Jessie said, before I had closed the door behind me.

A man is at a disadvantage talking to a woman as tall as he is, and I had tried long and hard to overcome this handicap.

"You don't like him, do you?" she asked.

"Woman," I asked, "can't I love you without liking him?"

She just stood looking at me, so I went on talking and saying more than I had intended. I said things she already knew, but possibly one thing she wanted to hear again. "Jessie," I said, "you know I don't know any card tricks. I don't like him. I never will. But I love you. Don't keep testing me, though, by giving me no choices. Jessie, don't let him ..." I stopped from going on because I knew I should have found a shorter way to say what I had already said.

"Don't let him what?" she asked. "What were you going to say?"

"I can't remember what I was going to say," I replied, "except that I feel I have lost touch with you."

"I am trying to help someone," she said. "Someone in my family. Don't you understand?"

I said, "I should understand."

"I am not able to help," she said.

"I should understand that, too," I said.

"We are talking too long," she said. "Why don't you and Paul go back to the Blackfoot and finish your fishing trip? You're no help here. But wherever you go, never lose touch with me."

Although she said we had talked too long, she took only one backward step. "Tell me," she asked, "why is he burned from head to foot?" When it comes to asking questions, Scottish daughters are almost complete recapitulations of their mothers.

I told her what I had told her mother, and she looked like her mother while she listened.

"Tell me," she said, "just before you brought Neal in, did you happen to see the whore run through town with an armful of clothes?"

"At a distance," I told her.

"Tell me," she asked, "if my brother comes back next summer, will you try to help me help him?"

It took a long time to say it, but I said it. I said, "I will try."

Then she said, "He won't come back." Then she added, "Tell me, why is it that people who want help do better without it—at least, no worse. Actually, that's what it is, no worse. They take all the help they can get, and are just the same as they always have been."

"Except that they are sunburned," I said.

"That's no different," she said.

"Tell me," I asked her, "if your brother comes back next summer, will we both try to help him?"

"If he comes back," she nodded. I thought I saw tears in her eyes but I was mistaken. In all my life, I was never to see her cry. And also he was never to come back.

Without interrupting each other, we both said at the same time, "Let's never get out of touch with each other." And we never have, although her death has come between us.

She said, "Get out of the way," only this time she smiled when she said it. Then she started closing the door in my face.

When there was only a crack left, we kissed, and with one eye I tried to look around her. They had him greased from head to foot like a roasting ear of corn. They had enough bandages open to go on from there and wrap him up for a mummy.

I went down to Black Jack's and had a drink with Paul, and then we had another. He insisted on paying for both and on going back to the Blackfoot that night. He said, "I asked for a couple of days off, so I have another day coming." Then he insisted we go by way of Missoula and spend the night with father and mother. "Maybe," he said, "we can get the old man to go fishing with us tomorrow." Then he insisted on driving.

Our customary roles had been reversed, and I was the brother who was being taken fishing for the healing effects of cool waters. He knew I was being blamed for Neal, and he may well have thought my marriage was breaking up. He had heard me called a bastard, and he was out of the house when I and the three Scottish women publicly declared our love for each other, given the restrictions Scots put on such public declarations. Actually, I was feeling lordly with love and several times broke into laughter that I can't explain otherwise, but he could have thought I was trying to be brave about having made a mess of my life. I don't really know what he thought, but he was as tender as I usually tried to be to him.

On the way he said, "Mother will be glad to see us, too. But she gets excited when we show up without telling her ahead of time, so let's stop at Lincoln and telephone."

"You call her," I said. "She loves to hear you."

"Fine," he said, "but you ask father to come fishing with us."

So he made the arrangements for what turned out to be our last fishing trip together. He thought of all of us.

Even though we telephoned, Mother was excited when we got to Missoula. She tried to wring her hands in her apron, hug Paul, and laugh, all at the same time. Father stood in the background and just laughed. I still felt lordly and I just stood in the background. Whenever we had a family reunion, Mother and Paul were always the central attraction. He would lean back when he hugged her and laugh, but the best she could do was to hug and try to laugh.

It was late when we arrived in Missoula. We had been careful not to eat on the way, although there is a good restaurant in Lincoln, because we knew that, if we ate there, we would have to eat all over again in Missoula. Early in the dinner, Mother was especially nice to me, since she hadn't paid much attention to me so far, but soon she was back with fresh rolls, and she buttered Paul's.

"Here is your favorite chokecherry jelly," she said, passing it to him. She was a fine cook of wild berries and wild game, and she always had chokecherry jelly waiting for him. Somewhere along the line she had forgotten that it was I who liked chokecherry jelly, a gentle confusion that none of her men minded.

My father and mother were in retirement now, and neither one liked "being out of things," especially my mother, who was younger than my father and was used to "running the church." To them, Paul was the reporter, their chief contact with reality, the recorder of the world that was leaving them and that they had never known very well anyway. He had to tell them story after story, even though they did not approve of some of them. We sat around the table a long time. As we started to get up, I said to Father, "We'd appreciate it if you would go fishing with us tomorrow."

"Oh," my father said and sat down again, automatically unfolded his napkin, and asked, "Are you sure, Paul, that you want me? I can't fish some of those big holes anymore. I can't wade anymore."

Paul said, "Sure I want you. Whenever you can get near fish, you can catch them."

To my father, the highest commandment was to do whatever his sons wanted him to do, especially if it meant to go fishing. The minister looked as if his congregation had just asked him to come back and preach his farewell sermon over again.

It was getting to be after their bedtime, and it had been a

long day for Paul and me, so I thought I'd help Mother with
the dishes and then we'd turn in for the night. But I really
knew that things weren't going to be that simple, and they
knew it, too. Paul gave himself a stretch as soon as it was not
immediately after dinner, and said, "I think I'll run over town
and see some old pals. I'll be back before long, but don't wait
up for me."

I helped my mother with the dishes. Although only one had
left, all the voices had gone. He had stayed long enough after
dinner for us to think he would be happy spending an
evening at home. Each of us knew some of his friends, and all
of us knew his favorite pal, who was big and easy and nice to
us, especially to Mother. He had just got out of prison. His
second stretch.

From the time my mother stood looking at the closed doors
until she went to bed, she said only, "Goodnight." She said it
over her shoulder near the head of the stairs to both my
father and me.

I never could tell how much my father knew about my
brother. I generally assumed that he knew a good deal
because there is a substantial minority in every church
congregation who regard it as their Christian duty to keep the
preacher informed about the preacher's kids. Also, at times,
my father would start to talk to me about Paul as if he were
going to open up a new subject and then he would suddenly
put a lid on it before the subject spilled out.

"Did you hear what Paul did lately?" he asked.

I told him, "I don't understand you. I hear all kinds of
things about Paul. Mostly, I hear he's a fine reporter and a
fine fisherman."

"No, no," my father said. "But haven't you heard what he
does afterwards?"

I shook my head.

Then I think he had another thought about what he was
thinking, and swerved from what he was going to say.
"Haven't you heard," he asked me, "that he has changed his

spelling of our name from Maclean to MacLean. Now he spells it with a capital L."

"Oh, sure," I said. "I knew all about that. He told me he got tired of nobody spelling his name right. They even wrote his paychecks with a capital L, so he finally decided to give up and spell his name the way others do."

My father shook his head at my explanation, its truth being irrelevant. He murmured both to himself and to me, "It's a terrible thing to spell our name with a capital L. Now somebody will think we are Scottish Lowlanders and not Islanders."

He went to the door and looked out and when he came back he didn't ask me any questions. He tried to tell me. He spoke in the abstract, but he had spent his life fitting abstractions to listeners so that listeners would have no trouble fitting his abstractions to the particulars of their lives.

"You are too young to help anybody and I am too old," he said. "By help I don't mean a courtesy like serving choke-cherry jelly or giving money.

"Help," he said, "is giving part of yourself to somebody who comes to accept it willingly and needs it badly.

"So it is," he said, using an old homiletic transition, "that we can seldom help anybody. Either we don't know what part to give or maybe we don't like to give any part of ourselves. Then, more often than not, the part that is needed is not wanted. And even more often, we do not have the part that is needed. It is like the auto-supply shop over town where they always say, 'Sorry, we are just out of that part.'"

I told him, "You make it too tough. Help doesn't have to be anything that big."

He asked me, "Do you think your mother helps him by buttering his rolls?"

"She might," I told him. "In fact, yes, I think she does."

"Do you think you help him?" he asked me.

"I try to," I said. "My trouble is I don't know him. In fact, one of my troubles is that I don't even know whether he needs help. I don't know, that's my trouble."

"That should have been my text," my father said. "We are willing to help, Lord, but what if anything is needed?

"I still know how to fish," he concluded. "Tomorrow we will go fishing with him."

I lay waiting a long time before finally falling asleep. I felt the rest of the upstairs was also waiting.

Usually, I get up early to observe the commandment observed by only some of us—to arise early to see as much of the Lord's daylight as is given to us. I several times heard my brother open my door, study my covers, and then close my door. I began waking up by remembering that my brother, no matter what, was never late for work or fishing. One step closer to waking and I remembered that this was the trip when my brother was taking care of me. Now it began to seep into me that he was making my breakfast, and, when this became a matter of knowledge, I got up and dressed. All three were sitting at the table, drinking tea and waiting.

Mother said, as if she had wakened to find herself Queen for a Day, "Paul made breakfast for us." This made him feel good enough to smile early in the morning, but when he was serving me I looked closely and could see the blood vessels in his eyes. A fisherman, though, takes a hangover as a matter of course—after a couple of hours of fishing, it goes away, all except the dehydration, but then he is standing all day in water.

We somehow couldn't get started that morning. After Paul and I had left home, Father put away his fishing tackle, probably thinking he was putting it away for good, so now he couldn't remember where. Mother had to find most of the things for him. She knew nothing about fishing or fishing tackle, but she knew how to find things, even when she did not know what they looked like.

Paul, who usually got everyone nervous by being impatient to be on the stream, kept telling Father, "Take it easy. It's turned cooler. We'll make a killing today. Take it easy." But my father, from whom my brother had inherited his impatience to have his flies on water, would look at me visibly loathing himself for being old and not able to collect himself.

My mother had to go from basement to attic and to most closets in between looking for a fishing basket while she made lunches for three men, each of whom wanted a different kind of sandwich. After she got us in the car, she checked each car door to see that none of her men would fall out. Then she dried her hands in her apron, although her hands were not wet, and said, "Thank goodness," as we drove away.

I was at the wheel, and I knew before we started just where we were going. It couldn't be far up the Blackfoot, because we were starting late, and it had to be a stretch of water of two or three deep holes for Paul and me and one good hole with no bank too steep for Father to crawl down. Also, since he couldn't wade, the good fishing water had to be on his side of the river. They argued while I drove, although they knew just as well as I did where we had to go, but each one in our family considered himself the leading authority on how to fish the Blackfoot River. When we came to the side road going to the river above the mouth of Belmont Creek, they spoke in unison for the first time. "Turn here," they said, and, as if I were following their directions, I turned to where I was going anyway.

The side road brought us down to a flat covered with ground boulders and cheat grass. No livestock grazed on it, and grasshoppers took off like birds and flew great distances, because on this flat it is a long way between feeding grounds, even for grasshoppers. The flat itself and its crop of boulders are the roughly ground remains of one of geology's great disasters. The flat may well have been the end of the ice age lake, half as big as Lake Michigan, that in places was two thousand feet deep until the glacial dam broke and this hydraulic monster of the hills charged out on to the plains of eastern Washington. High on the mountains above where we stopped to fish are horizontal scars slashed by passing icebergs.

I had to be careful driving toward the river so I wouldn't

high-center the car on a boulder and break the crankcase. The flat ended suddenly and the river was down a steep bank, blinking silver through the trees and then turning to blue by comparing itself to a red and green cliff. It was another world to see and feel, and another world of rocks. The boulders on the flat were shaped by the last ice age only eighteen or twenty thousand years ago, but the red and green precambrian rocks beside the blue water were almost from the basement of the world and time.

We stopped and peered down the bank. I asked my father, "Do you remember when we picked a lot of red and green rocks down there to build our fireplace? Some were red mudstones with ripples on them."

"Some had raindrops on them," he said. His imagination was always stirred by the thought that he was standing in ancient rain spattering on mud before it became rocks.

"Nearly a billion years ago," I said, knowing what he was thinking.

He paused. He had given up the belief that God had created all there was, including the Blackfoot River, on a six-day work schedule, but he didn't believe that the job so taxed God's powers that it took Him forever to complete.

"Nearly *half* a billion years ago," he said as his contribution to reconciling science and religion. He hurried on, not wishing to waste any part of old age in debate, except over fishing. "We carried those big rocks up the bank," he said, "but now I can't crawl down it. Two holes below, though, the river comes out in the open and there is almost no bank. I'll walk down there and fish, and you fish the first two holes. I'll wait in the sun. Don't hurry."

Paul said, "You'll get 'em," and all of a sudden Father was confident in himself again. Then he was gone.

We could catch glimpses of him walking along the bank of the river which had been the bottom of the great glacial lake. He held his rod straight in front of him and every now and then he lunged forward with it, perhaps reenacting some glacial race memory in which he speared a hairy ice age mastodon and ate him for breakfast.

Paul said, "Let's fish together today." I knew then that he was still taking care of me, because we almost always split up when we fished. "That's fine," I said. "I'll wade across and fish the other side," he said. I said, "Fine," again, and was doubly touched. On the other side you were backed against cliffs and trees, so it was mostly a roll-casting job, never my specialty. Besides, the river was powerful here with no good place to wade, and next to fishing Paul liked swimming rivers with his rod in his hand. It turned out he didn't have to swim here, but as he waded sometimes the wall of water rose to his upstream shoulder while it would be no higher than his hip behind him. He stumbled to shore from the weight of water in his clothes, and gave me a big wave.

I came down the bank to catch fish. Cool wind had blown in from Canada without causing any electric storms, so the fish should be off the bottom and feeding again. When a deer comes to water, his head shoots in and out of his shoulders to see what's ahead, and I was looking all around to see what fly to put on. But I didn't have to look further than my neck or my nose. Big clumsy flies bumped into my face, swarmed on my neck and wiggled in my underwear. Blundering and soft-bellied, they had been born before they had brains. They had spent a year under water on legs, had crawled out on a rock, had become flies and copulated with the ninth and tenth segments of their abdomens, and then had died as the first light wind blew them into the water where the fish circled excitedly. They were a fish's dream come true—stupid, succulent, and exhausted from copulation. Still, it would be hard to know what gigantic portion of human life is spent in this same ratio of years under water on legs to one premature, exhausted moment on wings.

I sat on a log and opened my fly box. I knew I had to get a fly that would match these flies exactly, because when a big hatch like this or the salmon fly is out, the fish won't touch anything else. As proof, Paul hadn't had a strike yet, so far as I could see.

I figured he wouldn't have the right fly, and I knew I had it. As I explained earlier, he carried all his flies in his hat-band.

He thought that with four or five generals in different sizes he could imitate the action of nearly any aquatic or terrestrial insect in any stage from larval to winged. He was always kidding me because I carried so many flies. "My, my," he would say, peering into my fly box, "wouldn't it be wonderful if a guy knew how to use ten of all those flies." But I've already told you about the Bee, and I'm still sure that there are times when a general won't turn a fish over. The fly that would work now had to be a big fly, it had to have a yellow, black-banded body, and it had to ride high in the water with extended wings, something like a butterfly that has had an accident and can't dry its wings by fluttering in the water.

It was so big and flashy it was the first fly I saw when I opened my box. It was called a Bunyan Bug, tied by a fly tyer in Missoula named Norman Means, who ties a line of big flashy flies all called Bunyan Bugs. They are tied on big hooks, No. 2's and No. 4's, have cork bodies with stiff horsehair tied crosswise so they ride high in the water like dragonflies on their backs. The cork bodies are painted different colors and then are shellacked. Probably the biggest and flashiest of the hundred flies my brother made fun of was the Bunyan Bug No. 2 Yellow Stone Fly.

I took one look at it and felt perfect. My wife, my mother-in-law, and my sister-in-law, each in her somewhat obscure style, had recently redeclared their love for me. I, in

my somewhat obscure style, had returned their love. I might
never see my brother-in-law again. My mother had found my
father's old tackle and once more he was fishing with us. My
brother was taking tender care of me, and not catching any
fish. I was about to make a killing.

It is hard to cast Bunyan Bugs into the wind because the
cork and horsehair make them light for their bulk. But,
though the wind shortens the cast, it acts at the same time to
lower the fly slowly and almost vertically to the water with no
telltale splash. My Stone Fly was still hanging over the water
when what seemed like a speedboat went by it, knocked it
high into the air, circled, opened the throttle wide on the
returning straight away, and roared over the spot marked X
where the Stone Fly had settled. Then the speedboat turned
into a submarine, disappearing with all on board including
my fly, and headed for deep water. I couldn't throw line into
the rod fast enough to keep up with what was disappearing
and I couldn't change its course. Not being as fast as what was
under water, I literally forced it into the air. From where I
was I suppose I couldn't see what happened, but my heart was
at the end of the line and telegraphed back its impressions as
it went by. My general impression was that marine life had
turned into a rodeo. My particular information was that a
large Rainbow had gone sun-fishing, turning over twice in the
air, hitting my line each time and tearing loose from the fly
which went sailing out into space. My distinct information was
that it never looked around to see. My only close-at-hand
information was that when the line was reeled in, there was
nothing on the end of it but some cork and some hairs from a
horse's tail.

The stone flies were just as thick as ever, fish still swirled
in quiet water, and I was a little smarter. I don't care much
about taking instructions, even from myself, but before I
made the next cast I underlined the fact that big Rainbows
sometimes come into quiet waters because aquatic insects
hatch in or near quiet waters. "Be prepared," I said to myself,
remembering an old war song. I also accepted my own advice

to have some extra coils of line in my left hand to take some of
the tension off the first run of the next big Rainbow swirling
in quiet water.

So on this wonderful afternoon when all things came
together it took me one cast, one fish, and some reluctantly
accepted advice to attain perfection. I did not miss another.

From then on I let them run so far that sometimes they
surged clear across the river and jumped right in front of
Paul.

When I was young, a teacher had forbidden me to say
"more perfect" because she said if a thing is perfect it can't be
more so. But by now I had seen enough of life to have
regained my confidence in it. Twenty minutes ago I had felt
perfect, but by now my brother was taking off his hat and
changing flies every few casts. I knew he didn't carry any such
special as a Bunyan Bug No. 2 Yellow Stone Fly. I had five or
six big Rainbows in my basket which began to hurt my
shoulder so I left it behind on shore. Once in a while I looked
back and smiled at the basket. I could hear it thumping on the
rocks and falling on its side. However I may have violated
grammar, I was feeling more perfect with every Rainbow.

Just after my basket gave an extra large thump there was an
enormous splash in the water to the left of where I was
casting. "My God," I thought before I could look, "there's
nothing that big that swims in the Blackfoot," and, when I
dared look, there was nothing but a large circle that got
bigger and bigger. Finally the first wave went by my knees. "It
must be a beaver," I thought. I was waiting for him to surface
when something splashed behind me. "My God," I said again,
"I would have seen a beaver swim by me under water." While
I was wrenching my neck backwards, the thing splashed right
in front of me, too close for comfort but close enough so I
could watch what was happening under water. The silt was
rising from the bottom like smoke from the spot where
lightning had struck. A fair-sized rock was sitting in the spot
where the smoke was rising.

While I was relating my past to the present rock, there was

another big splash in front of me, but this time I didn't bother to jump.

Beaver, hell! Without looking, I knew it was my brother. It didn't happen often in this life, only when his fishing partner was catching fish and he couldn't. It was a sight, however rare, that he could not bear to watch. So he would spoil his partner's hole, even if it was his brother's. I looked up just in time to see a fair-sized boulder come out of the sky and I ducked too late to keep it from splashing all over me.

He had his hat off and he shook his fist at me. I knew he had fished around his hat band before he threw the rocks. I shook my fist back at him, and waded to shore, where my basket was still thumping. In all my life, I had got the rock treatment only a couple of times before. I was feeling more perfect than ever.

I didn't mind that he spoiled the hole before I had filled my basket, because there was another big hole between us and father. It was a beautiful stretch of water, against cliffs and in shadows. The hole I had just fished was mostly in sunlight— the weather had become cooler, but was still warm enough so that the hole ahead in shadows should be even better than the one in sunlight and I should have no trouble finishing off my basket with a Bunyan Bug No. 2 Yellow Stone Fly.

Paul and I walked nearly the length of the first hole before we could hear each other yell across the river. I knew he hated to be heard yelling, "What were they biting on?" The last two words, "biting on," kept echoing across the water and pleased me.

When the echoes ceased, I yelled back, "Yellow stone flies." These words kept saying themselves until they subsided into sounds of the river. He kept turning his hat round and round in his hands.

I possibly began to get a little ashamed of myself. "I caught them on a Bunyan Bug," I yelled. "Do you want one?"

"No," he yelled before "want one" had time to echo. Then "want one" and "no" passed each other on the back turns.

"I'll wade across with one," I said through the cup of my hands. That's a lot to say across a river, and the first part of it returning met the last part of it just starting. I didn't know whether he had understood what I had said, but the river still answered, "No."

While I was standing in quiet, shady water, I half noticed that no stone flies were hatching, and I should have thought longer about what I saw but instead I found myself thinking about character. It seems somehow natural to start thinking about character when you get ahead of somebody, especially about the character of the one who is behind. I was thinking of how, when things got tough, my brother looked to himself to get himself out of trouble. He never looked for any flies from me. I had a whole round of thoughts on this subject before I returned to reality and yellow stone flies. I started by thinking that, though he was my brother, he was sometimes knot-headed. I pursued this line of thought back to the Greeks who believed that not wanting any help might even get you killed. Then I suddenly remembered that my brother was almost always a winner and often because he didn't borrow flies. So I decided that the response we make to character on any given day depends largely on the response fish are making to character on the same day. And thinking of the response of fish, I shifted rapidly back to reality, and said to myself, "I still have one more hole to go."

I didn't get a strike and I didn't see a stone fly and it was the same river as the one above, where I could have caught my limit a few minutes before if my brother hadn't thrown rocks in it. My prize Bunyan Bug began to look like a fake to me as well as to the fish. To me, it looked like a floating mattress. I cast it upstream and let it drift down naturally as if it had died. Then I popped it into the water as if it had been blown there. Then I made it zigzag while retrieving it, as if it were trying to launch itself into flight. But it evidently retained the appearance of a floating mattress. I took it off, and tried several other flies. There were no flies in the water for me to match, and by the same token there were no fish jumping.

I began to cast glances across the river under my hat brim. Paul wasn't doing much either. I saw him catch one, and he just turned and walked to shore with it, so it couldn't have been much of a fish. I was feeling a little less than more perfect.

Then Paul started doing something he practically never did, at least not since he had been old enough to be cocky. He suddenly started fishing upstream, back over the water he had just fished. That's more like me when I feel I haven't fished the hole right or from the right angle, but, when my brother fished a hole, he assumed nothing was left behind that could be induced to change its mind.

I was so startled I leaned against a big rock to watch.

Almost immediately he started hauling them in. Big ones, and he didn't spend much time landing them either. I thought he gave them too little line and took them in too fast, but I knew what he was up to. He expected to make a killing in this hole, and he wasn't going to let any one fish thrash around in the water until it scared the rest off. He had one on now and he held the line on it so tight he was forcing it high in the air. When it jumped, he leaned back on his rod and knocked the fish into the water again. Full of air now, it streaked across the top of the water with its tail like the propeller of a seaplane until it could get its submarine chambers adjusted and submerge again.

He lost a couple but he must have had ten by the time he got back to the head of the hole.

Then he looked across the river and saw me sitting beside my rod. He started fishing again, stopped, and took another look. He cupped his hands and yelled, "Do you have George's No. 2 Yellow Hackle with a feather not a horsehair wing?" It was fast water and I didn't get all the words immediately. "No. 2" I caught first, because it is a hell of a big hook, and then "George," because he was our fishing pal, and then "Yellow." With that much information I started to look in my box, and let the other words settle into a sentence later.

One bad thing about carrying a box loaded with flies, as I

do, is that nearly half the time I still don't have the right one.

"No," I admitted across the water, and water keeps repeating your admissions.

"I'll be there," he called back and waded upstream.

"No," I yelled after him, meaning don't stop fishing on my account. You can't convey an implied meaning across a river, or, if you can, it is easy to ignore. My brother walked to the lower end of the first hole where the water was shallow and waded across.

By the time he got to me, I had recovered most of the pieces he must have used to figure out what the fish were biting. From the moment he had started fishing upstream his rod was at such a slant and there was so much slack in his line that he must have been fishing with a wet fly and letting it sink. In fact, the slack was such that he must have been letting the fly sink five or six inches. So when I was fishing this hole as I did the last one—with a cork-body fly that rides on top of the water—I was fighting the last war. "No. 2" hook told me of course it was a hell of a big insect, but "yellow" could mean a lot of things. My big question by the time he got to me was, "Are they biting on some aquatic insect in a larval or nymph stage or are they biting on a drowned fly?"

He gave me a pat on the back and one of George's No. 2 Yellow Hackles with a feather wing. He said, "They are feeding on drowned yellow stone flies."

I asked him, "How did you think that out?"

He thought back on what had happened like a reporter. He started to answer, shook his head when he found he was wrong, and then started out again. "All there is to thinking," he said, "is seeing something noticeable which makes you see something you weren't noticing which makes you see something that isn't even visible."

I said to my brother, "Give me a cigarette and say what you mean."

"Well," he said, "the first thing I noticed about this hole was that my brother wasn't catching any. There's nothing more noticeable to a fisherman than that his partner isn't catching any.

"This made me see that I hadn't seen any stone flies flying around this hole."

Then he asked me, "What's more obvious on earth than sunshine and shadow, but until I really saw that there were no stone flies hatching here I didn't notice that the upper hole where they were hatching was mostly in sunshine and this hole was in shadow."

I was thirsty to start with, and the cigarette made my mouth drier so I flipped the cigarette into the water.

"Then I knew," he said, "if there were flies in this hole they had to come from the hole above that's in the sunlight where there's enough heat to make them hatch.

"After that, I should have seen them dead in the water. Since I couldn't see them dead in the water, I knew they had to be at least six or seven inches under the water where I couldn't see them. So that's where I fished."

He leaned against a big rock with his hands behind his head to make the rock soft. "Wade out there and try George's No. 2," he said, pointing at the fly he had given me.

I didn't catch one right away, and I didn't expect to. My side of the river was the quiet water, the right side to be on in the hole above where the stone flies were hatching, but the drowned stone flies were washed down in the powerful water on the other side of this hole. After seven or eight casts, though, a small ring appeared on the surface. A small ring usually means that a small fish has risen to the surface, but it can also mean a big fish has rolled under water. If it is a big fish under water, he won't look so much like a fish as an arch of a rainbow that has appeared and disappeared.

Paul didn't even wait to see if I landed him. He waded out to talk to me. He went on talking as if I had time to listen to him and land a big fish. He said, "I'm going to wade back again and fish the rest of the hole." Sometimes I said, "Yes," and when the fish went out of the water, speech failed me, and when the fish made a long run I said at the end of it, "You'll have to say that over again."

Finally, we understood each other. He was going to wade the river again and fish the other side. We both should fish fairly fast, because Father probably was already waiting for us. Paul threw his cigarette in the water and was gone without seeing whether I landed the fish.

Not only was I on the wrong side of the river to fish with drowned stone flies, but Paul was a good enough roll caster to have already fished most of my side from his own. But I caught two more. They also started as little circles that looked like little fish feeding on the surface but were broken arches of big rainbows under water. After I caught these two, I quit. They made ten, and the last three were the finest fish I ever caught. They weren't the biggest or most spectacular fish I ever caught, but they were three fish I caught because my brother waded across the river to give me the fly that would catch them and because they were the last fish I ever caught fishing with him.

After cleaning my fish, I set these three apart with a layer of grass and wild mint.

Then I lifted the heavy basket, shook myself into the shoulder strap until it didn't cut any more, and thought, "I'm through for the day. I'll go down and sit on the bank by my father and talk." Then I added, "If he doesn't feel like talking, I'll just sit."

I could see the sun ahead. The coming burst of light made it look from the shadows that I and a river inside the earth were about to appear on earth. Although I could as yet see only the sunlight and not anything in it, I knew my father was sitting somewhere on the bank. I knew partly because he and I shared many of the same impulses, even to quitting at about the same time. I was sure without as yet being able to see into what was in front of me that he was sitting somewhere in the sunshine reading the New Testament in Greek. I knew this both from instinct and experience.

Old age had brought him moments of complete peace. Even when we went duck hunting and the roar of the early morning shooting was over, he would sit in the blind wrapped in an old army blanket with his Greek New Testament in one hand and his shotgun in the other. When a stray duck happened by, he would drop the book and raise the gun, and, after the shooting was over, he would raise the book again, occasionally interrupting his reading to thank his dog for retrieving the duck.

The voices of the subterranean river in the shadows were different from the voices of the sunlit river ahead. In the shadows against the cliff the river was deep and engaged in profundities, circling back on itself now and then to say things over to be sure it had understood itself. But the river ahead came out into the sunny world like a chatterbox, doing its best to be friendly. It bowed to one shore and then to the other so nothing would feel neglected.

By now I could see inside the sunshine and had located my father. He was sitting high on the bank. He wore no hat. Inside the sunlight, his faded red hair was once again ablaze and again in glory. He was reading, although evidently only by sentences because he often looked away from the book. He did not close the book until some time after he saw me.

I scrambled up the bank and asked him, "How many did you get?" He said, "I got all I want." I said, "But how many did you get?" He said, "I got four or five." I asked, "Are they any good?" He said, "They are beautiful."

He was about the only man I ever knew who used the word "beautiful" as a natural form of speech, and I guess I picked up the habit from hanging around him when I was little.

"How many did you catch?" he asked. "I also caught all I want," I told him. He omitted asking me just how many that was, but he did ask me, "Are they any good?" "They are beautiful," I told him, and sat down beside him.

"What have you been reading?" I asked. "A book," he said. It was on the ground on the other side of him. So I would not have to bother to look over his knees to see it, he said, "A good book."

Then he told me, "In the part I was reading it says the Word was in the beginning, and that's right. I used to think water was first, but if you listen carefully you will hear that the words are underneath the water."

"That's because you are a preacher first and then a fisherman," I told him. "If you ask Paul, he will tell you that the words are formed out of water."

"No," my father said, "you are not listening carefully. The water runs over the words. Paul will tell you the same thing. Where is Paul anyway?"

I told him he had gone back to fish the first hole over again. "But he promised to be here soon," I assured him. "He'll be here when he catches his limit," he said. "He'll be here soon," I reassured him, partly because I could already see him in the subterranean shadows.

My father went back to reading and I tried to check what we had said by listening. Paul was fishing fast, picking up one here and there and wasting no time in walking them to shore. When he got directly across from us, he held up a finger on each hand and my father said, "He needs two more for his limit."

I looked to see where the book was left open and knew just enough Greek to recognize λόγος as the Word. I guessed from it and the argument that I was looking at the first verse of John. While I was looking, Father said, "He has one on."

It was hard to believe, because he was fishing in front of us on the other side of the hole that Father had just fished. Father slowly rose, found a good-sized rock and held it behind his back. Paul landed the fish, and waded out again for number twenty and his limit. Just as he was making the first cast, Father threw the rock. He was old enough so that he threw awkwardly and afterward had to rub his shoulder, but the rock landed in the river about where Paul's fly landed and at about the same time, so you can see where my brother learned to throw rocks into his partner's fishing water when he couldn't bear to see his partner catch any more fish.

Paul was startled for only a moment. Then he spotted Father on the bank rubbing his shoulder, and Paul laughed, shook his fist at him, backed to shore and went downstream until he was out of rock range. From there he waded into the water and began to cast again, but now he was far enough away so we couldn't see his line or loops. He was a man with a wand in a river, and whatever happened we had to guess from what the man and the wand and the river did.

As he waded out, his big right arm swung back and forth. Each circle of his arm inflated his chest. Each circle was faster and higher and longer until his arm became defiant and his chest breasted the sky. On shore we were sure, although we could see no line, that the air above him was singing with loops of line that never touched the water but got bigger and bigger each time they passed and sang. And we knew what was in his mind from the lengthening defiance of his arm. He was not going to let his fly touch any water close to shore where the small and middle-sized fish were. We knew from his arm and chest that all parts of him were saying, "No small one for the last one." Everything was going into one big cast for one last big fish.

From our angle high on the bank, my father and I could see where in the distance the wand was going to let the fly first touch water. In the middle of the river was a rock iceberg, just its tip exposed above water and underneath it a rock house. It met all the residential requirements for big fish—powerful water carrying food to the front and back doors, and rest and shade behind them.

My father said, "There has to be a big one out there."

I said, "A little one couldn't live out there."

My father said, "The big one wouldn't let it."

My father could tell by the width of Paul's chest that he was going to let the next loop sail. It couldn't get any wider. "I wanted to fish out there," he said, "but I couldn't cast that far."

Paul's body pivoted as if he were going to drive a golf ball three hundred yards, and his arm went high into the great arc and the tip of his wand bent like a spring, and then everything sprang and sang.

Suddenly, there was an end of action. The man was immobile. There was no bend, no power in the wand. It pointed at ten o'clock and ten o'clock pointed at the rock. For a moment the man looked like a teacher with a pointer illustrating something about a rock to a rock. Only water moved. Somewhere above the top of the rock house a fly was swept in water so powerful only a big fish could be there to see it.

Then the universe stepped on its third rail. The wand jumped convulsively as it made contact with the magic current of the world. The wand tried to jump out of the man's right hand. His left hand seemed to be frantically waving good-bye to a fish, but actually was trying to throw enough line into the rod to reduce the voltage and ease the shock of what had struck.

Everything seemed electrically charged but electrically unconnected. Electrical sparks appeared here and there on the river. A fish jumped so far downstream that it seemed outside the man's electrical field, but, when the fish had jumped, the man had leaned back on the rod and it was then that the fish had toppled back into the water not guided in its reentry by itself. The connections between the convulsions and the sparks became clearer by repetition. When the man leaned back on the wand and the fish reentered the water not altogether under its own power, the wand recharged with convulsions, the man's hand waved frantically at another departure, and much farther below a fish jumped again. Because of the connections, it became the same fish.

The fish made three such long runs before another act in

the performance began. Although the act involved a big man and a big fish, it looked more like children playing. The man's left hand sneakily began recapturing line, and then, as if caught in the act, threw it all back into the rod as the fish got wise and made still another run.

"He'll get him," I assured my father.

"Beyond doubt," my father said. The line going out became shorter than what the left hand took in.

When Paul peered into the water behind him, we knew he was going to start working the fish to shore and didn't want to back into a hole or rock. We could tell he had worked the fish into shallow water because he held the rod higher and higher to keep the fish from bumping into anything on the bottom. Just when we thought the performance was over, the wand convulsed and the man thrashed through the water after some unseen power departing for the deep.

"The son of a bitch still has fight in him," I thought I said to myself, but unmistakably I said it out loud, and was embarrassed for having said it out loud in front of my father. He said nothing.

Two or three more times Paul worked him close to shore, only to have him swirl and return to the deep, but even at that distance my father and I could feel the ebbing of the underwater power. The rod went high in the air, and the man moved backwards swiftly but evenly, motions which when translated into events meant the fish had tried to rest for a moment on top of the water and the man had quickly raised the rod high and skidded him to shore before the fish thought of getting under water again. He skidded him across the rocks clear back to a sandbar before the shocked fish gasped and discovered he could not live in oxygen. In belated despair, he rose in the sand and consumed the rest of momentary life dancing the Dance of Death on his tail.

The man put the wand down, got on his hands and knees in the sand, and, like an animal, circled another animal and waited. Then the shoulder shot straight out, and my brother stood up, faced us, and, with uplifted arm proclaimed himself the victor. Something giant dangled from his fist. Had

Romans been watching they would have thought that what was dangling had a helmet on it.

"That's his limit," I said to my father.

"He is beautiful," my father said, although my brother had just finished catching his limit in the hole my father had already fished.

This was the last fish we were ever to see Paul catch. My father and I talked about this moment several times later, and whatever our other feelings, we always felt it fitting that, when we saw him catch his last fish, we never saw the fish but only the artistry of the fisherman.

While my father was watching my brother, he reached over to pat me, but he missed, so he had to turn his eyes and look for my knee and try again. He must have thought that I felt neglected and that he should tell me he was proud of me also but for other reasons.

It was a little too deep and fast where Paul was trying to wade the river, and he knew it. He was crouched over the water and his arms were spread wide for balance. If you were a wader of big rivers you could have felt with him even at a distance the power of the water making his legs weak and wavy and ready to swim out from under him. He looked downstream to estimate how far it was to an easier place to wade.

My father said, "He won't take the trouble to walk downstream. He'll swim it." At the same time Paul thought the same thing, and put his cigarettes and matches in his hat.

My father and I sat on the bank and laughed at each other. It never occurred to either of us to hurry to the shore in case he needed help with a rod in his right hand and a basket loaded with fish on his left shoulder. In our family it was no great thing for a fisherman to swim a river with matches in his hair. We laughed at each other because we knew he was getting damn good and wet, and we lived in him, and were swept over the rocks with him and held his rod high in one of our hands.

As he moved to shore he caught himself on his feet and then was washed off them, and, when he stood again, more of him showed and he staggered to shore. He never stopped to shake himself. He came charging up the bank showering molecules of water and images of himself to show what was sticking out of his basket, and he dripped all over us, like a young duck dog that in its joy forgets to shake itself before getting close.

"Let's put them all out on the grass and take a picture of them," he said. So we emptied our baskets and arranged them by size and took turns photographing each other admiring them and ourselves. The photographs turned out to be like most amateur snapshots of fishing catches—the fish were white from overexposure and didn't look as big as they actually were and the fishermen looked self-conscious as if some guide had to catch the fish for them.

However, one closeup picture of him at the end of this day remains in my mind, as if fixed by some chemical bath. Usually, just after he finished fishing he had little to say unless he saw he could have fished better. Otherwise, he merely smiled. Now flies danced around his hatband. Large drops of water ran from under his hat on to his face and then into his lips when he smiled.

At the end of this day, then, I remember him both as a distant abstraction in artistry and as a closeup in water and laughter.

My father always felt shy when compelled to praise one of his family, and his family always felt shy when he praised them. My father said, "You are a fine fisherman."

My brother said, "I'm pretty good with a rod, but I need three more years before I can think like a fish."

Remembering that he had caught his limit by switching to George's No. 2 Yellow Hackle with a feather wing, I said without knowing how much I said, "You already know how to think like a dead stone fly."

We sat on the bank and the river went by. As always, it was making sounds to itself, and now it made sounds to us. It would be hard to find three men sitting side by side who knew better what a river was saying.

On the Big Blackfoot River above the mouth of Belmont

Creek the banks are fringed by large Ponderosa pines. In the slanting sun of late afternoon the shadows of great branches reached from across the river, and the trees took the river in their arms. The shadows continued up the bank, until they included us.

A river, though, has so many things to say that it is hard to know what it says to each of us. As we were packing our tackle and fish in the car, Paul repeated, "Just give me three more years." At the time, I was surprised at the repetition, but later I realized that the river somewhere, sometime, must have told me, too, that he would receive no such gift. For, when the police sergeant early next May wakened me before daybreak, I rose and asked no questions. Together we drove across the Continental Divide and down the length of the Big Blackfoot River over forest floors yellow and sometimes white with glacier lilies to tell my father and mother that my brother had been beaten to death by the butt of a revolver and his body dumped in an alley.

My mother turned and went to her bedroom where, in a house full of men and rods and rifles, she had faced most of her great problems alone. She was never to ask me a question about the man she loved most and understood least. Perhaps she knew enough to know that for her it was enough to have loved him. He was probably the only man in the world who had held her in his arms and leaned back and laughed.

When I finished talking to my father, he asked, "Is there anything else you can tell me?"

Finally, I said, "Nearly all the bones in his hand were broken."

He almost reached the door and then turned back for reassurance. "Are you sure that the bones in his hand were broken?" he asked. I repeated, "Nearly all the bones in his hand were broken." "In which hand?" he asked. "In his right hand," I answered.

After my brother's death, my father never walked very well again. He had to struggle to lift his feet, and, when he did get them up, they came down slightly out of control. From time to time Paul's right hand had to be reaffirmed; then my father would shuffle away again. He could not shuffle in a straight line from trying to lift his feet. Like many Scottish ministers before him, he had to derive what comfort he could from the faith that his son had died fighting.

For some time, though, he struggled for more to hold on to. "Are you sure you have told me everything you know about his death?" he asked. I said, "Everything." "It's not much, is it?" "No," I replied, "but you can love completely without complete understanding." "That I have known and preached," my father said.

Once my father came back with another question. "Do you think I could have helped him?" he asked. Even if I might have thought longer, I would have made the same answer. "Do you think I could have helped him?" I answered. We stood waiting in deference to each other. How can a question be answered that asks a lifetime of questions?

After a long time he came with something he must have wanted to ask from the first. "Do you think it was just a stick-up and foolishly he tried to fight his way out? You know what I mean—that it wasn't connected with anything in his past."

"The police don't know," I said.

"But do you?" he asked, and I felt the implication.

"I've said I've told you all I know. If you push me far enough, all I really know is that he was a fine fisherman."

"You know more than that," my father said. "He was beautiful."

"Yes," I said, "he was beautiful. He should have been—you taught him."

My father looked at me for a long time—he just looked at me. So this was the last he and I ever said to each other about Paul's death.

Indirectly, though, he was present in many of our conversations. Once, for instance, my father asked me a series of questions that suddenly made me wonder whether I understood even my father whom I felt closer to than any man I have ever known. "You like to tell true stories, don't you?" he asked, and I answered, "Yes, I like to tell stories that are true."

Then he asked, "After you have finished your true stories sometime, why don't you make up a story and the people to go with it?

"Only then will you understand what happened and why.

"It is those we live with and love and should know who elude us."

Now nearly all those I loved and did not understand when I was young are dead, but I still reach out to them.

Of course, now I am too old to be much of a fisherman, and now of course I usually fish the big waters alone, although some friends think I shouldn't. Like many fly fishermen in western Montana where the summer days are almost Arctic in length, I often do not start fishing until the cool of the evening. Then in the Arctic half-light of the canyon, all existence fades to a being with my soul and memories and the sounds of the Big Blackfoot River and a four-count rhythm and the hope that a fish will rise.

Eventually, all things merge into one, and a river runs through it. The river was cut by the world's great flood and runs over rocks from the basement of time. On some of the rocks are timeless raindrops. Under the rocks are the words, and some of the words are theirs.

I am haunted by waters.

Logging and Pimping and "Your Pal, Jim"

The first time I took any real notice of him was on a Sunday afternoon in a bunkhouse in one of the Anaconda Company's logging camps on the Blackfoot River. He and I and some others had been lying on our bunks reading, although it was warm and half-dark in the bunkhouse this summer afternoon. The rest of them had been talking, but to me everything seemed quiet. As events proved in a few minutes, the talking had been about "The Company," and probably the reason I hadn't heard it was that the lumberjacks were registering their customary complaints about the Company—it owned them body and soul; it owned the state of Montana, the press, the preachers, etc.; the grub was lousy and likewise the wages, which the Company took right back from them anyway by overpricing everything at the commissary, and they had to buy from the commissary, out in the woods where else could they buy. It must have been something like this they were saying, because all of a sudden I heard him break the quiet: "Shut up, you incompetent sons of bitches. If it weren't for the Company, you'd all starve to death."

At first, I wasn't sure I had heard it or he had said it, but he had. Everything was really quiet now and everybody was watching his small face and big head and body behind an elbow on his bunk. After a while, there were stirrings and one by one the stirrings disappeared into the sunlight of the door.

Not a stirring spoke, and this was a logging camp and they were big men.

Lying there on my bunk, I realized that actually this was not the first time I had noticed him. For instance, I already knew his name, which was Jim Grierson, and I knew he was a socialist who thought Eugene Debs was soft. Probably he hated the Company more than any man in camp, but the men he hated more than the Company. It was also clear I had noticed him before, because when I started to wonder how I would come out with him in a fight, I discovered I already had the answer. I estimated he weighed 185 to 190 pounds and so was at least 35 pounds heavier than I was, but I figured I had been better taught and could reduce him to size if I could last the first ten minutes. I also figured that probably I could not last the first ten minutes.

I didn't go back to my reading but lay there looking for something interesting to think about, and was interested finally in realizing that I had estimated my chances with Jim in a fight even before I thought I had noticed him. Almost from the first moment I saw Jim I must have felt threatened, and others obviously felt the same way—later as I came to know him better all my thinking about him was colored by the question, "Him or me?" He had just taken over the bunkhouse, except for me, and now he was tossing on his bunk to indicate his discomfort at my presence. I stuck it out for a while, just to establish homestead rights to existence, but now that I couldn't read anymore, the bunkhouse seemed hotter than ever, so, after carefully measuring the implications of my not being wanted, I got up and sauntered out the door as he rolled over and sighed.

By the end of the summer, when I had to go back to school, I knew a lot more about Jim, and in fact he and I had made a deal to be partners for the coming summer. It didn't take long to find out that he was the best lumberjack in camp. He was probably the best with the saw and ax, and he worked with a kind of speed that was part ferocity. This was back in 1927, as I remember, and of course there was no such thing as a chain saw then, just as now there is no such thing as a logging camp or a bunkhouse the whole length of the Blackfoot River, although there is still a lot of logging going on there. Now the saws are one-man chain saws run by light high-speed motors, and the sawyers are married and live with their families, some of them as far away as Missoula, and drive more than a hundred miles a day to get to and from work. But in the days of the logging camps, the men worked mostly on two-man crosscut saws that were things of beauty, and the highest paid man in camp was the man who delicately filed and set them. The two-man teams who pulled the saws either worked for wages or "gyppoed." To gyppo, which wasn't meant to be a nice-sounding word and could be used as either a noun or a verb, was to be paid by the number of thousands of board feet you cut a day. Naturally, you chose to gyppo only if you thought you could beat wages and the men who worked for wages. As I said, Jim had talked me into being his partner for next summer, and we were going to gyppo and make big money. You can bet I agreed to this with some misgivings, but I was in graduate school now and on my own financially and needed the big money. Besides, I suppose I was flattered by being asked to be the partner of the best sawyer in camp. It was a long way, though, from being all flattery. I also knew I was being challenged. This was the world of the woods and the working stiff, the logging camp being a world especially overbearing with challenges, and, if you expected to duck all challenges, you shouldn't have wandered into the woods in the first place. It is true, too, that up to a point I liked being around him—he was three years older than I was, which at times is a lot, and he had seen parts of life with which I, as the son of a Presbyterian minister, wasn't exactly intimate.

A couple of other things cropped up about him that summer that had a bearing on the next summer when he and I were to gyppo together. He told me he was Scotch, which figured, and that made two of us. He said that he had been brought up in the Dakotas and that his father (and I quote) was "a Scotch son of a bitch" who threw him out of the house when he was fourteen and he had been making his own living ever since. He explained to me that he made his living only partly by working. He worked just in the summer, and then this cultural side of him, as it were, took over. He holed up for the winter in some town that had a good Carnegie Public Library and the first thing he did was take out a library card. Then he went looking for a good whore, and so he spent the winter reading and pimping—or maybe this is stated in reverse order. He said that on the whole he preferred southern whores; southern whores, he said, were generally "more poetical," and later I think I came to know what he meant by this.

So I started graduate school that autumn, and it was tough and not made any easier by the thought of spending all next summer on the end of a saw opposite this direct descendant of a Scotch son of a bitch.

But finally it was late June and there he was, sitting on a log across from me and looking as near like a million dollars as a lumberjack can look. He was dressed all in wool—in a rich Black Watch plaid shirt, gray, short-legged stag pants, and a beautiful new pair of logging boots with an inch or so of white sock showing at the top. The lumberjack and the cowboy followed many of the same basic economic and ecological patterns. They achieved a balance if they were broke at the end of the year. If they were lucky and hadn't been sick or anything like that, they had made enough to get drunk three or four times and to buy their clothes. Their clothes were very expensive; they claimed they were robbed up and down the line and probably they were, but clothes that would stand their work and the weather had to be something special. Central to both the lumberjack's and the cowboy's outfit were the boots, which took several months of savings.

The pair that Jim had on were White Loggers made, as I remember, by a company in Spokane that kept your name and measurements. It was a great shoe, but there were others and they were great, too—they had to be. The Bass, the Bergman, and the Chippewa were all made in different parts

of the country, but in the Northwest most of the jacks I remember wore the Spokane shoe.

As the cowboy boot was made all ways for riding horses and
working steers, the logger's boot was made for working on
and around logs. Jim's pair had a six-inch top, but there were
models with much higher tops—Jim happened to belong to
the school that wanted their ankles supported but no tie on
their legs. The toe was capless and made soft and somewhat
waterproof with neat's-foot oil. The shoe was shaped to walk
or "ride" logs. It had a high instep to fit the log, and with a
high instep went a high heel, not nearly so high as a cowboy's
and much sturdier because these were walking shoes; in fact,
very fine walking shoes—the somewhat high heel threw you
slightly forward of your normal stance and made you feel you
were being helped ahead. Actually, this feeling was their
trademark.

Jim was sitting with his right leg rocking on his left knee,
and he gestured a good deal with his foot, raking the log I was
sitting on for emphasis and leaving behind a gash in its side.
The soles of these loggers' boots looked like World War I,
with trenches and barbwire highly planned—everything
planned, in this case, for riding logs and walking. Central to
the grand design were the caulks, or "corks" as the jacks called
them; they were long and sharp enough to hold to a heavily
barked log or, tougher still, to one that was dead and had no
bark on it. But of course caulks would have ripped out at the
edges of a shoe and made you stumble and trip at the toes, so
the design started with a row of blunt, sturdy hobnails around
the edges and maybe four or five rows of them at the toes.
Then inside came the battlefield of caulks, the real barbwire,
with two rows of caulks coming down each side of the sole and
one row on each side continuing into the instep to hold you
when you jumped crosswise on a log. Actually, it was a beautiful if somewhat primitive design and had many uses—for
instance, when a couple of jacks got into a fight and one went
down the other was almost sure to kick and rake him with his

boots. This treatment was known as "giving him the leather" and, when a jack got this treatment, he was out of business for a long time and was never very pretty again.

Every time Jim kicked and raked the log beside me for emphasis I wiped small pieces of bark off my face.

In this brief interlude in our relations it seemed to me that his face had grown a great deal since I first knew him last year. From last year I remembered big frame, big head, small face, tight like a fist; I even wondered at times if it wasn't his best punch. But sitting here relaxed and telling me about pimping and spraying bark on my face, he looked all big, his nose too and eyes, and he looked handsome and clearly he liked pimping—at least for four or five months of the year— and he especially liked being bouncer in his own establishment, but even that, he said, got boring. It was good to be out in the woods again, he said, and it was good to see me—he also said that; and it was good to be back to work—he said that several times.

Most of this took place in the first three or four days. We started in easy, each one admitting to the other that he was soft from the winter, and, besides, Jim hadn't finished giving me this course on pimping. Pimping is a little more complicated than the innocent bystander might think. Besides selecting a whore (big as well as southern, i.e., "poetical") and keeping her happy (taking her to the Bijou Theater in the afternoons) and hustling (rounding up all the Swedes and Finns and French Canadians you had known in the woods), you also had to be your own bootlegger (it still being Prohibition) and your own police fixer (it being then as always) and your own bouncer (which introduced a kind of sporting element into the game). But after a few days of resting every hour we had pretty well covered the subject, and still nobody seemed interested in bringing up socialism.

I suppose that an early stage in coming to hate someone is just running out of things to talk about. I thought then it didn't make a damn bit of difference to me that he liked his whores big as well as southern. Besides, we were getting in shape a little. We started skipping the rest periods and took only half an hour at lunch and at lunch we sharpened our axes on our Carborundum stones. Slowly we became silent, and silence itself is an enemy to friendship; when we came back to camp each went his own way, and within a week we weren't speaking to each other. Well, this in itself needn't have been ominous. Lots of teams of sawyers work in silence because that is pretty much the kind of guys they are and of course because no one can talk and at the same time turn out thousands of board feet. Some teams of sawyers even hate each other and yet work together year after year, something like the old New York Celtic basketball team, knowing the other guy's moves without troubling to look. But our silence was different. It didn't have much to do with efficiency and big production. When he broke the silence to ask me if I would like to change from a six- to a seven-foot saw, I knew I was sawing for survival. A six-foot blade was plenty long enough for the stuff we were sawing, and the extra foot would have been only that much more for me to pull.

It was getting hot and I was half-sick when I came back to camp at the end of the day. I would dig into my duffel bag and get clean underwear and clean white socks and a bar of soap and go to the creek. Afterwards, I would sit on the bank until I was dry. Then I would feel better. It was a rule I had learned my first year working in the Forest Service—when exhausted and feeling sorry for yourself, at least change socks. On weekends I spent a lot of time washing my clothes. I washed them carefully and I expected them to be white, not gray, when they had dried on the brush. At first, then, I relied on small, home remedies such as cleanliness.

I had a period, too, when I leaned on proverbs, and tried to pass the blame back on myself, with some justification. All winter I had had a fair notion that something like this would happen. Now I would try to be philosophical by saying to myself, "Well, pal, if you fool around with the bull, you have to expect the horn."

But, when you are gored, there is not much comfort in proverbs.

Gradually, though, I began to fade out of my own picture

of myself and what was happening and it was he who controlled my thoughts. In these dreams, some of which I had
during the day, I was always pulling a saw and he was always
at the other end of it getting bigger and bigger but his face
getting smaller and smaller—and closer—until finally it must
have come through the cut in the log, and with no log between us now, it threatened to continue on down the saw until
it ran into me. It sometimes came close enough so that I could
see how it got smaller—by twisting and contracting itself
around its nose—and somewhere along here in my dream I
would wake up from the exertion of trying to back away from
what I was dreaming about.

In a later stage of my exhaustion, there was no dream—or
sleep—just a constant awareness of being thirsty and of a
succession of events of such a low biological order that normally they escaped notice. All night sighs succeeded grunts
and grumblings of the guts, and about an hour after everyone
was in bed and presumably asleep there were attempts at
homosexuality, usually unsuccessful if the statistics I started
to keep were at all representative. The bunkhouse would become almost silent. Suddenly somebody would jump up in his
bed, punch another somebody, and mutter, "You filthy son of
a bitch." Then he would punch him four or five times more,
fast, hard punches. The other somebody never punched
back. Instead, trying to be silent, his grieved footsteps returned to bed. It was still early in the night, too early to start
thinking about daybreak. You lay there quietly through the
hours, feeling as if you had spent all the previous day drinking out of a galvanized pail—eventually, every thought of
water tasted galvanized.

After two or three nights of this you came to know you
could not be whipped. Probably you could not win, but you
could not be whipped.

I'll try not to get technical about logging, but I have to give
you some idea of daylight reality and some notion of what was
going on in the woods while I was trying to stay alive. Jim's
pace was set to kill me off—it would kill him eventually too,

but first me. So the problem, broadly speaking, was how to throw him off this pace and not quite get caught doing it, because after working a week with this Jack Dempsey at the other end of the saw I knew I'd never have a chance if he took a punch at me. Yet I would have taken a punching from him before I would ever have asked him to go easier on the saw. You were no logger if you didn't feel this way. The world of the woods and the working stiff was pretty much made of three things—working, fighting, and dames—and the complete lumberjack had to be handy at all of them. But if it came to the bitter choice, he could not remain a logger and be outworked. If I had ever asked for mercy on the saw I might as well have packed my duffel bag and started down the road.

So I tried to throw Jim off pace even before we began a cut. Often, before beginning to saw, sawyers have to do a certain amount of "brushing out," which means taking an ax and chopping bushes or small jack pines that would interfere with the sawing. I guess that by nature I did more of this than Jim, and now I did as much of it as I dared, and it burned hell out of him, especially since he had yelled at me about it early in the season when we were still speaking to each other. "Jesus," he had said, "you're no gyppo. Any time a guy's not sawing he's not making money. Nobody out here is paying you for trimming a garden." He would walk up to a cut and if there was a small jack pine in the way he would bend it over and hold it with his foot while he sawed and he ripped through the huckleberry bushes. He didn't give a damn if the bushes clogged his saw. He just pulled harder.

As to the big thing, sawing, it is something beautiful when you are working rhythmically together—at times, you forget what you are doing and get lost in abstractions of motion and power. But when sawing isn't rhythmical, even for a short time, it becomes a kind of mental illness—maybe even something more deeply disturbing than that. It is as if your heart isn't working right. Jim, of course, had thrown us off basic rhythm when he started to saw me into the ground by making the stroke too fast and too long, even for himself. Most of the time I followed his stroke; I had to, but I would pick periods when I would not pull the saw to me at quite the speed or distance he was pulling it back to him. Just staying slightly off beat, not being quite so noticeable that he could yell but still letting him know what I was doing. To make sure he knew, I would suddenly go back to his stroke.

I'll mention just one more trick I invented with the hope of weakening Jim by frequent losses of adrenalin. Sawyers have many little but nevertheless almost sacred rules of work in order to function as a team, and every now and then I would almost break one of these but not quite. For instance, if you are making a cut in a fallen tree and it binds, or pinches, and you need a wedge to open the cut and free your saw and the wedge is on Jim's side of the log, then you are not supposed to reach over the log and get the wedge and do the job. Among sawyers, no time is wasted doing Alphonse-Gaston acts; what is on your side is your job—that's the rule. But every now and then I would reach over for his wedge, and when our noses almost bumped, we would freeze and glare. It was like a closeup in an early movie. Finally, I'd look somewhere else as if of all things I had never thought of the wedge, and you can be sure that, though I reached for it, I never got to it first and touched it.

Most of the time I took a lot of comfort from the feeling that some of this was getting to him. Admittedly, there were times when I wondered if I weren't making up a good part of this feeling just to comfort myself, but even then I kept doing things that in my mind were hostile acts. The other lumberjacks, though, helped to make me feel that I was real. They all acknowledged I was in a big fight, and quietly they encouraged me, probably with the hope they wouldn't have to take him on themselves. One of them muttered to me as we started out in the morning, "Some day that son of a bitch go out in the woods, he no come back." By which I assumed he meant I was to drop a tree on him and forget to yell, "Timber!" Actually, though, I had already thought of this.

Another good objective sign was that he got in a big argument with the head cook, demanding pie for breakfast. It sounds crazy, for anybody who knows anything knows that the head cook runs the logging camp. He is, as the jacks say, "the guy with the golden testicles." If he doesn't like a jack because the jack has the bad table manners to talk at meal time, the cook goes to the woods foreman and the jack goes down the road. Just the same, Jim got all the men behind him and then put up his big argument and nobody went down the road and we had pie every morning for breakfast—two or three kinds—and nobody ever ate a piece, nobody, including Jim.

Oddly, after Jim won this pie fight with the cook, things got a little better for me in the woods. We still didn't speak to each other, but we did start sawing in rhythm.

Then, one Sunday afternoon this woman rode into camp, and stopped to talk with the woods foreman and his wife. She was a big woman on a big horse and carried a pail. Nearly every one in camp knew her or of her—she was the wife of a rancher who owned one of the finest ranches in the valley. I had only met her but my family knew her family quite well, my father occasionally coming up the valley to preach to the especially congregated Presbyterians. Anyway, I thought I had better go over and speak to her and maybe do my father's cause some good, but it was a mistake. She was still sitting on her big horse and I had talked to her for just a couple of minutes, when who shows up but Jim and without looking at me says he is my partner and "pal" and asks her about the pail. The woods foreman takes all our parts in reply. First, he answers for her and says she is out to pick huckleberries, and then he speaks as foreman and tells her we are sawyers and know the woods well, and then he replies to himself and speaks for us and assures her that Jim would be glad to show her where the huckleberries are, and it's a cinch he was. In the camp, the men were making verbal bets where nothing changes hands that Jim laid her within two hours. One of the jacks said, "He's as fast with dames as with logs." By late afternoon she rode back into camp. She never stopped. She was hurried and at a distance looked white and didn't have any huckleberries. She didn't even have her empty pail. Who the hell knows what she told her husband?

At first I felt kind of sorry for her because she was so well known in camp and was so much talked about, but she was riding "High, Wide, and Handsome." She was back in camp every Sunday. She always came with a gallon pail and she always left without it. She kept coming long after huckleberry season passed. There wasn't a berry left on a bush, but she came with another big pail.

The pie fight with the cook and the empty huckleberry pail were just what I needed psychologically to last until Labor Day weekend, when, long ago, I had told both Jim and the foreman I was quitting in order to get ready for school. There was no great transformation in either Jim or me. Jim was still about the size of Jack Dempsey. Nothing had happened to reduce this combination of power and speed. It was just that something had happened so that most of the time now we sawed to saw logs. As for me, for the first (and only) time in my life I had spent over a month twenty-four hours a day doing nothing but hating a guy. Now, though, there were times when I thought of other things—it got so that I had to say to myself, "Don't ever get soft and forget to hate this guy for trying to kill you off." It was somewhere along in here, too, when I became confident enough to develop the theory that he wouldn't take a punch at me. I probably was just getting wise to the fact that he ran this camp as if he were the best fighter in it without ever getting into a fight. He had us stiffs intimidated because he made us look bad when it came to work and women, and so we went on to feel that we were also about to take a punching. Fortunately, I guess, I always realized this might be just theory, and I continued to act as if he were the best fighter in camp, as he probably was, but, you know, it still bothers me that maybe he wasn't.

When we quit work at night, though, we still walked to camp alone. He still went first, slipping on his Woolrich shirt over the top piece of his underwear and putting his empty lunch pail under his arm. Like all sawyers, we pulled off our shirts first thing in the morning and worked all day in the tops of our underwear, and in the summer we still wore wool underwear, because we said sweat made cotton stick to us and wool absorbed it. After Jim disappeared for camp, I sat down on a log and waited for the sweat to dry. It still took me a while before I felt steady enough to reach for my Woolrich shirt and pick up my lunch pail and head for camp, but now I knew I could last until I had said I would quit, which some- times can be a wonderful feeling.

One day toward the end of August he spoke out of the silence and said, "When are you going to quit?" It sounded as if someone had broken the silence before it was broken by Genesis.

I answered and fortunately I had an already-made answer; I said, "As I told you, the Labor Day weekend."

He said, "I may see you in town before you leave for the East. I'm going to quit early this year myself." Then he added, "Last spring I promised a dame I would." I and all the other jacks had already noticed that the rancher's wife hadn't shown up in camp last Sunday, whatever that meant.

The week before I was going to leave for school I ran into him on the main street. He was looking great—a little thin, but just a little. He took me into a speakeasy and bought me a drink of Canadian Club. Since Montana is a northern border state, during Prohibition there was a lot of Canadian whiskey in my town if you knew where and had the price. I bought the second round, and he bought another and said he had enough when I tried to do the same. Then he added, "You know, I have to take care of you." Even after three drinks in the afternoon, I was a little startled, and still am.

Outside, as we stood parting and squinting in the sunlight, he said, "I got a place already for this dame of mine, but we've not yet set up for business." Then he said very formally, "We would appreciate it very much if you would pay us a short visit before you leave town." And he gave me the address and, when I told him it would have to be soon, we made a date for the next evening.

The address he had given me was on the north side, which is just across the tracks, where most of the railroaders lived. When I'was a kid, our town had what was called a red-light district on Front Street adjoining the city dump which was always burning with a fitting smell, but the law had more or less closed it up and scattered the girls around, a fair proportion of whom sprinkled themselves among the railroaders. When I finally found the exact address, I recognized the house next to it. It belonged to a brakeman who married a tramp and thought he was quite a fighter, although he never won many fights. He was more famous in town for the story that he came home one night unexpectedly and captured a guy coming out. He reached in his pocket and pulled out three dollars. "Here," he told the guy, "go and get yourself a good screw."

Jim's place looked on the up-and-up—no shades drawn and the door slightly open and streaming light. Jim answered and was big enough to blot out most of the scenery, but I could see the edge of his dame just behind him. I remembered she was supposed to be southern and could see curls on her one visible shoulder. Jim was talking and never introduced us. Suddenly she swept around him, grabbed me by the hand, and said, "God bless your ol' pee hole; come on in and park your ol' prat on the piano."

Suddenly I think I understood what Jim had meant when he told me early in the summer that he liked his whores southern because they were "poetical." I took a quick look around the "parlor," and, sure enough, there was no piano, so it was pure poetry.

Later, when I found out her name, it was Annabelle, which fitted. After this exuberant outcry, she backed off in silence and sat down, it being evident, as she passed the light from a standing lamp, that she had no clothes on under her dress.

When I glanced around the parlor and did not see a piano I did, however, notice another woman and the motto of Scotland. The other woman looked older but not so old as she was supposed to be, because when she finally was introduced she was introduced as Annabelle's mother. Naturally, I wondered how she figured in Jim's operation and a few days later I ran into some jacks in town who knew her and said she was still a pretty good whore, although a little sad and flabby. Later that evening I tried talking to her; I don't think there was much left to her inside but it was clear she thought the world of Jim.

I had to take another look to believe it, but there it was on the wall just above the chair Jim was about to sit in—the motto of Scotland, and in Latin, too—*Nemo me impune lacesset.* Supposedly, only Jim would know what it meant. The whores wouldn't know and it's for sure his trade, who were Scandinavian and French-Canadian lumberjacks, wouldn't. So he sat on his leather throne, owner and chief bouncer of the establishment, believing only he knew that over his head it said: "No one will touch me with impunity."

But there was one exception. I knew what it meant, having been brought up under the same plaque, in fact an even tougher-looking version that had Scotch thistles engraved around the motto. My father had it hung in the front hall where it would be the first thing seen at all times by anyone entering the manse—and in the early mornings on her way to the kitchen by my mother who inherited the unmentioned infirmity of being part English.

Jim did most of the talking, and the rest of us listened and sometimes I just watched. He sure as hell was a good-looking guy, and now he was all dressed up, conservatively in a dark gray herringbone suit and a blue or black tie. But no matter the clothes, he always looked like a lumberjack to me. Why not? He was the best logger I ever worked with, and I barely lived to say so.

Jim talked mostly about sawing and college. He and I had talked about almost nothing during the summer, least of all about college. Now, he asked me a lot of questions about college, but it just wasn't the case that they were asked out of envy or regret. He didn't look at me as a Scotch boy like himself, not so good with the ax and saw but luckier. He looked at himself, at least as he sat there that night, as a successful young businessman, and he certainly didn't think I was ever going to do anything that he wanted to do. What his being a socialist meant to him I was never to figure out. To me, he emerged as all laissez-faire. He was one of those people who turn out not to have some characteristic that you thought was a prominent one when you first met them. Maybe you only thought they had it because what you first saw or heard was at acute angle, or maybe they have it in some form but your personality makes it recessive. Anyway, he and I never talked politics (admitting that most of the time we never talked at all). I heard him talking socialism to the other jacks—yelling it at them would be more exact, as if they didn't know how to saw. Coming out the back door of the Dakotas in the twenties he had to be a dispossessed socialist of some sort, but his talk to me about graduate school was concerned mostly with the question of whether, if hypothetically he decided to take it on, he could reduce graduate study to sawdust, certainly a fundamental capitalistic question. His educational experiences in the Dakotas had had a lasting effect. He had gone as far as the seventh grade, and his teachers in the

Dakotas had been big and tough and had licked him. What he was wondering was whether between seventh grade and graduate school the teachers kept pace with their students and could still lick him. I cheered him up a lot when I told him, "No, last winter wasn't as tough as this summer." He brought us all another drink of Canadian Club, and, while drinking this one, it occurred to me that maybe what he had been doing this summer was giving me his version of graduate school. If so, he wasn't far wrong.

Nearly all our talk, though, was about logging, because logging was what loggers talked about. They mixed it into everything. For instance, loggers celebrated the Fourth of July—the only sacred holiday in those times except Christmas—by contests in logrolling, sawing, and swinging the ax. Their work was their world, which included their games and their women, and the women at least had to talk like loggers, especially when they swore. Annabelle would occasionally come up with such a line as, "Somebody ought to drop the boom on that bastard," but when I started fooling around to find out whether she knew what a boom was, she switched back to pure southern poetry. A whore has to swear like her working men and in addition she has to have pretty talk.

I was interested, too, in the way Jim pictured himself and me to his women—always as friendly working partners talking over some technical sawing problem. In his creations we engaged in such technical dialogue as this: "'How much are you holding there?' I'd ask; 'I'm holding an inch and a half,' he'd say; and I'd say, 'God, I'm holding two and a half inches.'" I can tell you that outside of the first few days of the summer we didn't engage in any such friendly talk, and any sawyer can tell you that the technical stuff he had us saying about sawing may sound impressive to whores but doesn't make any sense to sawyers and had to be invented by him. He was a great sawyer, and didn't need to make up anything, but it seemed as if every time he made us friends he had to make up lies about sawing to go with us.

I wanted to talk a little to the women before I left, but when

I turned to Annabelle she almost finished me off before I got started by saying, "So you and I are partners of Jim?" Seeing that she had made such a big start with this, she was off in another minute trying to persuade me she was Scotch, but I told her, "Try that on some Swede."

Her style was to be everything you wished she were except what you knew she wasn't. I didn't have to listen long before I was fairly sure she wasn't southern. Neither was the other one. They said "you all" and "ol'" and had curls and that was about it, all of which they probably did for Jim from the Dakotas. Every now and then Annabelle would become slightly hysterical, at least suddenly exuberant, and speak a line of something like "poetry"—an alliterative toast or rune or foreign expression. Then she would go back to her quiet game of trying to figure out something besides Scotch that she might persuade me she was that I would like but wouldn't know much about.

Earlier in the evening I realized that the two women were not mother and daughter or related in any way. Probably all three of them got strange pleasures from the notion they were a family. Both women, of course, dressed alike and had curls and did the southern bit, but fundamentally they were not alike in bone or body structure, except that they were both big women.

So all three of them created a warm family circle of lies.

The lumberjack in herringbone and his two big women in only dresses blocked the door as we said good-bye. "So long," I said from outside. "Au revoir," Annabelle said. "So long," Jim said, and then he added, "I'll be writing you."

And he did, but not until late in autumn. By then probably all the Swedish and Finnish loggers knew his north-side place and he had drawn out his card from the Missoula Public Library and was rereading Jack London, omitting the dog stories. Since my address on the envelope was exact, he must have called my home to get it. The envelope was large and square; the paper was small, ruled, and had glue on the top edge, so it was pulled off some writing pad. His handwriting was large but grew smaller at the end of each word.

I received three other letters from him before the school year was out. His letters were only a sentence or two long. The one- or two-sentence literary form, when used by a master, is designed not to pass on some slight matter but to put the world in a nutshell. Jim was my first acquaintance with a master of this form.

His letters always began, "Dear partner," and always ended, "Your pal, Jim."

You can be sure I ignored any shadow of suggestion that I work with him the coming summer, and he never openly made the suggestion. I had decided that I had only a part of my life to give to gyppoing and that I had already given generously. I went back to the United States Forest Service and fought fires, which to Jim was like declaring myself a charity case and taking the rest cure.

So naturally I didn't hear from him that summer—undoubtedly, he had some other sawyer at the end of the saw whom he was reducing to sawdust. But come autumn and there was a big square envelope with the big handwriting that grew smaller at the end of each word. Since it was early autumn, he couldn't have been set up in business yet. Probably he had just quit the woods and was in town still looking things over. It could be he hadn't even drawn a library card yet. Anyway, this was the letter:

> *Dear partner,*
>
> *Just to let you know I have screwed a dame that weighs 300 lbs.*
>
> > *Your pal,*
> > *Jim*

A good many years have passed since I received that letter, and I have never heard from or about Jim since. Maybe at three hundred pounds the son of a bitch was finally overpowered.

USFS 1919: *The Ranger, the Cook, and a Hole in the Sky*

> And then he thinks he knows
> The hills where his life rose . . .
> —Matthew Arnold,
> "The Buried Life"

I was young and I thought I was tough and I knew it was beautiful and I was a little bit crazy but hadn't noticed it yet. Outside the ranger station there were more mountains in all directions than I was ever to see again—oceans of mountains—and inside the station at this particular moment I was ahead in a game of cribbage with the ranger of the Elk Summit District of the Selway Forest of the United States Forest Service (USFS), which was even younger than I was and enjoyed many of the same characteristics.

It was mid-August of 1919, so I was seventeen and the Forest Service was only fourteen, since, of several possible birthdays for the Forest Service, I pick 1905, when the Forest Division of the Department of the Interior was transferred to the Department of Agriculture and named the United States Forest Service.

In 1919 it was twenty-eight miles from the Elk Summit Ranger Station of the Selway Forest to the nearest road, fourteen miles to the top of the Bitterroot Divide and fourteen straight down Blodgett Canyon to the Bitterroot Valley only a few miles from Hamilton, Montana. The fourteen miles

125

going down were as cruel as the fourteen going up, and far more dangerous, since Blodgett Canyon was medically famous for the tick that gave Rocky Mountain Fever, with one chance out of five for recovery. The twenty-eight-mile trail from Elk Summit to the mouth of Blodgett Canyon was a Forest Service trail and therefore marked by a blaze with a notch on top; only a few other trails in the vast Elk Summit district were so marked. Otherwise, there were only game trails and old trappers' trails that gave out on open ridges and meadows with no signs of where the game or trappers had vanished. It was a world of strings of pack horses or men who walked alone—a world of hoof and foot and the rest done by hand. Nineteen nineteen across the Bitterroot Divide in northern Idaho was just before the end of most of history that had had no four-wheel drives, no bulldozers, no power saws and nothing pneumatic to take the place of jackhammers and nothing chemical or airborne to put out forest fires.

Nowadays you can scarcely be a lookout without a uniform and a college degree, but in 1919 not a man in our outfit, least of all the ranger himself, had been to college. They still picked rangers for the Forest Service by picking the toughest guy in town. Ours, Bill Bell, was the toughest in the Bitterroot Valley, and we thought he was the best ranger in the Forest Service. We were strengthened in this belief by the rumor that Bill had killed a sheepherder. We were a little disappointed that he had been acquitted of the charges, but nobody held it against him, for we all knew that being acquitted of killing a sheepherder in Montana isn't the same as being innocent.

As for a uniform, our ranger always wore his .45 and most of our regular crew also packed revolvers, including me. The two old men in the outfit told the rest of us that "USFS" stood for "Use 'er Slow and Fuck 'er Fast." Being young and literal, I put up an argument at first, pointing out that the beginning letters in their motto didn't exactly fit USFS—that their last word "Fast" didn't begin with S as "Service" did. In fact, being thickheaded, I stuck with this argument quite a while, and could hear my voice rise. Each time, they spit through the parting in their moustaches and looked at me as if I were too young to say anything that would have any bearing on such a subject. As far as they were concerned, their motto fitted the United States Forest Service exactly, and by the end of the summer I came to share their opinion.

Although our ranger, Bill Bell, was the best, he did not shine at cribbage. He put down his cards and said, "Fifteen-two, fifteen-four, fifteen-six, and a pair are eight." As usual, I spread out his hand and counted after him. All he had was an eight and a pair of sevens, a hand he always counted as eight. Maybe the eight card gave him the idea. "Bill," I told him, "that's a six hand. Fifteen-two, fifteen-four, and a pair are six." Being wrong always made Bill Bell feel somebody was insulting him. "Damn it," he said, "can't you see that eight card? Well, eight plus seven . . . ." The cook, still wiping dishes, looked over Bill's shoulder and said, "That's a six hand." Bill folded up his cards and tossed them into the pile—whatever the cook said was always right with Bill, which didn't make me like the cook any better. It is always hard to like a spoiled cook, and I disliked this one particularly.

Even so, I had no idea how much I was going to dislike him before the summer was over, or, for that matter, how big a thing another card game was going to be. By the middle of that summer when I was seventeen I had yet to see myself become part of a story. I had as yet no notion that life every now and then becomes literature—not for long, of course, but long enough to be what we best remember, and often enough so that what we eventually come to mean by life are those moments when life, instead of going sideways, backwards, forward, or nowhere at all, lines out straight, tense and inevitable, with a complication, climax, and, given some luck, a purgation, as if life had been made and not happened. Right then, though, I wasn't thinking of Bill as being the hero of any story—I was just getting tired of waiting for him to make the next deal. Before he did, he licked his fingers so he wouldn't deal two or three cards at a time.

It was hard to figure out how Bill could be so different

when he had a rope in his hands—with a rope he was an artist, and he usually was doing something with one. Even when he was sitting in the ranger station he would whirl little loops and "dab" them over a chair; either that or tie knots, beautiful knots. While the crew talked, he threw loops or tied knots. He was a sort of "Yeah" or "No" guy to human beings—now and then he talked part of a sentence or a sentence or two—but to his horses and mules he talked all the time, and they understood him. He never talked loud to them, especially not to mules, which he knew are like elephants and never forget. If a mule got balky when he was shoeing him, he never reached for anything—he just led him out in the sun and tied up one front foot and let him stand there for a couple of hours. You can't imagine what a Christianizing effect it has, even on a mule, to stand for a couple of hours in the hot sun minus a foot.

Bill was built to fit his hands. He was big all over. Primarily he was a horseman, and he needed an extra large horse. He was not the slender cowboy of the movies and the plains. He was a horseman of the mountains. He could swing an ax or pull a saw, run a transit and build trail, walk all day if he had to, put on climbing spurs and string number nine telephone wire, and he wasn't a bad cook. In the mountains you work to live, and in the mountains you don't care much whether your horse can run fast. Where's he going to run? Bill's horse was big and long-striding, and could walk all day over mountain trails at five miles an hour. He was a mountain horse carrying a mountain man. Bill called him Big Moose. He was brown and walked with his head thrown back as if he wore horns.

Every profession has a pinnacle to its art. In the hospital it is the brain or heart surgeon, and in the sawmill it is the sawyer who with squinting eyes makes the first major cut that turns a log into boards. In the early Forest Service, our major artist was the packer, as it usually has been in worlds where there are no roads. Packing is an art as old as the first time man moved and had an animal to help him carry his belongings. As such, it came ultimately from Asia and from there across

Northern Africa and Spain and then up from Mexico and to us probably from Indian squaws. You can't even talk to a packer unless you know what a cinch (*cincha*) is, a latigo, and a manty (*manta*). With the coming of roads, this ancient art has become almost a lost art, but in the early part of this century there were still few roads across the mountains and none across the "Bitterroot Wall." From the mouth of Blodgett Canyon, near Hamilton, Montana, to our ranger station at Elk Summit in Idaho nothing moved except on foot. When there was a big fire crew to be supplied, there could be as many as half a hundred mules and short-backed horses heaving and grunting up the narrow switchbacks and dropping extra large amounts of manure at the sharp turns. The ropes tying the animals together would jerk taut and stretch their connected necks into a straight line until they looked like dark gigantic swans circling and finally disappearing into a higher medium.

Bill was our head packer, and the Forest Service never had a better one. But right now he was having a hard time figuring out which of his three remaining cards he should play. He would like to have taken off his black Stetson and scratched his head, but the first thing he did when he dressed in the morning was to put on his black hat, and it was the last thing he took off when he went to bed. In between he did not like to remove it. Before he got around to pushing it back on his head and playing a card, I found myself thinking of some of the trips I had taken with him across the Bitterroot Divide.

As head packer, Bill rode in front of the string, a study in angles. With black Stetson hat at a slant, he rode with his head turned almost backward from his body so he could watch to see if any of the packs were working loose. Later in life I was to see Egyptian bas-reliefs where the heads of men are looking one way and their bodies are going another, and so it is with good packers. After all, packing is the art of balancing packs and then seeing that they ride evenly—otherwise the animals will have saddle sores in a day or two and be out of business for all or most of the summer.

Up there in front with Bill, you could see just about anything happen. A horse might slip or get kicked out of the string and roll frightened downhill until he got tangled around a tree trunk. You might even have to shoot him, collect the saddle, and forget the rest of what was scattered over the landscape. But mostly what you were watching for took Bill's trained eye to see—a saddle that had slipped back so far the animal couldn't breathe, or a saddle that had slipped sideways. In an outfit that large, there are always a few "shad bellies" that no cinch can hang on to and quite a few "bloaters" that blow up in the morning when the cinch touches them and then slowly deflate. Who knows what? The trouble may have started back in the warehouse where the load cargoer couldn't tell weight or didn't give a damn and now an animal was trying to keep steady across the Bitterroot Divide with lopsided packs. Or maybe the packs balanced, but some assistant packer had tied one higher than the other. Or had tied a sloppy diamond hitch and everything slipped. The Bitterroot Divide, with its many switchbacks, granite boulders, and bog holes, brought out every weakness in a packer, his equipment, and his animals. To take a pack string of nearly half a hundred across the Bitterroot Divide was to perform a masterpiece in that now almost lost art, and in 1919 I rode with Bill Bell and saw it done.

The divide was just as beautiful as the way up. In August it was blue with June lupine. Froth dropped off the jaws of the horses and mules, and, snorting through enlarged red nostrils, the animals shook their saddles, trying without hands to rearrange their loads. Not far to the south was El Capitan, always in snow and always living up to its name. Ahead and to the west was our ranger station—and the mountains of Idaho, poems of geology stretching beyond any boundaries and seemingly even beyond the world.

Six miles or so west of the divide is a lake, roughly two-thirds of the way between Hamilton and Elk Summit, that is the only place where there is water and enough grass to hold a big bunch of horses overnight. K. D. Swan, the fine photographer of the early Forest Service, should have been there to record the design of the divide—ascending in triangles to the sky and descending in ovals and circles to an oval meadow and an oval lake with a moose knee-deep beside lily pads. It was triangles going up and ovals coming down, and on the divide it was springtime in August.

The unpacking was just as beautiful—one wet satin back after another without saddle or saddle sore, and not a spot of white wet flesh where hair and hide had rubbed off. Perhaps one has to know something about keeping packs balanced on the backs of animals to think this beautiful, or to notice it at all, but to all those who work come moments of beauty unseen by the rest of the world.

So, to a horseman who has to start looking for horses before daybreak, nothing is so beautiful in darkness as the sound of a bell mare.

While I was sitting there thinking of how Bill was a major artist and how even the knots he tied were artistic, he had somehow got ahead of me in the cribbage game, at which he was a chump. At least, I was a lot better than he was at cribbage, once the favorite indoor pastime of the woods. We even played it outdoors, and often on the trail one of us would carry a deck of cards and a cribbage board in his pack sack, and in the middle of the morning and afternoon we would straddle a log and have a game.

Bill really wasn't ahead, but I was going to lose unless he played like a Chinaman. We both were in striking distance of 121, which is the end of the game in cribbage, and I had the advantage of counting first. I needed only eight points, which normally I should have been able to make with a decent hand plus the "pegging." But I had a lousy hand, just a pair of fours, and a pair is worth only two points, so I would have to peg six to make 121, and that's a lot. In case you don't know cribbage, about all Bill had to do to stop me from pegging six was not to pair anything I put down. I started the pegging by playing one of my fours, and, so help me, he had a four in his hand and he snapped it down. "I'll take two for a pair of fours," he said. As I told you, all I had in my hand was a pair of fours. I put down the third four, and in cribbage three of a kind counts six, so I had 121 and the ball game, and a start toward discovering that somehow artists aren't sharp at cards.

Actually, I had heard rumors in Hamilton, which was Bill's headquarters in the Bitterroot Valley, that the local small-town gamblers could hardly wait for Bill to get his monthly check. Among the local housemen and shills he was supposedly noted for playing poker as if he breathed through gills. Knowing how Bill hated to lose, I was somewhat surprised that he hadn't also been acquitted of shooting a shill.

Knowing Bill, I also knew that he was sore at me, at least for the moment, so I thought, "Let's see if a change of games won't change the luck." Of course, three can play a lot more card games than two. As the cook was finishing dishes, I asked him, "Why don't you cut in on a nickel-and-dime game? Poker? Pinochle? You and Bill name it."

I'll never forget that cook; in fact, he was to become one of my longest memories. Even out in the woods, he wore low canvas shoes. He turned his shoes toward me and said, "I never play cards against the men I work with." This wasn't the first time the cook had made this stately speech to me, so I started disliking him all over again. His name may have been Hawkins, but I really think it was Hawks and in memory I made it into Hawkins because in some book there was a character I didn't like by the name of Hawkins.

Bill and I played one more game of cribbage trying to get over being sore, but we weren't successful. I picked up the cards and put them in their case and the case on the only shelf in the cabin. Before I reached the door the cook had picked them up and was sitting at the table shuffling. He dealt out four hands. Then he went around the first three hands again, quickly giving each hand one or two cards as if each hand had asked to draw. He paused, however, before giving himself cards. Then with one motion he picked them all up. After shuffling, he dealt out five hands, sometimes four, never three, lest I get the idea that he would play with Bill and me. I stood there watching him shuffling and dealing. It was worth watching. After about five minutes, he picked up all the cards with one swoop, stuck them in the case and the case on the shelf and started for bed. I closed the door and started for the tent where the crew slept. I liked him less than ever.

There were only four of us in the "regular crew," plus the lookouts who were stationed on the high peaks, plus the ranger and the cook. The regular crew was hired by the month (sixty dollars per) for the summer—the ranger was the only one in the district who was hired all year. Earlier in the season, there had been a big fire in the district and an emergency crew of over a hundred men had been hired on the streets of Butte and Spokane, but the fire had been put out and the emergency crew sent back to town. Our small regular crew now was building trail about three miles from the station—grade A trail, too, with about a twenty-foot right-of-way and no more than a six-percent grade. A twenty-foot swath through the wilderness with no trees or brush left standing and, instead of going over an outcropping of rocks with a short steep pitch in the trail, we blasted through the rocks to keep the trail from gaining more than six feet of altitude every hundred feet. Tons of dynamite and we could have taken a hay wagon down our mountain boulevard. Of course, all we needed were trails wide enough to get pack horses through without the packs getting caught between trees, and in a few years the Forest Service revised the specifications and gave orders for the back country to be opened with as many trails as possible. Still, it is proper when young to strive for gigantic perfection that doesn't make sense, and today somewhere in the jungles of Idaho is a mile or two of overgrown boulevard leading nowhere, not even to a deserted Mayan temple.

Of the regular crew of four, two were old men and two were young punks. There was Mr. McBride and his red-headed son. Mr. McBride was a jack-of-all-trades who had worked at different ranches in the Bitterroot Valley and his son was trying to be like his father. Mr. Smith was the old man of the crew and was always worried about his bowels. He was addressed as "Mr. Smith." He was dignified and took small, aged steps on large legs that made his feet look tiny. He had been a miner and he naturally was our powder man, and a good one. Since there were four of us and Mr. McBride had a son, Mr. Smith looked upon me as his. That's how I was elected to the dynamite, which made me sick. Before I had started the job I had heard stories that if you touch dynamite and then your face you will get a headache. Maybe I was carried away by the story, because as long as I worked on the powder I always had headaches. Maybe, though, at seventeen I wasn't quite big enough to swing a double jackhammer all day.

When you are blasting, naturally you first make a hole in the rock for your powder. Nowadays it is done with a pneumatic drill; then it was done by hand and jackhammer. If you worked in a team of two it was called "double jacking." One man held the drill, and every time the other man hit the head of it with the jackhammer the man holding the drill would turn it slightly until the bit completed a circle. This was the outline for the hole, and the same thing went on until the hole was dug, stopping only when the man holding the drill said, "Mud." Then the hammer man gratefully rested while the man holding the drill took a very small dipper and cleaned out the hole. Otherwise, the man with the hammer kept swinging, and, if by chance just once he missed the small head of the drill and the hammer glanced off he would muti-late the hand or arm of the man holding the drill. Sometimes it seemed that Mr. Smith had forgotten how to say "Mud," and I would look down and see the heads of two or three drills, on each of which Mr. Smith had the same hand, the skin of which was already freckled by age. I no longer think that rubbing my face gave me the headaches.

This morning the headache started earlier than usual. I can't give you any very clear reason why I disliked the cook so much. I was honest enough with myself to say that I might be jealous of him. Although I was only seventeen, this was my third summer in the Forest Service, two of them working for Bill, and he had started to show me how to pack, and in return I would do him favors like coming back to camp in the morning to pack out lunch to the crew. I couldn't figure how this cook had moved into first place. Everything he said or did was just perfect, as far as Bill was concerned. Besides, I didn't like his looks—he looked like a bluejay, cocky, with his head on a slant and a tuft of hair on top of it. A bluejay with low canvas shoes. Mostly, though, I didn't need reasons to dislike him. When you get older, you become rational more or less, but when you are young you know. I knew this cook was a forty-cent piece.

It wasn't helping my headache either to think of the ranger being sore at me. I said to myself, "Take it easy, and keep your big mouth shut. It's nothing and it will blow over." Then I repeated to myself, "Keep your big mouth shut," but I knew I wouldn't. I had formed principles to compensate for having started work when I was fifteen. I had missed a lot, I knew— the swimming hole, summer girls, and a game called tennis which was played in white flannels with cuffs. I would say to myself, "You decided to go into the woods, so the least you can do is be tough." I hadn't felt this way at fifteen when I first worked for Bill, but that was the way I felt now at seventeen. Even though Bill was my model and an artist—maybe because he was—at seventeen something in me was half-looking for trouble with him.

Before noon who should come along but the cook packing our lunch. He said to me, "The ranger wants you to come back to camp after you eat."

When I got back to camp, Bill was in the cabin we used as a warehouse, building the packs for the string that was going to Hamilton soon. I didn't ask him why he had sent for me and he didn't say. I just started helping him build and balance the packs, and tried to keep my mind on what I was doing, partly because building packs is never a mechanical job. Not even when you're packing the simplest stuff like tin cans, which go into boxes called "panyards," made of rawhide, wood, or canvas, that are hung on the prongs of the saddle. You can't forget to wrap each can in toilet paper, or the labels on the cans will rub off and you won't be able to tell peaches from peas. And the heaviest cans have to go to the bottom, or the pack will shift. Then each of the two side packs has to weigh the same and together (with the top pack) they shouldn't weigh more than 175 pounds for a horse or 225 for a mule—at least, those were the Forest Service regulations then, but they were twenty-five pounds too heavy if the animals weren't to be bone heaps by the middle of the summer. I don't care who you are, I'll bet you that without a scale you can't build two packs weighing the same and together weighing 150 or 200 pounds when a top pack has been added.

After we had packed for a while, I forgot to wonder why the ranger had sent for me. Maybe it was just to help him box things up. Then, while we were working with our heads bent, I heard the cook come by jingling the knives and forks the crew had used for lunch.

Still working on a pack, I heard myself say, "I don't like that son of a bitch."

Bill lifted a pack and put it down. Inside I heard myself say, "Keep your big mouth shut." Outside, I heard myself add, "Some day I am going to punch the piss out of him." Bill stood up and said, "Not in this district you won't." He looked at me for a long time, and I looked back still crouched over my pack. I figured that at this moment crouching was a good position. Finally, we both went back to work.

Bending and lifting, he began to tell me about how the morning had gone. "The lookout on Grave Peak quit this

morning." "Yeah?" I said. "Yeah," he said. "He came off that
mountain in about three jumps." It was nearly twelve miles to
the top of the peak. "Do you know what he said to me?" he
asked. "No," I said. I wasn't happy about how this was going
to end. "The lookout said, 'Give me my time. This is too tough
a job for me, fighting fire in the day and sleeping with rattlesnakes at night.'" After lifting the pack again for weight, he
went on, "Seems that he put his hand on the bed to pull back
the blanket and he felt something shaped like a fire hose. Do
you believe it?"

At Bear Creek, where I first worked for Bill, there had been
a lot of rattlers on those bare mountainsides. On a steep
sidehill trail, the up side can be as high as your hand, so you
could almost brush those rattlesnakes as you swung along.
And, being cold-blooded, they could be attracted to the
warmth of a bed at night. But I hadn't seen a rattlesnake this
summer in Elk Summit, although it was the adjoining district.

"No, I don't believe it." I said. "Why not?" he asked. "It's
too high up there for rattlesnakes," I said. "Are you sure?" he
asked, and I told him I wasn't sure but I thought so. Still
working with the packs he said, "Why don't you go up on the
lookout for a couple of weeks and find out?"

I didn't ask him when; I knew he meant now. I lifted the
two packs until I thought they were balanced, and then
started for the door. He added, "If you spot any fires, call
them in. And, if there's a big rain or snow, close up camp and
come back to the station."

I knew it would be dark before I got to Grave Peak, so I
asked the cook to make me a sandwich. I had a big blue
bandanna handkerchief, and I put the sandwich in the handkerchief and tied the handkerchief to my belt in the middle of
my back. I picked up my razor, toothbrush, and comb, and
my favorite ax and Carborundum stone. Then I strapped on
my .32-20 and started up the high trail. I knew I had been
sent into exile.

It was twelve miles and all up, but I never stopped to rest or eat the sandwich. Bill seemed to be watching all the time. By walking hard I kept even with daylight until near the end. Then darkness passed over me from below—just the dazzling peak above told me where I was going.

For the first few days, I was too tired to think about my troubles. I was still half-sick from the dynamite and I still dragged from that big fire we had fought in late July, so I spent most of my time just looking the place over and getting things squared away.

Modern lookouts live on top of their peaks in what are called "birdcages"—glass houses on towers with lightning rods twisted around them so that the lookouts are not afraid of lightning striking them, and for twenty-four hours a day can remain on the towers to watch for lightning to strike and smoke to appear. This, of course, is the way it should be, but in 1919 birdcages, as far as we knew, were only for birds. We watched from the open peak and lived in a tent in a basin close to the peak where usually there was a spring of water. From my camp to the lookout was a good half-hour climb, and I spent about twelve hours a day watching mountains.

Near the top there were few trees and nearly all of them had been struck by lightning. It had gone around them, like a snake of fire. But I was to discover that, on a high mountain, lightning does not seem to strike from the sky. On a high mountain, lightning seems to start somewhat below you and very close by, seemingly striking upward and outward. Once it was to knock me down, toss branches over me and leave me sick.

The basin where my tent was pitched was covered with chunks of cliff that had toppled from above. I did not see a rattlesnake, but I shared the basin with a grizzly bear who occasionally came along flipping over fallen pieces of dis-integrated cliff as he looked for disproportionately small grubs. When I saw him coming, I climbed the highest rock and tried to figure out how many hundreds of grubs he had to eat for a square meal. When he saw me, he made noises in his mouth as if he were shifting his false teeth. In a thicket on top of a jack pine, I found the skeleton of a deer. Your guess is as good as mine. Mine is that the snow in the high basin was deep enough to cover the trees, and the deer was crossing the crust and broke through or was killed and eventually the snow melted. There was a tear in my tent so when it rained I could keep either my food or my bed dry, but not both.

Since this was not my first hitch as a lookout, I knew what to watch for—a little cloud coming up a big mountain, usually in the late afternoon when the dews had long dried and the winds were at their height. And usually it detached itself from the mountain and went on up into the sky and became just a little cloud. Once in a while it would disappear on the mountain, and then you didn't know what you had seen—probably a cloud but maybe a puff of smoke and the wind had changed and you couldn't see it now, so you marked it on your map to watch for several days. In a lightning storm you marked every strike to watch, and sometimes it was a week later before one of them became a little cloud again and then got bigger and began to boil. When a cloud began to boil, then it wasn't a cloud, especially if it reflected red on the bottom. It could mean fire even when the cloud was two or three miles down the canyon from where it was first seen, because, if there were no wind, smoke could drift a long way behind a ridge before rising again where it would show. So that's the way a fire first looks to a lookout: something—you don't know what—usually in late afternoon, that may go away and not come again and, if it comes back and is smoke, it may be quite a long way from the fire.

A possible late-afternoon cloud has no resemblance to what a fire looks like if it gets out of control, and it was often impossible in those early years to get men quickly on a fire when it was in the back country where there were no roads and sometimes not even trails, and of course long before there were planes stationed in Missoula ready to drop chemicals and smoke jumpers.

Instead, when a fire got out of control the Forest Service hired a hundred or so bindle stiffs off the streets of Butte or

Spokane at thirty cents an hour (forty-five cents for straw bosses), shipped them to some rail station near the end of a branch line, and walked them the final thirty-five or forty miles over "the wall." By the time they reached the fire, it had spread all over the map, and had jumped into the crowns of trees, and for a lot of years a prospective ranger taking his exam had said the last word on crown fires. Even by my time he was a legend. When asked on his examination, "What do you do when a fire crowns?" he had answered, "Get out of the way and pray like hell for rain."

Our big fire that summer had been big enough so that I was still tired and my eyes still ached from smoke and no sleep, and big enough so that for years it crowned in my dreams, but it wasn't in the class of those fires of 1910 that burned out the Coeur d'Alene and great pieces of the Bitterroot. The smoke from those fires drifted seven hundred miles to Denver, and in my home town of Missoula the street lights had to be turned on in the middle of the afternoon, and curled ashes brushed softly against the lamps as if snow were falling heavily in the heat of August. Of course, no other fires on record were as big as those of 1910, but the one of 1919 was the biggest I was ever on.

It came in a rage and a crown to the top of the ridge. You may know, when a fire gets big enough it generates its own wind. The heat from the fire lightens the air, which rises in the sky, and the cooler air from above swoops down to replace it, and soon a great circular storm enrages the fire and the sky is a volcanic eruption of burning cones and branches descending in streamers of flames. The fire stands on the ridge, roaring for hell to arrive as reinforcement. While you are trying to peer through it to see the inferno on its way, suddenly somebody yells, "God, look behind. The son of a bitch has jumped the gulch." One hundred and eighty degrees from where you have been looking for the inferno and half-way up the opposite ravine a small smoke is growing big where one of those burning cones or branches dropped out of the sky and trapped you with a fire in your rear. Then what do you do?

Of course, the men who had been brought in from Butte or Spokane were dead tired and barefoot long before they reached the fire. At the hiring hall in Butte and Spokane each had to have a good pair of boots and a jacket to be employed, so they took turns in the alley changing the one good pair they had. Now all but one of them had marched across the Bitterroot wall in poor street shoes, and, not being able to keep ahead of the pack train, they ate twenty-eight miles of dust. They were bums off the street, miners out of the holes for the summer with the hope of avoiding tuberculosis, winos, and Industrial Workers of the World, who had been thick in Butte and Spokane during World War I. Since it was only the summer after the war, we ordinary working stiffs were still pretty suspicious of IWWs. Those of us who belonged to the regular crew (that is, who were paid sixty dollars a month instead of thirty cents an hour) said that IWW meant "I Won't Work," and we were also sure that they were happy to see our country burn. For whatever reason, we had to spend as much time patrolling them as we did the fire. First we had to get them to the top of the opposite ridge before the new fire arrived there, and a lot of them only wanted to lie down and go to sleep with the great fire coming from behind. It was the first time I ever saw that sometimes death has no meaning to men if they can lie down and sleep. We kicked them up the hill, while they begged to be left lying where they were, and we beat the new fire to the top. Then we made a "fire trench," just a scraping two or three feet wide to remove anything that would burn, like dry needles or duff. In front of the fire trench we built piles of dry twigs and then we waited for the wind to turn and blow back toward the new fire coming up the side of the ravine. We waited until the foreman gave us the signal before we lit the piles of twigs and sent fires burning back into the main one. This is known as "backfiring" and for once it worked, although if the wind had shifted again to its original direction, all we would have done was give the fire a head start on us. We did not sleep for three days. Some of us had to carry drinking water in warm canvas sacks up a

thousand-foot ridge. The rest of us slowly extended the fire
trench down the sides of the fire. The bottom of it we let go
for a while—a fire doesn't go very far or fast downhill.

We had done a good job in heading off the fire. What you
do in the first couple of hours after you hit a fire is what
counts, and if it isn't right you had better take that young
ranger's advice and give yourself over to prayer. Bill and the
man he had made fire foreman had both experience and gift,
and it takes gift as well as having been there before to know
where to hit a fire hard enough to turn it in its tracks. When
it's less than 110 degrees and nothing is about to burn you to
death or roar at you and your lungs will still breathe the heat
and your eyes aren't closed with smoke, it's easy to state the
simple principles of a science, if that's what it is. All you're
trying to do is to force the fire into some opening at the top of
the ridge that's covered with shale and rocks or, if such open-
ings don't abound in your vicinity, to force it into a thin stand
of alpine pine or something that doesn't burn very fast. But
with the inferno having arrived and the smoke so thick you
can see only two or three men ahead of you, it's gift and guts,
not science, that tells you where the head of the fire is, and
where an open ridge is that can't be seen, and where and
when the wind will turn and whether your men have what it
takes to stand and wait. Don't forget this last point when you
place your men—it isn't just horses that panic when the barn
burns. But we were placed right and either we had guts or we
were too sick to care. Anyway, we stood and the wind stayed
with us and we crowded the big fire with our backfires and
turned it into the timberline.

But every time we got the fire under control, something
strange would happen—the fire would jump our fire trench,
usually at some fairly ordinary place, so we became sure that
IWWs were rolling burning logs over the trench and starting
the fire off again. If they were, it was probably just to keep
their jobs going, but that wasn't what we thought, and anyway
it didn't matter much what we thought—the fire kept jumping the line everywhere until I and the red-headed kid were

picked to patrol the fire. The fire foreman told us to carry revolvers. That's all we were told. I still ask myself why the two youngest in the outfit were given this assignment. Did they think we were so young that we would make a big show of ourselves but would freeze in the clutch and wouldn't shoot? Or did they think we were so young we were crazy enough to shoot almost sight unseen? Or did they think that nobody, especially the IWWs, could answer these questions? Anyway we patrolled miles and miles through burning branches and feathered ashes so light they rose ahead of us as we approached. We didn't look for trouble and we didn't find any. Also, we didn't pray, but finally the rains came. The other kid being red-headed, I think he would have shot. That wouldn't have left me much choice.

I don't suppose Bill would have sent me up to the lookout if he knew how much I needed a couple of days of rest, a thought that gave me a good deal of pleasure. Still being sore at him, I reported by telephone to the ranger station the fewest number of times required—three times a day. The telephone, in a coffin-shaped box, was nailed to the tent pole and had a crank on it. Two longs rang the ranger station, and one long and a short was my call, but nobody called me from the station. There was one woman on a distant lookout and her call was two longs and a short, and I am sure the rest of us lookouts often stood poised ready to ring two longs and a short, but never did. Instead we looked at her mountain and thought it looked different from other mountains, and we took off our telephone receivers and listened to her voice when it was her turn to report to the station. She was married and talked every night to her husband in Kooskia, but we did not listen to avoid feeling sorry for ourselves.

After a few days of resting and not mending the tent, I started to feel tough again. I knew I had been sent up here as punishment. I was expected to sit still and watch mountains and long for company and something to do, like playing crib-bage, I suppose. I was going to have to watch mountains for sure, that was my job, but I would not be without company. I already knew that mountains live and move. Long ago when I had had a child sickness and nobody could tell what it was or how to treat it, my mother put me outside in a bed with mosquito netting over it, and I lay there watching mountains until they made me well. I knew that, when needed, mountains would move for me.

About the same time, I began to have another feeling, although one related to the feeling that I wasn't going to let Bill punish me by making me watch mountains. Somewhere along here I first became conscious of the feeling I talked about earlier—the feeling that comes when you first notice your life turning into a story. I began to sense the difference between what I would feel if I were just nearing the end of a summer's work or were just beginning a story. If what were coming was going to be like life as it had been, a summer's job would be over soon and I would go home and tell my pals about the big fire and packing my .32-20 on the fire line and the dynamite. Looking down from Grave Peak, though, I was no longer sure that the big fire was of any importance in what was starting to happen to me. It was becoming more important that I didn't like the damn cook, who was nobody, not even a good or bad cook, and could do nothing well except shuffle cards. Faintly but nevertheless truly I was becoming part of a plot and being made the opponent of my hero, Bill Bell, in fact, mysteriously making myself his opponent. The cook began to look like the mysterious bad guy; even I became mysterious to myself—I was going to show a ranger and a cook that I couldn't be defeated by being made to watch mountains, which were childhood friends of mine.

It doesn't take much in the way of body and mind to be a lookout. It's mostly soul. It is surprising how much our souls are alike, at least in the presence of mountains. For all of us, mountains turn into images after a short time and the images turn true. Gold-tossed waves change into the purple backs of monsters, and so forth. Always something out of the moving deep, and nearly always oceanic. Never a lake, never the sky.

But no matter what images I began with, when I watched long enough the mountains turned into dreams, and still do, and it works the other way around—often, waking from dreams, I know I have been in the mountains, and I know they have been moving—sometimes advancing threateningly, sometimes creeping hesitantly, sometimes receding endlessly. Both mountains and dreams.

In the late afternoon, of course, the mountains meant all business for the lookouts. The big winds were veering from the valleys toward the peaks, and smoke from little fires that had been secretly burning for several days might show up for the first time. New fires sprang out of thunder before it sounded. By three-thirty or four, the lightning would be flexing itself on the distant ridges like a fancy prizefighter, skipping sideways, ducking, showing off but not hitting anything. By four-thirty or five, it was another game. You could feel the difference in the air that had become hard to breathe. The lightning now came walking into you, delivering short smashing punches. With an alidade, you marked a line on the map toward where it struck and started counting, "Thousand-one, thousand-two," and so on, putting in the "thousand" to slow your count to a second each time. If the thunder reached you at "thousand-five," you figured the lightning had struck about a mile away. The punches became shorter and the count closer and you knew you were going to take punishment. Then the lightning and thunder struck together. There was no count.

But what I remember best is crawling out of the tent on summer nights when on high mountains autumn is always approaching. To a boy, it is something new and beautiful to piss among the stars. Not under the stars but among them. Even at night great winds seem always to blow on great mountains, and tops of trees bend, but, as the boy stands there with nothing to do but to watch, seemingly the sky itself bends and the stars blow down through the trees until the Milky Way becomes lost in some distant forest. As the cosmos brushes by the boy and disappears among the trees, the sky is continually replenished with stars. There would be stars enough to brush by him all night, but by now the boy is getting cold.

Then the shivering organic speck of steam itself disappears.

By figuring backward, I knew it was the twenty-fifth of August when an unusually hot electrical storm crashed into the peak and was followed by an unusually high wind. The wind kept up all night and the next day, and I tightened all the ropes on my tent. Cold rode in with the wind. The next night after I went to bed it began to snow. It was August 27, and the stuff was damp and heavy and came down by the pound. Most of it went through the tear in my tent but there was enough left over so that by morning you could track elk in the snow.

I didn't think much of the immediate prospects of building a fire and cooking breakfast, so first I climbed to the top of the peak. When I looked, I knew I might never again see so much of the earth so beautiful, the beautiful being something you know added to something you see, in a whole that is different from the sum of its parts. What I saw might have been just another winter scene, although an impressive one. But what I knew was that the earth underneath was alive and that by tomorrow, certainly by the day after, it would be all green again. So what I saw because of what I knew was a kind of death with the marvelous promise of less than a three-day resurrection. From where I stood to the Bitterroot wall, which could have been the end of the world, was all windrows of momentary white. Beyond the wall, it seemed likely, eternity went on in windrows of Bitterroot Mountains and summer snow.

Even before I got back to camp it had begun to melt. Hundreds of shrubs had been bent over like set snares, and now they sprang up in the air throwing small puffs of white as if hundreds of snowshoe rabbits were being caught at the same instant.

While I was making breakfast, I heard the ticktock of a clock repeating, "It's time to quit; it's time to quit." I heard it almost as soon as it began, and almost that soon I agreed. I said to myself, "You fought a big fire and packed a big gun," and I said, "You slit waxy sticks of dynamite and stuck detonation caps in them and jumped back to watch them sizzle," and then I said, "You helped Bill pack and you watched mountains by yourself. That's a summer's work. Get your time and quit." I said these things several times to impress them on myself. I knew, in addition, that the fire season was over; in fact, the last thing the ranger had told me was to come in if it snowed. So I rang two longs for the ranger station; I rang two longs until I almost pulled the crank off the telephone, but in my heart I knew that the storm had probably blown twenty trees across the line between the peak and the station. Finally, I told myself to stay there until tomorrow when most of the snow would be gone and then to walk to the station and get my time and start over the hill to Hamilton.

What I neglected to tell myself is that it is almost impossible to quit a ranger who is sore because you do not like his cook, or to quit a story once you have become a character in it. The rest of the day I straightened up the camp, finally mended the tent, and listened to the ticktock get louder. I put the boxes of tin cans in trees where the grizzly bear couldn't get them. I had seen him split them open with one snap to a can.

It was nearly ten o'clock the next morning before I started for the ranger station. There was no use starting until the sun had done some more melting. Besides, I had decided to take along the tree-climbing outfit with the faint hope that maybe the storm had blown only two or three trees across the telephone line, so in addition to my ax and my own little odds and ends, I was walking bow-legged with climbing spurs and climbing belt and was carrying insulators and number nine telephone wire. I doubt if I had dropped more than a thousand feet of altitude before I was out of the snow. Also, by then I had chopped two trees that had fallen across the line and had made one splice in the wire. I should have known from the count that I would never clean out twelve miles of telephone line in a day, but now that I was going to quit I

developed a pious feeling, wishing to end in the act of con-
scientiously performing my duty, so I kept the climbing spurs
on and followed the telephone right-of-way, watching the line
dip from tree to tree. When you are following line this way
you lose all sense of the earth, and all that exists is this extended pencil line in your eye. I wouldn't have seen a rattlesnake unless he had wings and was flying south for the winter.
As far as I was concerned, there were no rattlesnakes in Elk
Summit district, and, if there were any, they would be holed
up because it was late in the season and had just snowed. You
could have examined my thoughts clear to the bottom of the
heap and never found a snake track.

I don't need to tell you how a rattlesnake sounds—you can't
mistake one. Sometimes you can think that a big winged
grasshopper is a rattlesnake, but you can never think that a
rattlesnake is anything else. I stayed in the air long enough to
observe him streaking for the brush, an ugly bastard, short,
not like a plains rattler, and much thicker behind his head.

I don't know how far I jumped, but I was mad when I
lit—mad at myself for jumping so high. I took off my climbing spurs, picked up my ax, and started into the brush after
him. I remembered about the crazy sheepherder in the valley
who had been bitten that summer by a rattler and, instead of
taking it easy and caring for the bite, had chased the rattler
until he killed him—and himself. I also remembered the crew
talking about it and saying that, even for a sheepherder, he
must have been crazy. I must have been crazier, because after
remembering I went into the brush after him. I went in too
fast and couldn't find him.

We talk nowadays about a "happening," which is a good
term to describe the next section of my life. In my mind it
didn't occur successively and can't be separated: the snake was
coiled about four feet in front of me I stuck the ax down
between him and me he hit the ax handle the ax handle rang
like a bell that had been struck and there was no punctuation
between any of this. Then time started again because it was
after this happening that I felt my hands sting from holding

the ax handle the way your hands sting when you are a kid holding a baseball bat and not paying any attention and another kid with a bat comes sneaking up and hits your bat with his.

The snake lay there as if he had never left his coil. He whirred and watched. He just barely left the next move up to me, and I made it fast. I almost set a record for a standing backward jump. It was getting so that I was doing most of my thinking in the air. I decided if I got to the ground again that I would try to take some of the sting out of my hands by chopping a few more fallen trees but instead when I lit I stood frozen trying to picture the snake as he struck because part of the picture was missing. All I could recall was about a foot and a half of his tail end lying on the ground. His head and all his upper part weren't in the picture. Where they should have been was just a vertical glaze. As I backed off farther, I came to the conclusion that about a foot and a half of him stayed on the ground as a platform to strike from and what struck was too fast to see. The bastard still whirred, so I backed off even farther before I strapped on my climbing spurs. This time when I started to follow the line, I kept one eye and a good part of another on where I was putting my feet.

If you have ever strung much wire, you know there is an important difference between the climbers used on telephone poles and on trees. Tree spurs are about two inches longer, because when you are climbing trees your spurs first have to penetrate the bark before they can start getting any hold in the wood, which is all fine and dandy as long as the trees have bark. But pretty soon the line crossed an old fire burn, maybe one of those 1910 burns, and the only trees standing were long dead and had no bark on them—and were as hard as ebony. I could get only about half an inch of spur in them and so I rocked around on the tips of my spurs and prayed the half inch would hold. The higher I climbed these petrified trees, the more I prayed. Before long, the line crossed a gulch 250 yards or more wide, and it was natural but tough luck that the line on one side of the gulch was down. A span of 250 yards of number nine line is a hell of a lot of weight for a dead tree to hold up in a storm, and one of the trees, rotted at the roots, had come down. I chopped out the line that had got wound around the tree when it fell and I spliced the line and added a few feet to it and picked a new tree to hang it on. Then I almost left the line lying there and started for the ranger station, because I didn't want to climb a dead tree while carrying that weight of line, but whenever I started to duck out like that the ranger was sure to be watching. So I put the wire over my climbing belt and the belt around the tree, and started up with my rear end sticking straight out to punch as much spur into that calcified tree as possible. You've seen linemen at work and know it's a job for rear ends that stick out and you should know why, even if you've never had climbers on. And when you're hanging line on trees instead of poles, you have an extra hazard to overcome—you have to lean even farther back on your rear end and swing a little ax to chop off the limbs as you go up, because your belt is around that tree and it has to go up if you are. Also going up with you are at least 250 yards of number nine wire, getting heavier and tauter every time you stick half an inch of spur into this totem pole of Carborundum. Below on the tree are the sharp stubs of branches you have chopped.

Less than half way up, the line had become so taut it would have pulled me out of the tree if I hadn't been strapped to it by the belt. The half inch of spur became less and less. Then I heard the splinter. Maybe I would have felt better if I had had no belt and the wire had just flipped me over the cliff into the gulch. Anyway, with my spurs torn out of the totem pole I came down about ten or twelve feet, and then my belt caught on something, and I dangled there and smelled smoke from the front of my shirt, my belly having passed over ten feet of the snag ends of chopped branches. I worked the belt loose and fell ten or twelve feet more, and so on. I never could push far enough away from the tree to jab my spurs into it again, and when I finally reached the ground I felt as if an Indian had started a fire by rubbing two sticks together, using me for one of the sticks.

I was afraid to look at my lower quarters to see what was still with me. Instead, I studied the snags of those branches to see which of my private parts were to hang there forever and slowly turn to stone. Finally, I could tell by the total distribution of pain that all of me was still on the same nervous system.

I was suddenly destitute of piety, and knew that I had done all the telephone repair work that I was going to do that day. I tried to tie my outfit into one pack, but all I was thinking about was how thick that mountain rattler was behind his head. And how warm I was in front.

It was downhill to the ranger station, and I arrived there late in the afternoon, still not altogether cooled off. As I expected, Bill was in the warehouse, and he didn't look up when I came in. He said, "Why did you leave the peak?" He knew damn well why I came in—he had told me to come in if it snowed. I said, "There are rattlers up there." He grinned and seemed pleased with himself and the snake. I didn't mention anything about tree climbing, although the front of my shirt was torn.

He wasn't building packs—he was just pulling things together at the end of the season. We didn't say much of anything to each other because I was sore about the snake and he was enjoying himself, but after a while we both got our minds on what we were doing and we both were enjoying ourselves. Maybe one of the chief reasons you become a packer is that you like to handle groceries—and tools. By this time in the season most of the slabs of bacon are moldy and a lot of the tools have broken handles or need their points or edges sharpened, but that's all right. It's a good feeling to pick up an honest mattock that's lost its edge from chopping roots and rocks while making a fire trench, and moldy bacon gives a feeling of having been more than ready to be of service. Finally Bill said, "Why do you go back with the trail crew? They've been doing without you, and I need somebody around camp to help me straighten out the stuff now that the season is over." Then he said, as if he had put the two things together in his mind, "How about a game of cribbage at the station tonight?" I said I would if he needed me and to myself I said I'd put off for a day or two telling him that I was going to quit. More and more, I sensed I was slipping out of life and being drawn into a story. I couldn't quit even when it was time to quit.

The cribbage I especially wasn't crazy about. Here he was, a big black hat and a blue shirt and a cold Bull Durham cigarette hanging on his lip and in his logging boots a double tongue with a fancy fringe cut in it; in addition to all this splendor, he was the best packer going and we thought the best ranger, and he could handle big crews of fire fighters as if he personally owned them and the Bitterroot Mountains, and maybe he had killed a sheepherder, and yet he couldn't play cribbage. And, if the rumors from Hamilton were true about his poker, he couldn't play cards and he couldn't keep away from them. But my immediate burden was this two-handed face-to-face cribbage, and I couldn't get anybody in the outfit to join and make a third so we could play something else. I've already told you about the cook turning me down, and you can bet I tried the crew before I tried him.

The crew was like nearly every other crew I ever worked with in the woods. They were misers on the job. They wouldn't buy shoelaces as long as they could tie more knots in the old ones; they wouldn't bet a nickel on a card game; they learned to sew great ugly patches on their shirts; they spent all Sunday darning their socks and patching the patches on their shirts; they hoarded and Christianized—all so they would have a bigger roll to lose the first night they hit town. The closer we got to quitting time, of course, the more they hoarded and Christianized. When I went to the crew's tent to find my bedroll and air it before night, I ran into the whole bunch, and it was good to see them, especially Mr. Smith, who gave me a thump on the back, but I didn't try to tempt them into any forms of sin like a dime-limit poker game. I knew I was stuck with cribbage, and I could hear Bill counting an eight and a pair of sevens: "fifteen-two, fifteen-four, fifteen-six, and a pair make eight."

That evening I learned never to quit hating a guy just because I hadn't seen him for a while. Bill and I were a little guarded with each other, but my two weeks in exile had cleaned away some of our bad feelings. Sending me to Siberia, though, hadn't given Bill any greater insight into cards, and I knew that unless we changed the game we would soon be in trouble again. I am sure that feeling was right; where I was wrong was in forgetting to keep on hating the cook. He was almost through wiping the dishes, the food had tasted pretty good, especially after two weeks of my own cooking, and three men seemed as if they should be friendly when we had just been through an August snowstorm.

As one of those people who often are among the first to hear what they are saying, I heard myself say, overloaded with friendship, "Here, give me a towel and let's finish the dishes. Then, how about joining us in a game of something? The season is almost over and the three of us have never sat down to a game."

He jerked away the towel I was reaching for. In his canvas shoes, he rose on his toes, sank back on his heels, and rose again. Until this time I hadn't been old enough to realize that you can't hate a guy without expecting him to return the compliment. Up to now, I thought you could hate somebody as if it were your own business. "How many times do I have to tell you—I don't play cards against guys I work with." The cards lay rejected in my hand. He rolled the towel in a wad and threw it on the dishrack. "Here, give me those cards," he said, and grabbed them out of my hand and sat down at the table and began to shuffle. The cards seemed to burst into flames. He said, "Sit down," and I obeyed, with my hand still open where the cards had been.

Then he did two things.

First, he flashed through the cards and picked out the four aces. Then he stuck them in the pack. Then he asked me to cut the deck. Then he dealt out hands to Bill, me, and himself. "Turn them over," he said to me. Mine was just a hand. So was Bill's. In his hand were all four aces.

He started out the same way the next time—he picked out

the four aces, stuck them into the deck, shuffled, had me cut, and then dealt out hands to the three of us. "Turn them over," he said, and there wasn't a single ace in any hand. He slapped the deck of cards in front of me. "Here," he said, "find the four aces." And he went back to finish the dishes.

It wasn't like me to be obedient, but I was. I fumbled through the deck and never found an ace. Then I tried to conduct a more thorough search and then I gave up. As he spread his dish towel to dry, he said over his shoulder, "Look in your shirt pocket." They were there, all four of them. I spread them out to count them. I was to have plenty of reason to remember this trick.

"He's a cardshark," Bill said, with a smile on his face, something like the smile that was there when I had told him the rattler had almost bitten me.

After a while, Bill added, "He's an artist." Well, I was a little dazed, I admit, and there was no denying he was a cardshark, and in the center circle of male magic sits the cardshark, but Bill's calling him an artist was something I wouldn't accept. I said to myself—fortunately not out loud this time—"Still, there's something wrong with this guy. I still think he's a forty-cent piece."

He came over and sat down next to me at the table again and began to shuffle and deal. Now, he was only practicing by himself. Usually he dealt one round and said one sentence. If he wanted more emphasis, he would shuffle, cut, and deal four hands and then say one sentence. Something like this. "I'll tell you once and for all about my card playing . . ." (one round). "I play cards for a living . . ." (one round). "I have to get out in the summer for my health . . ." (one round). "I can't do hard work because I have to keep my hands soft . . ." (one round). "So I cook and wash dishes . . ." (one round). "I practice every night before I go to bed." Then he played a whole poker game again before he finished, "I never play cards against men I work with."

With one movement he picked up the four hands, and we all started for bed.

"By the way," Bill said as I went out the door, "I have a scheme—I'll tell you about it tomorrow." Before I went to sleep I had the scheme fairly well figured out. Just fairly well.

The truth is that I don't think he had it figured out too well himself at the time—maybe never. It became obvious as we talked in the warehouse the next morning that he was talking to shape things in his own mind. From the beginning I was the one to pick up the money, and he would "cover me," whatever that meant. At the beginning, too, he thought he would need only two others, and he made what to me was a strange pick—Mr. Smith and a Canadian soldier who had been gassed and had been sent out to recover in the high mountains. Although he wore the first pair of hornrim glasses I ever saw, and with a braided cord attached, he turned out to be almost as gifted in communing with livestock as Bill himself. He could talk to all horses and mules and heal them, no matter what their trouble was. He must have had something for Bill to pick him for the rough work ahead, even though sometimes he coughed so bad that we would take the whiskey away from him and drink it ourselves on the theory that there was no use wasting fairly good moonshine on a dying man. Bill's picking him had to be a case of one horseman believing in another. At first, then, Bill was going to count on the three of us and himself, but before the morning was over he had decided on the whole crew. "It's a pretty good crew," he said. "We can't leave any of them out." As for the cook, I was warned again never to put a hand on him.

He estimated that it would take us another week or more to get the station in shape at the end of the season, and to load the pack string, mostly with surplus tools from the big fire. The cook, he said, would ride to Hamilton. The rest of us would walk. No wonder the cook wore low canvas shoes in the woods.

The first night in town we were to meet at the Oxford, a pool and card parlor that by report was Hamilton's best. He was betting all his roll on the cook. As for the rest of us, we could get in on a sure thing if we liked and just as much as we wanted to contribute. That was up to me and to them—me to tell them and all of us to contribute. I was told again—several times—that I was to pick up the money in case trouble started, and I was told again that he would "cover me."

"Wear your own gun, too," he said to me. "God," I said, "Bill, I can't do that. I've nothing but that .32-20 on a .45 frame. That's as big as horse artillery. I'd be arrested before I got to the bar." "Well," he said, "expect trouble." After a while I asked, "Bill, you don't have any side arm, do you, but the big .45? Do you think you can get into a gambling joint wearing that?" He said, "I said I'll cover you."

Early in the morning I had started putting pieces together by remembering the rumors that in Hamilton Bill was regarded as nature's gift to the local gamblers. It was said that they even matched to see which one would pluck him when he came to town. So now we were going to have a big melodrama that might be called "The Ranger's Revenge." I was to go out and invite the crew to make the stake bigger so those Hamilton boys who had done Bill in would be done in bigger themselves. And a couple of weeks ago I had been sent into exile because I said I was going to take a punch at the cook. And when the time came the cook was going to ride into Hamilton, while we walked.

"Well," I said to myself, "it all fits." But I bet twenty dollars on the son of a bitch myself, and normally I hoarded my money just like the rest of them.

It took the crew some time to warm up to the idea of staking the cook. To start with, they didn't like the cook much better than I did. Then, too, in the struggle between instincts, it's hard to know whether miserliness or greed will have the edge. The crew still would rather darn their socks than lose a dime, but they couldn't bear to miss a sure thing. Finally, I told them about finding the four aces in my shirt pocket. "That's simple to explain but hard to do," Mr. Smith said. Since he had spent most of his life around mining camps, he knew all about cards, but wasn't much good with them himself and practically never played. "He palmed them," he said. "What the hell is palming?" I asked. He got a card and showed us how you hold the edges of a card between your first finger and your little finger and then bend your fingers and reach with your thumb and push or pull the card from your palm to the back of your hand or vice versa, at the same time turning your wrist so the card can't be seen by someone in front of you. "So what he did," Mr. Smith said, "was to have the cards in the back of his hand and to show you the palm, and, as he went by your shirt pocket, he bent his fingers and put the cards in it." He tried to show us but he was clumsy and we could always see the card, though we got the idea. We all tried to palm but we were clumsier than Mr. Smith. In fact, I tried for several years to get fairly good, but never did. Mr. Smith said to convince us, "You've seen this in vaudeville." In those days the Pantages circuit made the rounds of Spokane, Butte, and Missoula, so we had all seen a magician hold out a card in his palm and then toss it in the air where it disappeared. "Do you mean," Mr. McBride asked, "the cook is good enough to be in vaudeville?" "He might be," said Mr. Smith. "Here we're just trying to palm one card, but he may have palmed all those four aces at once." Someone reverently said, "Jesus!" and they all bet.

Besides, they too began to get the feeling that they were all to have parts in a sort of pulp-magazine plot, and they liked the feeling. If they seemed to feel a lot better than I did about having a part in a story, maybe that was because they liked their part better than I thought I was going to like mine. Anyway, when I collected the "hat pool," it turned out the average bet was more than what I had bet—even a little more than half a month's wages. Once their bets became official by my handing over their money to Bill, they gathered every night to see the cook shuffle, peering in a semicircle around the table like a bunch of rail birds at a race track watching their favorite horse work out. Now that they had bet on him, they even spoke of "having a piece of him."

Although, as Bill had suggested, I was working around the station and not with the trail crew, I knew that they weren't

getting much done either. For them as for me, quitting time
had come and we were all through for the season. It wasn't
only because we felt carried away by being in our own story.
Anyone who has done seasonal work knows that as regular as
the seasons themselves is the return of this feeling at the end
of each season, "It's time to quit. It's time to quit." Even Mr.
Smith seemed to have lost his passion for dynamite.

We started trying to have some fun, more or less getting in
practice for the first night in town. Now I know that it's common to picture loggers and cowboys as always whooping it up,
full of bad whiskey and great jokes on greenhorns. I don't
know much about cowboys—they come from my wife's
country—but before I was through I worked with a lot of
crews in the woods, and day in and day out we weren't jokey,
and jokes on greenhorns were pretty standardized. For one
thing, we worked too hard and too long to be left bubbling
over with the comic spirit. For another thing, we worked too
often alone or in small groups to think it worth the time to be
funny. It's no trouble at all to be tragic when you're tired and
alone, but to be funny you have to be fresh and you have to
have time on your hands and you have to have an
audience—and you have to be funny. And, however much
you may love the woods, you can't claim it is full of natural
wits. Don't get me wrong—we had what we called our fun, but
only on what seemed like state occasions, and often then our
jokes were pretty much the same old jokes and often the
laugh was on us at the end. A state occasion was when a big
crew got together, especially if it was quitting time and no one
was working hard any more.

Even so, we began very gently to throw off our work-
ingman's puritanism and prepare for sin. We began with a
crew from the Engineers that had camped at the ranger station for a few days. They were mapping the back country
where, they said, "the government hadn't figured out yet
what they had stolen from the Indians." I went over to see
them right away, because I liked maps and what they stood
for, but the rest of our bunch were slower to take an interest

in this mapping crew. For one thing, they waited every night until the cook had finished shuffling cards. And for another, they had the practical woodsman's distrust of Forest Service maps. They were convinced that a lot of the back country was mapped in those early days by guys who sat in tents or in the Regional Office in Missoula in the winter and said, "No, it goes here." In fact, in those early days we never believed that a mountain was really there unless it had been located by the United States Geological Survey. So our bunch immediately got in an argument with the mapping crew. We pretended to ourselves that we were the Regional Office in Missoula. "Hell," we would say, "that creek doesn't go there. It goes here." Sometimes we were only trying to confuse them and sometimes we meant it.

At that time, though, the mapping crew was more troubled about the name of a creek than where it went. They had been over on the north fork of the Clearwater and of course had run into Wet Ass Creek. They had accurately located it, too. They may have compass-and-chained it; at least they had compass-and-paced it. But they were divided as to whether they should put down its real name on the map they were going to submit to the drafting room of the regional office. Well, the regional office has never cared much for jokes or poetry, so we sided loudly with those who were for its right name and argued that too much of the West had been named after some guy's home town in Minnesota or Massachusetts or even after the guy himself or after a bear or a deer. "There are only five thousand Deer Creeks in the country. Let's keep America's only Wet Ass Creek," we argued. The other bunch, who also would soon be spending a summer of money on a night with the whores of Hamilton, argued that many who worked in the Forest Service's drafting room in Missoula were women and would be offended by having to copy such language with their own pure hands.

We put it to a vote, and our side won, or, for the time being, we thought we had. Anyway, they all agreed to submitting its right name to the drafting room and we looked forward to its becoming a National Park—Wet Ass National Park, where all pilgrims from Brooklyn can stop their cars in the middle of the road to let their children feed the grizzlies and vice versa.

In the end, though, it turned out the joke was on us. On the next map of the Forest, it appeared all as one word and a final *e* had been added which henceforward was pronounced, and the *a* was made in Boston. Now, it doesn't mean anything but be sure you pronounce it right: Wĕ-tä′-sē Creek, just as if its headwaters were on Beacon Hill.

At the time, we liked our joke, and, on the temporary strength of it, tried others, but we were end-of-the-summer tired—for that matter, still tired from the big fire—and our jokes were tired, too. We even tried to take the Canadian on a snipe hunt and get him to hold the gunnysack open while we herded the snipe into it, but the Canadian hadn't been gassed in France just to get caught holding a gunnysack in Idaho. Besides, we were starting to get in practice for Hamilton, and we weren't thinking of making jokes when we got there. Instead, the crew had a still back in the woods and were making moonshine out of dried apricots, peaches, and prunes they stole from the warehouse. Old Mr. Smith had got hold of some Sterno and they would boil the pink stuff off the top and drink the rest and it would go right through them, sometimes before they could get to the toilet or to the brush. They were practicing up for Hamilton, and had a couple of days more to go. I'd decided I was going to leave next morning, and walk to Hamilton in one day and more or less set a record. So I wasn't drinking any of their stuff, not even their dried apricot brandy distilled in a lard pail. When I told them I was going to leave tomorrow, they said, "What the hell kind of a guy are you anyway? Aren't you going to stay with the crew and help us clean out the town? What about the cook winning all that money for us from those Hamilton tin-horn gamblers? What kind of a crew are we anyway if we don't clean out the town?"

All these were important matters, and you can be sure I'd thought about them. You just weren't a crew if you didn't "clean out the town" as your final act of the season. I don't know why, but it always happens if you're any good—and even if you're not much good—that when you work outside a town for a couple of months you get feeling a lot better than the town and very hostile toward it. The town doesn't even know about you, but you think and talk a lot about it. Old Mr. Smith would take another drink of that alcohol and other debris from the canned heat, and say, "We'll take that God damn town apart." Then with his dignity lost he would have to run for the toilet, yelling as he ran that we had to show them there were no guys as tough as those who worked for the USFS.

Besides, there was this big killing the cook was going to make for us. We spent part of every evening arguing about how much we'd win. The amounts varied depending upon whether we argued before or after we saw the cook deal, but we usually settled for a figure around what for each of us was a summer's wages. Secretly, we hoped for more.

But I was out to set a record. Ever since the ranger had realized that the cook was fancy with the cards and so had taken my place as his favorite, I'd felt a growing need to set a record. I wished that it could be in packing and that I could become known overnight as one of the Decker brothers, who had designed the latest packsaddle, but I couldn't live long in that pipe dream, and powder work made me sick, so it had to be walking. I knew I could outwalk anyone in our district, and at the moment I needed a little local fame, and I needed it bad.

Twenty-eight miles from Elk Summit to the mouth of Blodgett Canyon plus a few more miles to Hamilton is not outstanding distance, just as distance, but still it is a damn tough walk. For one thing, those were Forest Service miles, and, in case you aren't familiar with a "Forest Service mile," I'll give you a modern well-marked example. Our family cabin is near the Mission Glaciers and naturally one of the many nearby lakes is named Glacier Lake, which is at the end of the Kraft Creek Road, except that the final pitch is so steep

you have to make it on foot. Where the trail starts there is a
Forest Service sign reading: "Glacier Lake—1 Mi." Then you
climb quite a way on the trail toward Glacier Lake and you
come to another Forest Service sign reading: "Glacier
Lake—1.2 Mi." So a good working definition of a "Forest
Service mile" is quite a way plus a mile and two-tenths, and I
was going to walk over thirty Forest Service miles to Hamilton, about half of them up until I was above mountain goats
and the other half down and down until my legs would beg to
start climbing again and I wouldn't be able to comply. The
trail was full of granite boulders, and I would manage somehow so that Bill would hear that I had walked it in a day.

I said to Bill while he was counting his cribbage hand with
his lips, "When are you going to take the pack string and the
men into town?"

He finished counting before he said, "You will wait till we
get there." I didn't know whether he had asked or told me
something.

I picked up his hand and counted it over again. "I need the
whole crew," he said. I said, "Yes." "If you'll stay tomorrow,"
he said, "and help put the packs together, I'll try to get away
by noon the next day and camp on the divide that night. You
can start the same morning ahead of us."

It was Wednesday, and by his scheme we would work
Thursday and I would start Friday morning and he and the
men Friday noon.

"I'll meet you in town on Saturday," I said.

"Saturday night in Hamilton," he said, which was to become
one of my walking tunes.

Long before daylight I was using my feet like beetle feelers to
find my way across Horse Heaven Meadow. Don't look at me,
look at the map, because I don't have the kind of a mind that
could make up a name like that. Even if you want to drop the
Horse Heaven business, you still have a high mountain
meadow just before daybreak, full of snorts and spooks.
There are lots of horses out there but also a lot of other big

animals. Elk and deer for sure. Maybe bear. They wake in darkness and come down from the hills to drink, and then slowly feed toward higher ground until it gets hot and is time for them to lie down again. A clank in the darkness is the scariest of all sounds, but you know a second afterwards it has to be a hobbled horse. If you are listening for dainty sounds to signify deer, there is nothing daintier than a snort—but there are deer there. They snort, and then bound. Elk snort, and then crash. Bear bolt straight uphill in a landslide—no animal has such pistons for hindquarters.

I still walked in wonderland after daylight. Far ahead on gray cliffs I could see the white specks that were not spots in my eyes. The trail was already getting steep and I knew before noon I would be higher than the mountain goats and from experience I knew that there is nothing much higher on earth.

The first summer I worked in the Forest Service we had come out of Idaho over the Bitterroots by way of Lake Como, and the hunting season on mountain goats was open in Idaho but not in Montana, and also in those days we could buy a resident's license in Idaho if we worked for the Forest Service. So we all did, and camped for a few days near the divide to hunt. Bill said to me, "All you have to do is get above mountain goats. They never think anything is above them." So all I had to do was get above mountain goats, which is beyond where most men have been. But finally there was a goat standing below me near the edge of a cliff two hundred and fifty or so yards away. I knew that when you shoot downhill at such an angle, you have to shoot way under your target, but it was almost straight down and I didn't hold under him nearly enough. My bullet didn't even hit the cliff. It was just a loud sound bound for eternity. The goat only hightailed it behind a rock, and hid. Now nobody could see him from below but he was still in plain sight to me. So Bill had been right, and I thought afterwards it must be great to live believing that there is no danger from above. None of those goats could have been Presbyterians, or ever heard my father preach. This time, though, I held so far under him I was afraid I'd shoot my feet off and I still shot over him, but I did hit the rock, and I've often wondered where the bullet went from there. Likewise the goat, which may never again have been seen by man. I didn't get any more shots that season—man is evidently not entitled to miss a goat more than twice in the same year.

I walked head down because I wasn't getting anywhere when I watched, so I was aware of him first as a snort and then a stamp. He was in the trail in front of me and he was a big bull moose and he looked as if he had decided not to go any place. When you saw bull moose in Montana in those days you were probably near the Bitterroot Divide and close to one of those snowbank lakes left in the burrows of old glaciers.

This bull lowered his horns and then, possibly just for exercise, raised them. Some half-chewed marsh grass stuck out of his mouth. Finally, he reversed the order and stamped and then snorted. Reluctantly he turned and started down the trail, slowly at first but faster as he went along, as if the idea of retreating came very gradually to him. I watched those legs swinging those big feet that looked as if they had been shod, and I am almost sure he was a four-gaited animal, if you'll admit that for a short stretch I saw him single-foot. In wonderland, why shouldn't a moose single-foot as well as walk, trot, and pace?

Then I put my head down and started my one and only gait again. There was nothing but granite now and, as it became hard to climb and breathe, I needed somebody besides Bill to watch me. I began to think about my girl, and finally she appeared to me, as if her image had been resting in the woods with the deer.

Since my father was the Presbyterian minister in town, I had lived quite a few years under the impression that Roman Catholic girls were prettier than Protestant girls. About Jewish girls I was of a divided mind, probably because there were just two Jewish girls in my home town, one for each half of my mind. One was classy and played the piano and was several years older than I was and wouldn't even look my way. The other was younger than I was and ugly and would do anything to please me. She even made dates for me with other girls she thought I'd like. She had started me going with my present Irish Catholic girl, whose particular fascination was a deep scar in her forehead that half-closed a corner of her eye and made her look as if she was never quite looking at me. I discovered several years later that she had been screwing everybody in town, except me and possibly several other Protestants, and after that discovery I veered rapidly to red- (and black-) headed Protestant and Jewish girls, but at the time I conceived of her as my one and only. She watched me out of her deceptive eye, I thought admiringly, and I tore up the trail.

When I finally made the divide, I carefully studied the center of it, traced in my mind what I designated as the state line between Idaho and Montana and then made a small section of it real by pissing on it—a very short dehydrated state line. I always did this on big divides, especially on the Continental Divide where one is left wondering whether he is going to drain into the Atlantic or the Pacific. The divide here is not the Continental Divide, but it stirs the imagination.

Then I sat down and rested above the white goats. I looked back where I had worked three summers, and it looked strange. When you look back at where you have been, it often seems as if you have never been there or even as if there were no such place. Of the peaks in the sky, my old lookout, Grave Peak, of course, was the one I knew best. When I lived on it, it was a hard climb out of a basin full of big rocks and small grubs, a tent with a finally-mended hole, trees decapitated by lightning, no soft place to sit and one grizzly and one rattlesnake. But here from the divide, it was another reality. It was sculpture in the sky, devoid of any detail of life. There is a peak near my home town we call Squaw's Teat. It is not a great mountain but it has the right name for Grave Peak when viewed from the distance of the divide. From the divide the mountain I had lived on was bronze sculpture. It was all shape with nothing on it, just nothing. It was just color and shape and sky. It was as if some Indian beauty before falling asleep forever had decided to leave exposed what she thought was not quite her most beautiful part. So perhaps at a certain perspective what we leave behind is often wonderland, always different from what it was and generally more beautiful.

I was trying to keep from myself the fact that I had walked to the top too fast and was a lot tireder than I wanted to be. I had walked those fourteen miles to the rhythm of "It's time to quit. It's time to quit," but the tempo kept speeding up, especially after my girl began to watch me with a half-closed eye. Sitting there in the sun I began to feel chilled, so I crossed the divide and looked down Blodgett Canyon to see what it was like ahead.

You might never have heard the word geology and yet have known the instant you looked down Blodgett Canyon that you were looking at a gigantic, glacial classic. For thousands of years it must have been a monster of ice hissing in the cracks of mountains. Coming at me from almost straight below was a Jacob's ladder of switchbacks, rising out of what I later discovered geologists call a cirque but what to me looked like the original nest of a green coiled glacier. When it struck for the valley, the mountains had split apart. At the top where it writhed out of its course and returned, it left a peak or a series of pinnacles. When it reached its own mouth, the partially digested remains of mountains rolled out of its gorge all the way to the river.

It was a big world and not a very big boy and I thought it was time he shoved off, even though he hadn't taken a long enough rest.

I shook myself to get warm and started down the switchbacks. I'd intended to take it easy in getting started again, but going down switchbacks doesn't give you much choice and when you're young and out to set a local record you aren't going to take the long way around each switchback. Wherever the face of the mountain was open, I cut straight down, omitting all six-percent grades. I descended in avalanches. Avalanches beside me, avalanches in the rear of me, avalanches in front of me. On the fly, I watched over my shoulder to duck the big boulders. When my legs felt torn in front and I had to stop, I could hear rivulets of granite particles pursuing me and then giving up and then making one more try. After I hit the bottom of the basin and had been standing there for some time to let the spasms in my legs quiet and even after all the avalanches behind had come to a rest, one big granite chunk dropped from nowhere beside me. I looked up and could find no likely place but the middle of the sky.

At the bottom of the basin I was already lower than the white specks on the cliffs. On the cliffs there was only an occasional tree where a bird had dropped a seed in a crevice. At the top of the divide I had felt chilled in the sun. Here, at the bottom of the glacial basin my face was tightened with heat. Accompanied by avalanches from the sky, I had descended into the pit. The heat made one gigantic bounce from the solar system to the granite cliffs to me personally. Besides, it rose from what I walked on and I could feel that I was turning black under my face like Dante descending into the Inferno.

I had also made myself into something of a medical problem by refusing to drink water. Since I'd never before walked this far in a day and didn't want anybody to know until

I was sure I had, I took over all the thinking myself. I thought, when I go fishing on the Blackfoot River and it's hot and I start drinking from the river, pretty soon I can't stop drinking and pretty soon it doesn't even taste good and I end up waterlogged and half-sick. I reasoned, "You mustn't get sick, so you mustn't drink water." I can remember taking a sip when eating my sandwich, and, although I can't remember, I must have taken a few other sips, but I stood pledged to some kind of youthful and lofty denial of the flesh. I walked suffering all afternoon down that chasm where mountains had cried for centuries as their structure cracked. At the end, I walked in semidarkness, medically dehydrated.

For irony, a plunging stream accompanied me to the divide and another one followed me down. Blodgett Creek had started at the bottom of the basin right beside where I and the big boulder lit—springs all over with green sponges around them. I took off my woolen socks and waded in one of them to restore firmness to the flesh I walked on. The water was so cold my heart did something funny, so I stepped back on the sponge. On my way down the canyon, I stopped several times to wade in the creek. I watched little black trout who lived and breathed in it, but I fought, nobly I judged, not to take a drink of it myself.

I tried to think of various things, but by the time I was half way down the canyon I could think of nothing but drinking. I had pictured myself reaching across the green table for all those dollars, but my pressure on the dollars weakened and I felt them slip slowly out of my hands. The man in the tall black Stetson that I wanted to be like, had from time to time said to me, "And I'll cover you," but I still didn't know what he meant. I couldn't even retain my girl as part of my mental life. She watched me until she was just her half-closed eye, and then, as some years later, she gave me the big wink and was gone.

From time to time, I thought I was on the fire line and that the sky was swirling with burning cones and that the universe was upside down, with hell above. The trail ahead seemed full of light ashes rising off the ground because I drew near them.

At other times I felt sick and immediately afterwards thought I smelled dynamite.

But always I wanted a drink. I knew as a logger I should want a "boilermaker," a slug of whiskey with a bottle of beer as a chaser. Instead I wanted an ice-cream soda. I told myself that ice-cream sodas were for kids, but the image of a boilermaker left scars of dehydration. Besides, I liked ice-cream sodas and at seventeen was secretly curious how men could like the taste of whiskey. So I walked mile after mile with nothing in sight but ice-cream sodas that changed only to vary the color combinations—white vanilla, yellow lemon, and brown chocolate were my favorites, but once in a while I stuck in a strawberry flavor, just before chocolate. I filled the glasses nearly to the top with carbonated water, leaving not quite enough room for a dip of ice cream so that froth would run over. I drank all the ice-cream sodas I could make, always beginning by licking off the froth. I was a damn mess and childish, a fact I tried to keep from myself.

When I finally saw the light from the canyon's mouth, the cliff on the north side looked tipped beyond ninety degrees.

Even so, I wouldn't have been in too bad shape when I reached Hamilton if Hamilton had been where I remembered it was, a mile or two from the mouth of Blodgett Canyon. But after one good look I had to stop to absorb my disbelief. Hamilton is way out in the valley and upriver and must be five or six miles from the mouth of the canyon. Five or six miles, all gently sloping to the river, may be a breeze to you, but I sat by the side of the road and played mumblety-peg to steady my hands. I thought of the Bible and hoped that a pair of arms would enfold me and put me on a mule and lead me into Hamilton without any more thorns. There it was in plain view but farther away than seemed possible for a man to walk. This was the first time I had ever been in a fight when I took a terrible beating at the end. At seventeen I had been in a fair number of fights and had won most of them and naturally had lost some too, but always before when I was losing some big friend who maybe I hadn't

seen before would step in and stop the fight. I had never
before taken a beating with nobody there to stop the beating.
When you're watching a fight and you see a guy's legs buckle
and his hands drop and he doesn't even back away, it's easy to
say to another bystander, "Look at that gutless son of a bitch.
He won't even put up his hands to fight." It's different,
though, when you're the guy with nothing left in your legs
that will put up your hands, or back away.

I didn't try any of the hard positions in mumblety-peg,
nothing harder than to the nose and to both ears. It helped,
though, and gradually I figured out why I was here and
Hamilton was way out there. In the spring our crew had been
taken by truck from Hamilton to the mouth of Blodgett
Canyon as a start on our way to Idaho—in a truck, what's the
difference between a couple of miles and five or six? In the
spring, too, I hadn't looked back down Blodgett Canyon to
see how a glacier had made it and shoved its remains all the
way to the river. Hamilton was on the river, and now I
understood why I had four or five miles yet to go.

With that out of the way, I got up and snapped my
jackknife shut and began to walk. Sometimes all you have left
to win with is the knowledge of why you're taking the beating
and the realization that nobody else is going to save you from
it.

Since it never got closer while I watched, I didn't look until
it was there. I have always been grateful to Hamilton for
being, if not where I expected, at least where I could
understand.

At the time I was also grateful to Hamilton for being an
outwardly simple structure to comprehend after a long day.
The road from Blodgett Canyon turns at right angles and
joins the main street, and the main street of Hamilton is called
Main Street, and the streets that cross it at right angles are
named by number. I walked down Main Street to, I think, the
block between Third and Second where there was a
drugstore. I had two ice-cream sodas, a white vanilla and a
yellow lemon, and ordered a third, a chocolate soda, to

complete my favorite color sequence, but the drugstore clerk said, "Son, I don't think you should have another one now." I felt like going around behind the counter and shoving the drugstore clerk into his chocolate ice-cream freezer, especially for calling me "son," but I didn't and I can't claim to have thought better of it. I just felt strange all over.

Everything was going very fast, including the quitting time rhythm which I certainly had thought would slow and then stop when I got to town. Instead, everything I wanted to do all summer I wanted to do right now. I wanted to find the Chinese restaurant which all the Bitterrooters in the woods said was the best eating place in town, and I wanted to find this Oxford gambling joint and watch their shills at work and I more or less wanted to find a hotel and leave my pack and wash up and maybe lie down before going out on the town. This idea of lying down for a while interested me least of all, so I stopped somebody outside and asked where the Chinaman's was and I think it was in the same block, on Main between Third and Second.

The Chinaman behind the cash register wore a silky black coat, a white shirt, and a black string tie, and he studied me and my patches and pack and my hair that hadn't been cut in three months. He clearly didn't care for any Forest Service trade from Elk Summit, but without being asked I walked back near the kitchen and sat down at the smallest table in the room. I put my pack on the other chair for a guest. A white waitress came with a menu. Her voice was husky and she was the first woman I had smelled all summer, and she smelled like a woman. I couldn't read what was on the menu—maybe I didn't know the names of Chinese food or maybe I just couldn't see very well. The waitress came back several times and looked at me. I finally thought, "Probably I'm dirty," so I asked her where the men's room was and I washed in cold water and wiped myself with a cloth towel that came out about a foot at a time when I pushed a button. I wet my hair but my comb was in my pack so my hair was wet and stringy when I came back and, despite the cold water, I didn't feel any better.

She returned soon and still looked troubled and finally asked, "Do you think you should order now? Why not wait another hour or so before you eat?"

I would never have got to Hamilton if I felt that way about things. I said, "No, I want to order now." She must have known that she would have to order for me. She would ask, "Wouldn't you like to try ... ?" and then she would name something that ended with suey or mein. Each time I would say, "That would be just fine." I was overpolite in trying to show her that despite the way I looked I was really at home in such classy establishments as Chinese restaurants. I kept saying, "Yes, that would be just fine," until she stuck the pencil in her blouse and headed for the kitchen.

The moment I was alone I got very sick. I do not know whether I knew I was very sick. What I knew was that the world was made of two parts—inside and outside a Chinese restaurant—and that I was sure to feel better if only I could get to wherever I was not now. Later, I could look for the Oxford.

When the waitress finally came, I said, "Would you please give me my check?" She was frightened and said, "But you haven't even eaten yet." I said, "I know. Just bring me the check." She said, "Would you please wait a moment?" And she went, not to the kitchen, but to the cash register and talked to the Chinaman with the string tie.

Everything inside me was going sickeningly fast and everything outside was standing sickeningly still. I wondered how much longer I could wait for my check and then fresh air. I could even guess what they were whispering behind the cash register. Lumberjacks had pretty much the same joke that they played on Chinamen behind cash registers. Four or five jacks would finish eating together and then one would saunter to the front and say to the Chinaman, "He" (pointing in the general direction of the table) "is going to pay for mine. He" (pointing in the same general direction) "lost a bet to me." Then he would slide by, and this would go on until only one jack was left who would put down just enough money for his own dinner. "Hell, what do you mean me paying for those other guys? I don't even hardly know them." I was alone but clearly I was from the Forest Service and I had ordered dinner and now I was trying to get out of the restaurant before it was even served. It was a somewhat different lumberjack game, but it had to be a game between a lumberjack and a Chinaman that a Chinaman was supposed to lose. The waitress hurried past me to the kitchen, obviously not looking my way.

I couldn't wait any longer for anybody to talk to anybody else. I got up and thought I did pretty well to remember my pack. The kitchen door opened and I never knew before how many Chinamen work in the kitchen of a Chinese restaurant. Families of them, from children to old men, each outfitted with a butcher knife. They followed slowly behind me to the cash register. The waitress stood frightened by herself. She thought, Now I've done it.

I looked at the bill several times to be sure that it was not more than the silver dollar in my hand and then I put both on the counter next to the cash register and I remember thinking that my paying the bill was a kind of inscrutable joke on the Chinese. I reached out my hand for the change and knocked over the glass of toothpicks and then slid slowly to the floor in a cloud of toothpicks.

I do not remember hitting the floor.

The next thing I remember was a husky voice and the smell of woman, and when I opened my eyes I felt more than saw that the waitress was washing my face with a napkin and I immediately fell in love with her. Wherever I had been, I had been very lonely, and I immediately fell in love with her for bending over me. The Chinamen leaned forward in a circle, and were scared by what they saw. The Chinaman with the string tie was unhappy because it was happening in his place. The waitress made a big thing of smiling and said, "We've called the doctor."

I thought that would be quite a while, but when I opened my eyes next he had already listened to my chest and was lifting me up to listen to me through my back. When he saw I was awake, he asked questions. He was an old man, he wore a Stetson, and we all knew immediately that he was good. No one said a word unless the doctor asked him, and the doctor knew we all were scared and wanted to tell us not to be as soon as he could.

He pulled my shirt together and, before he started to button it, he said, "It was those God damn ice-cream sodas."

He talked to all of us, not just to me. He said it was this way. I had walked too far; it was very hot; and I didn't drink anything. Then I drank two God damn ice-cream sodas. This is the way he explained to us what happened medically. He said my blood from "the exertion" (he said "exertion") was mostly in the outside of me—in my legs and arms and muscles. Then I drank the two God damn ice-cream sodas and they were cold and so the blood all rushed to the inside of me and left my head empty and I fainted. He said, don't worry, take it easy for a day or so, and you'll feel as good as ever. All of us thought we understood everything and were greatly relieved.

He was a small-town doctor, and I have never asked a big-town doctor for his opinion of the small-town doctor's medical explanation. I am sure, though, that no big-town doctor ever said what the small-town doctor said to me next. He said: "You come to see me late tomorrow morning in my office, do you hear? If you don't come tomorrow, I'll charge you for tonight. If you come tomorrow, I won't charge you for tomorrow or tonight. All I want is to know that you are well."

Then the circle began to break up, and people helped me to find the change that had slipped out of my hand when I'd fallen. The doctor said to the Chinaman with the silk coat, "Get him to a hotel." I don't remember anything for a long time after that. Either I fainted again or I just went to sleep.

Even while I was waking I knew I should be in a hotel. I got up and checked my clothes and they were on a chair and my pack was in a corner and about the amount of money I should have had was in a pocket. I knew I had been asleep for a while but I also knew it was a long time until daybreak. I went back to bed to check on myself and the surroundings.

At first I tried to find out about myself, but before long the surroundings forced themselves upon my attention—not, however, until I realized this must be early morning of Saturday night in Hamilton. It was still too early in the morning to know how I would feel about the night when it got here, but I felt very bad about the night before when I fell in front of the cash register with toothpicks in my hair. As far as I knew, no one ever before had fainted except women and then only in books. I had actually never known a person who had fainted. Suddenly, I felt one of those great waves of sadness that rarely come over me. I had made it clear from Elk Summit only to lie down on the floor of a Chinese restaurant. Now nothing was left that could be mentioned to Bill about a day fourteen miles up and fourteen miles down with five or six miles still left to go. The coming night would be the last night when the ranger and the cook and the crew and I would be together. I got hold of myself and said, "I'd better be good tonight and that damn cook had better faint." I explored myself a little further: "I wish I felt a little better—I'm not feeling bad, but I'd be afraid to get up and walk down the hall and find out."

About here the surroundings took over. A big ass pushed the wall next to my bed and gave me a nudge. As the books would say, I sat bolt upright. It had to be an ass, but how the hell did it come through the wall? It was half-light in my room and I studied the wall. So help me, it was made of canvas. Likewise the other wall, but once in a while the wall beside my bed bulged as if the glacier that had made Blodgett Canyon was at work next door. Suddenly, I remembered things that aged Mr. Smith and Mr. McBride had told me. "This is just like an old-time western whorehouse," I thought, "with canvas partitions between the cribs." I watched and listened, and, after I saw and heard what was happening in the next room and was extending into part of mine, I said, "What the hell do I mean, like an old-time western whorehouse? This is the thing itself."

At first I thought that there had to be several people in the crib next door, but I finally added up everything and settled for a pimp and a whore screwing up and down the bed, occasionally swerving out of their course and then returning to leave peaks and pinnacles on my wall. It was only his ass that took the scenic route, unfortunately; hers must have kept on a straight course, and never nudged me, and I eventually came to understand why. She talked all the time in a monotone, and while they screwed she talked about how he had been out screwing other whores. I happened to be very sensitive to rhythm that year and I finally realized that I could scan what she was saying. If I allowed for understandable cæsuras, she was speaking blank verse.

That year I had taken an English course from the most famous teacher in our high school. She was very good, but perhaps was a little overwrought about poetry and students. Anyway, by early winter she decided her juniors could write a sonnet, so she assigned one. At that time, high school juniors in Montana could tell where a cinch ended and a latigo began, but had no such knowledge about an octave and a sestet, so after feeling steadily worse for several days I approached my mother with my problem, who looked at me carefully to be sure I had a problem, and then said, "After dishes, I will help you." So we sat down at a table and I held her left hand and she wrote the sonnet with her right hand, while her left hand trembled. Her sonnet was "On Milton's Blindness," something I had never heard of before. The poem was regarded as very good by the English teachers of Missoula County High School, and in May received the prize as the best poem of the year and was published in the school annual with a sterilized photograph of me adjoining it. My mother was very proud of me, but quietly insisted that I stay in after supper until I at least learned to scan, so again we sat at the table, this time with Milton or Shakespeare between us, and again I held her left hand and with her right hand she would beat out the accented syllables. Then we would write lines of our own iambic pentameter, and our blank verse, unlike Milton's or Shakespeare's, never had any little odds or ends left over. We wrote: "Ĭmmórtăl Míltŏn, búildĕr óf mў sóul," and other such lines that all Montana high school juniors could scan and tell was poetry. At least, if they could count to five.

At first I hadn't picked up the rhythm next door. Evidently she was just warming up and she spoke in just ordinary irritable profanity. "You lousy bastard," and so on. But then she started to dedicate a stave to each time he had double-crossed her, and each stave she ended with: "Yŏu aře ăs cróokĕd ás ă túb ŏf gúts." She liked this line and used it as a kind of refrain, and from it I picked up the scansion and realized for the first time that she was speaking iambic pentameter, but with skips and jumps here and there, more like Milton and Shakespeare than mother or me. Evidently her man not only had done her wrong but had gone around talking about it, because she had another set of staves she always ended with, "Yŏu're líke ă bábў crów, ăll móuth ănd aśs." I couldn't verify what she said about his mouth, because he was too busy ever to open it, but all you had to do to check his big ass was to watch my wall. It went down my wall like a wave, and back up it like a Rainbow trout.

I was about to consider her imagery when I must have fallen asleep, possibly lulled by her rhythms, and when I woke up, certainly much later, there was not a stir next door. I was nervous for having fallen asleep and wondered whether this business about a pimp and a whore and especially iambic pentameter wasn't a dream, a distorted continuation of my rhythm in my sickness. Outside in the hall a kind of marching was going on that faded and returned. I waited until it was in a fading cycle before sticking out my head, and, sure enough, it had to be him, though all that could be seen clearly was a hairy ass that could be recognized even by gaslight. When he turned at the end of the hall, there she was in his arms, with her little ass and knees draped in a V. Evidently, they were out for a stroll, taking a breather before the real work of the night began. They came up the hall toward me, and somehow I couldn't pull my neck in. They went right by my immovable nose and then made for their room. He was a man with his toes turned up and too much in love with his work to notice me, but she was just as nasty-looking a little whore as you will ever see, and, whatever she and this big ape were doing, clearly she could think of two or three other things at the same time, including me. She half twisted her neck off her shoulders just to give me the once over. Then, adding a twist to the twist, she said, "Go fuck yourself," so she still scanned, although no one will give her grade points in originality for declaiming one of the most famous lines in the English language.

The old lumberjacks used to talk about "a walking whorehouse," and now what they meant became clearer. I was about to say next, "All night whores flitted around the hotel," but I remembered in time that whores don't flit. One whore almost came through the other side of my wall. She came so close to coming through that somebody must have tried to throw her through.

You know, I wasn't very well while all this was happening, and eventually I fell asleep, not to waken until late in the morning, when, I thought, I was much refreshed. Anyway, I was all full of rhythms. To my quitting-time rhythm were permanently added those of my next-door neighbor. These were all iambic. But the one that now was pounding loudest was "Saturday night in Hamilton." I didn't know the name of this rhythm but it sounded something like "This is the forest primeval."

After dressing a little more shakily than expected, I took a tryout down the hall, and lay down again. Finally, I went out for breakfast and looked for some place that wasn't the Chinese restaurant for fear the waitress I fell in love with last night might not look any better in the daylight than I felt. I found a Greek restaurant, and never again went back to the

Chinese restaurant in order to preserve my first feelings about the waitress there. With a menu in front of me, I thought for a long time and finally ordered tea and toast. The expression on this new waitress's face suggested that she hadn't fallen in love with me at first sight and that this workmen's restaurant didn't welcome short orders, especially when they included tea instead of coffee. To make matters worse, I managed to put away the tea but not the toast.

Then I went looking for the doctor's office and found it in a building a block off Main Street where the rents were lower. The office was small and crowded and the air around which it had been built must have been the air which was still there. People sat on the exposed springs of couches, and the name of the doctor was Charles Richey, M.D., spelled backward on the window.

Dr. Richey did not practice a complicated branch of medicine. He wore his black Stetson in the office and spent about five minutes with each patient. He would stick his Stetson out of the inner office, point his finger at a patient and wiggle his finger. When it came my turn, he had his earphones on before I got through his door. He never said a word and he worried me when he went back to listen to the same spot on my chest. Finally, he jerked the phones out of his ears, and, like the night before, he tried to say something cheerful as soon as he was sure. He said, "You're all right." Then he asked me where I lived, and I told him Missoula and he told me I had better stay in Hamilton for another night. "Take it easy a little longer," he said, "and don't get in any fights."

I was an especially uncomplicated case and he had only one more thing to say to me. He said, "It was those God damn ice-cream sodas. After this, never drink anything but good whiskey."

It seemed like good advice and besides it came free, so, by way of expressing my gratitude, I have followed it ever since.

I tried to thank him but he was already wiggling his finger at another patient.

On the way back to my room, I kept an eye open for a different hotel, and saw one that said it was Deluxe at 25¢ per night (double that with bath). Just as I was to enter my old room to pack up, I noted that my neighbor's room was wide open and she was standing naked in front of a mirror trying on a hat. She was adding to her stature by wearing high-heeled shoes and tilting a very large hat this way and that, but when she saw me, she took off her hat so as not to impede her vision. What she said to me she had said once before, and so of course it still scanned. After I got into my own room, I had to lie down again. I lay there hoping that some day my next-door neighbor and the cook would meet socially. Concerning the outcome, I didn't care which one lost.

Later, I collected myself and my stuff, went downstairs and couldn't find anybody to pay. In that hotel they probably didn't charge by the room. I don't remember whether it was from the exertion of moving, but when I got to my new room I had to stretch out again. I rolled over and for the first time since I'd left home in the spring I felt the security of rubbing shoulders with a plaster wall and for the first time in several days I almost overslept. As I woke I knew I'd no time to enjoy in waking. I knew, even before looking at my watch, that Bill and the crew should be arriving or already had arrived from what should have been the camp on Big Sand Lake near the divide. I washed my face from a pitcher, but the water was stale, just like the knowledge that I would have nothing to say about walking from Elk Summit in a day.

By the time I got to the corral on the road to Blodgett Canyon that the Forest Service used to hold the stock, Bill was already unloading the string, and the cook and the Canadian were sitting in the shade of a deserted cabin that the Service had turned into a warehouse. Since the rest of the crew hadn't arrived, it was clear that the cook and the Canadian had ridden in and the rest of the crew, including Mr. Smith with tiny aged steps, were somewhere behind on foot. No one could kick about the Canadian riding and then just sitting there and not helping Bill unload—he was lucky to be alive after a horse had brought him down that canyon. As for the cook, you might feel like kicking him on to his feet but you'd restrain yourself if you knew anything about the woods. In the woods, the cooks are known as the kings of the camps, and they sit on the throne, because in the woods eating is what counts most in life. In the woods you work so damn hard you have to spend most of the rest of the time taking on fuel, and besides, if you're looking for your just rewards in the Forest Service, which has never been noted for wages, you'd better eat all you can while you're there and enjoy it, if possible.

So in the woods the rest of us do everything that has to be done, but the damn cook only cooks, and talks to the boss.

Without saying a word, Bill and I unloaded and unsaddled the string, and carried the packs, saddles, and drenched saddle blankets into the warehouse, right past the cook who sat in the shade swatting flies.

Finally, Bill and I had a conversation. In the Forest Service very few sentences are completed, either because you have to grunt or catch your breath or because guys who work in the woods aren't the kind who go running around finishing sentences. Bill was taking off the pack on one side of a mule and I was taking off the other.

He asked, "How did you . . . ?"

And, as the pack slipped on my shoulders, I grunted, "I made . . ."

Which, if we had the air and inclination to finish, would probably have sounded something like this. Question: "How did you make it walking from Elk Summit?" Answer: "I made it, but don't ask anything more."

We must have understood each other without finishing, because nothing further was said until the crew came straggling into the corral. They crawled through the corral bars and sat down in the shade near the cook and Canadian; then all of them together said nothing. I especially cared for Mr. Smith who cared for me, and it was painful to see how short his steps were and how white with perspiration his neck was above his bandanna handkerchief where it was usually dark with old veins.

While the crew rested, Bill and I fed the stock oats. It was

September, and you can't pack animals all summer over the
Bitterroot divide and expect them to survive on the grass they
pass on the way. Bill didn't say he was proud of them, but he
slapped each one on its rump as it snorted into its feed. At the
end of the summer, they looked fine.

After he finished with the animals, he turned to the men.
He and Mr. Smith did all the talking, although I don't think
they'd worked things out beforehand. Bill said, "We're one
crew, but don't let's hang together in one bunch until we get
to the Oxford. It would look bad."

Mr. Smith asked, "When do you want us, Bill?"

Bill said, "Drift into this Oxford place between nine-thirty
and ten."

Mr. Smith was showing remarkable recuperative powers
for his age. He took off the bandanna handkerchief and
wiped his neck. He seemed to be talking always to Bill and not
to us. "Bill," he said, "you take charge of the inside of that
poker room and I'll stand at the door and take care of
whatever tries to get in from the poolroom."

Bill said to me, "You're to get the money if anything goes
wrong." And then he added, as he always did, "I'll cover you."

Mr. McBride had something to say to Bill, and he had a
point. "Be sure we play for money and not for chips. We may
not be able to cash in any chips on the way out."

Bill said, "The rest of you help where we're hurting. You're
a good crew and we don't want too many plans."

Mr. Smith agreed, "That's right. For what we're doing, we
don't want too many plans."

Then the cook spoke up and added one of his stately
speeches. "You must realize," he said, "that I rarely make a
tricky deal. If I won only when I dealt I would have been dead
long ago. Except for one or two hands a night I am a
percentage player" (which was the first time I had ever heard
this phrase). "I am a very good percentage player, and I
should be ahead. But, if I am not, don't lose patience. There
will come one big hand and be ready."

So the cook had the last word, as I am sure he had planned.

He liked being the center of the drama, and he liked being Bill's favorite. Mr. Smith and I exchanged our dislike of him by a glance. Then we soon broke up, as directed, and on the way back to my room I stopped at my new restaurant where I was not well liked and asked the waitress if they had a small flour sack they could spare. She seemed to like me better and came back from the kitchen and said, no, they didn't have a flour sack but they had a ten-pound sugar sack and she showed it to me and the word SUGAR had not yet faded from being washed. I said, "That's fine. That's better than flour." In fact, SUGAR seemed just right, since I wanted the sack to put our big winnings in. It's funny how many non-funny jokes we make to ourselves.

I had been gone from my room for a long time, so when I got back I lay down on the bed and was still amused by my sugar sack when all of a sudden things fell apart. I say "all of a sudden," but for a long time I had only been pretending not to know that I was going to take a hell of a beating when I reached across the table to pick up the money. I always suspected that Bill was looking for trouble more than for money, but from time to time I would cheer myself up by underestimating the crew and thinking they were just greedy, not fighty, and would take their winnings and go off and get drunk. I had not fully realized how I was doomed until I had seen that the oldest men in the crew, Mr. Smith and Mr. McBride, were counting on a fight just as much as Bill was and, independently, had worked out an almost identical plan. In fact, when I said a temporary good-bye to Mr. Smith at the corral I discovered that the crew's fighting plans didn't stop with the tin-horn gamblers. He said, "We're going to clean out the town. First we'll take those tin-horn gamblers, then the ranch hands, and then the whores."

If we did all that we sure as hell would clean out the town as we knew it. As we knew the town, there were houses in it, but we weren't sure what if anything was inside them. The establishments open to us were inhabited by gamblers, ranch hands, and whores. Add a Chinese and a Greek restaurant and you have what the town was to us. You will note that Mr. Smith and I both said "ranch hands" and not "cowboys"—in the Forest Service we called cowboys ranch hands to show what we thought of them. I said to Mr. Smith, "The whores may be the toughest of all." He laughed through his moustache that was darker than his white hair; he was hoping this would be the case.

There shouldn't have been any doubt in my mind, though, that we were in for big trouble. After all I was finishing up my third summer in the Forest Service, so twice before I had gone through this autumn rite at quitting time. Twice before I had seen a catch-as-catch-can bunch of working stiffs transformed into blood brothers by the act of Cleaning Out the Town. Everybody got cleaned in this autumn rite of the early Forest Service—we cleaned up on the town and the town cleaned us out. When the rite was completed, all of it thereafter could be solemnized and capitalized—the Crew, Quitting Time, and Cleaning Out the Town. Everything about us was bigger than before, except our cash.

At the time, I thought the Big Fire was no longer important, but before all this became a story I realized the Big Fire is the Summer Festival and Cleaning Out the Town is the way it all ends in the autumn. It's as simple as this—you never forget the guys who helped you fight the big fire or clean out the town.

Lying on the bed, though, I couldn't see how I was going to avoid a beating. There's bound to be a fight, I knew now, and I'll have to reach over the table for the money. I'll need both hands to pick it up and put it in the sugar sack, which didn't seem funny now, and there will be my jaw sticking out for anybody to bruise with brass knuckles. I lay on the bed for some hours and couldn't think of any way to protect myself, and, worse still, I knew I'd thought often of this problem before and had kept burying it, because even in half-dreams no way came to me of defending myself. Now was my last chance to think, but after it became dark I still had no thoughts. Just sensations. Always I felt that in reaching for the money I was hit on the jaw from the side and couldn't see who had hit me. Next, I felt blood from inside my head slide down my throat.

I don't pretend I liked the beating or the blood, but it was not being able to lift a hand that sickened me most. It was like being a child again and being sent to a dark room and waiting for your father to come and whip you. It was a place of no ideas. Finally I said to myself, "At least don't lie here in the dark. Go over and take a look at the joint." I don't know whether I expected to get any new ideas, but at least I went to see.

The Oxford was the combination billiard, pool, and card parlor which for many westerners was the home away from home. The entering door led past the bar and tobacco stand; the guy behind the bar looked like he was trying to look like the owner. I bought a bottle of homebrew beer, but if I'd asked for a shot of moonshine I probably could have got it. Then I sauntered through the big door into the game room. It retreated to the rear in geometric patterns. The farther back it went the higher the stakes, the deeper the sin and the lower the social order. The large rectangles of billiard and pool tables in front become shortened by distance into round card tables. The ceilings were concealed in darkness; each green cloth-covered table glared under its own light shade. The big room narrowed into one small, slightly raised room in which was one glaring green table surrounded almost by darkness. Here at the end of space was the poker table.

I worked slowly to the rear, pretending to walk casually and trying to drink the flat beer. The billiard table was for the sporting elite who could pay twenty-five cents an hour. The table was in good shape and the two players were good and were playing three-cushion billiards. The spectator next to me clapped when they made a hard shot and in a whisper told me that one of the players was the best barber in town and the other was vice-president of the bank. Then, in an even lower whisper and in greater awe, he told me that by common

agreement they quit playing every night at nine because each
had a woman he spent a couple of hours with before going
home to his wife.

The pool players and tables were so bad nobody was
watching. The balls must have been made of concrete and the
rubber in the cushions was dead, so the players, to get any
bounce, shot too hard, If you fired a rifle and jerked up
your head and shoulder the way they did when they shot
their cue ball, you'd have missed Grave Peak at a hundred
yards. When they miscued, they said, "God damn it," and
chalked the tips of their cues. You can tell poor pool players
anywhere—they're the ones who are always saying, "God
damn it," and are always chalking their cues and always
jerking their heads when they shoot—something chalk won't
cure. On the rifle range, it's called "flinching." I kept moving,
and came to the first card tables.

The Oxford was no exception. The first card tables are
always for the regular local players—not the gamblers but the
clothing-store clerks and delivery men who married when
they were young and can't afford to lose but can't stay away
from cards. So they pretend with the help of the house that
they're not gambling and certainly not losing. They play slow
games in which they lose steadily but never, as in poker, lose a
bundle of cash on a turn of a card. The ones I watched were
playing "pan" and pinochle, and they were playing for "chits,"
not chips. They had paid real money for their chits, as if they
were chips, but when they traded them back the house would
give them only trade tokens that would allow them to buy
homebrew beer or play pool. The house was even pretending
that it wasn't charging them for using the table, but while I
stood there a houseman came by and picked a chit out of the
pot. If you count the number of times the houseman picks a
chit out of a pot in a year, you'll probably find that it's
not the gamblers but the deliverymen pretending they aren't
gambling who keep small town gambling joints going financially.

I pretended to be drinking from my bottle of beer when I

passed the poker room so that they couldn't get a good look at me. There were three of them, also engaged in pretending. They were pretending to play poker against each other, and they were studying their cards and stroking their piles of chips with their left hands. It was a cinch they were all housemen and were just keeping a game going as a decoy for some working stiff with a pay check from the Forest Service or a sheep ranch. They were all dressed alike, and were all dressed like Bill Bell—black Stetson hats, blue shirts, and yellow strings from sacks of Bull Durham hanging out of their shirt pockets. I wondered if all the guys in the Bitterroot who thought they were tough wore some kind of uniform, because even the doctor wore a small black Stetson. They pretended that no one was standing in the doorway, as, faceless, they studied their cards under their hat brims; then almost as one the hat brims raised slightly and they peered from underneath. What made it a cinch they were all shills working for the house was that nobody watched them play. Any westerner knows that when nobody watches the poker game, the poker game isn't real. The poker game is Magnetic North, and when even a sheepherder with his summer's pay is drawn into the magnetic field, a circle forms around it.

Not wanting them to get a good look at me, I kept moving. But then I didn't get a good look at them either—mostly what I saw down the sides of my tipped beer bottle were the brims of their hats and their hunched shoulders shielding their cards. Their black hats were black but not like Bill's black hat, gray with dust. Hunched shoulders always look big, but one pair looked at least as big as Bill's. I began to think of him as Biggest Brim, and the other two as Big Brim and Bigger Brim, just like olives, the smallest grade always being marked Large. Not much else of them was allowed to show except their hands, which looked as if they were trying to be clumsy to get me into the game.

Something had made me crawl out of bed and go spying, although I hadn't learned much. My first view of the tin-horn gamblers in the flesh wasn't a great deal different from my mental image of tin-horn gamblers—they were faceless but had an eye on me. I had learned just one thing for sure—that it was a long way from the poker room in the rear to the front door, and I made a note, if we had to back out fighting, to watch sideways for anybody who might be swinging the butt of a pool cue.

I was nervous and much too early and, although still not feeling well, I began to realize I hadn't eaten much of anything since leaving Elk Summit. I crossed the street to the Greek restaurant with the waitress who didn't like me. The waitress was on shift, gave my table a swish with her apron and said, as if there'd always been complete understanding between us, "You're going to eat something tonight. You haven't eaten anything since you came to town."

I said, "I was thinking the same thing myself."

"I'll get some soup while you're looking the menu over," she said. "Be sure to order meat. It'll make you strong again."

I thought about her all the time she was in the kitchen. I wasn't exactly prepared for this sudden motherly change in events, and when you're hurt you don't forgive quickly. Looking at the soup, as she put it down, she said, "I think I know where Bill Bell's dog is."

The soup came up in steam and I was glad it smelled good because that meant I was better, so for a moment I really didn't hear what she said. When I did, I asked, "Do you know Bill Bell?" Then she didn't hear. "You must order something with a lot of meat." She helped me think things over, and after a lot of thought we decided on what anyone probably would have—a hamburger, rare and with onions, on a theory we both shared, that rare and onions make you strong. When she came back from the kitchen after ordering, she said, "I don't know Bill Bell but I know where his dog is. Did you like your soup?" "It was good and hot," I said, and left it up to her to go on.

As she lifted the soup bowl and brushed off the bits of crackers from the table, she said, "I come from a sheep ranch near Darby, and I've heard his dog is on a sheep ranch near Hamilton. I can tell you where."

This time she was gone quite a while, waiting for the hamburger to get done. I knew that she was probably right about Bill's dog. Like Bill himself, the dog was one of the legends of the Bitterroot Valley. He had a name, but everybody called him "Bill's Dog." He liked Bill best among humans but he had an even higher commitment—he was committed to sheep. He would follow Bill into the woods in the spring and he liked especially to be around Bill when he was working with livestock or twirling his rope in the evening, but by the middle of July he would get an inner call and be gone, and when autumn came Bill would find him at some sheep camp.

As a sheep dog he specialized on coyotes. Coyotes are wily animals, but wily animals including ourselves and coyotes have more set patterns than we think. The sheep camp is usually on a creek bottom or near a spring, and one coyote usually appears on top of a nearby ridge and barks like hell and makes a big show of himself, and the sheep dog, following his usual pattern, takes out after the coyote and the coyote of course disappears over the hill. Then it so happens that when the dog comes sailing over the ridge with his tongue hanging out, there are three or four coyotes waiting to meet him. The first coyote didn't know that just what Bill's Dog was looking for was three or four coyotes.

Bill's Dog looked as if he were divided into two parts, his head and shoulders being pit bull and the remaining half with which he ran being greyhound. Probably nothing in the valley touched him for speed and ferocity. Actually, he wasn't so much committed to sheep as he was to sheep camps where he could kill coyotes. Every sheep camp in the valley regarded it a privilege to entertain him.

The waitress came back and asked, "When is Bill going to leave tomorrow for Elk Summit?" "It's a guess," I told her, "but I'd guess around noon." "I'll try to get his dog to him in the morning," she said, "but if I don't make it, here's a piece of paper that tells the ranch where he is and how to get there. Will you give the note to Bill?"

I nodded and put it in my shirt pocket. "So you don't know

Bill?" I asked. I cut the hamburger sandwich into four pieces
and even then it was big and I had to open my mouth wide.
She said, "No, I come from Darby and I ran away to go to
Missoula." Missoula was my town. It is the biggest town
around, and is near the mouth of the Bitterroot River. Darby
is a small town about seventy miles up the Bitterroot River,
and Hamilton is in between in both distance and size, but
closer to Darby than to Missoula. "But," she said, "I got a job
here in Hamilton slinging hash, and somehow I never got as
far as Missoula."

Since I was still trying to open my mouth wide, she went on.
"I'm a Bitterrooter, so even if I don't know Bill Bell I know all
about him and his dog."

She had dark red hair and perhaps her teeth were a little
too far apart but she looked good and she looked strong and
it was not hard to imagine her on a sheep ranch. Her face and
neck were covered with outdoor freckles and they got even
thicker as they disappeared toward her breasts.

"I know you work for Bill," she said, and then she said as if
she'd tried to say it before, "and I know you're in for big
trouble tonight."

I put down the remaining quarter of the sandwich. "How
do you know that?" I asked.

"Men eat here," she said. I looked at the clock and told her,
"I have to be going." She said, "You haven't finished your
sandwich." I assured her, "It was good, but I have to be on my
way."

"All right," she said, "but don't forget about Bill's Dog." "I
won't," I told her.

"Be sure now," she said, "not to forget about Bill's Dog. I
want you to think about him tonight."

"You sound smart," I told her.

"No," she said, "I haven't been to Missoula yet."

The Bitterroot girl who followed me to the door was about
my age, and we both felt it. "So long and good luck," she said.
Then she called after me, "Don't forget to tell Bill that I gave

him the slip of paper, but you're not supposed to look at it."

"I'll tell him," I called back, and then I put all my life out of my mind except around a poker table.

I focused so intensely I still remember all that happened as if it were last night.

There was no one in the barroom except the guy behind the bar, who looked as if he were about to lose the place he may have owned. For a moment I thought there was no sound at all in the next room. Then suddenly a crash was followed by several thuds as the life went out of concrete pool balls when they hit dead cushions. Evidently one pair of pool players was left.

"Hey, punk," the barkeep snarled, "where do you think you're going?"

I was late and worried because there was just one set of sounds in the next room, so I tried to slide past by being polite.

"I'm supposed to meet with some friends in there," I said.

"Come over here," he said. Then I got really worried, because I should have been standing right behind the cook, but I went part way to the bar, close enough to see a Smith & Wesson .38 on the lower counter where he washed the glasses. No revolver had been there when I bought my homemade beer. He stopped looking at me long enough to take a drink from a shot glass sitting by the revolver.

"Have a shot of moonshine," he said to me. "Thanks," I said, and shook my head. "It's on the house," he said, and I said "Thanks" again.

He said, actually pointing at me, "You're with Bill Bell, aren't you? You were in here not long ago."

I said, "I work for him."

"He's in there," he told me. "What's he doing in there?" I asked.

"Why don't you look in there and tell me?" he asked.

I could see that I would be here forever if I kept on being

polite. I said, "Why don't you look in there yourself? You've got a gun and it's only twenty feet to the door where you can look."

He said, "I'm afraid to leave the front of the place alone. Somebody might come in and steal something." I took another look and when I saw it actually wasn't twenty feet to the door, I realized he was scared. I don't like guys who look big and tough but aren't and also happen to have a gun. When they're tough all the way through, it's easier to figure out what the gun will do.

I walked those less than twenty feet softly and looked.

Just as sound had said, in all the big room there were only two pool players, probably a couple of ranch hands who had worked with cattle so long they didn't notice any more what went on among humans. Otherwise, it was as if the earth had tilted and everybody had slid into the back room. You could hardly see the poker table, but everybody was peering at it and watching in silence.

You know, watching a poker game isn't like watching most other card games where all is silent while the hand is played and then there's a round of relaxation and comment after the cards have been thrown into the pile. In this usual kind of card game everybody sees all the cards by the time the cards are thrown in, so nobody's giving anything away by talking when the game's over. But in draw poker half or more of the game is psychology, and you toss your hand face down into the pile so no one can see what cards you held unless you're willing to stay in the game and bet that you're the winner. Hand after hand in poker is played with nothing showing at the end but a pair of whatever it took to open the betting, and nobody would be allowed to watch the game if he gave an indication of what the cards were that had been tossed face down into the pile. In draw poker, you pay for every card you see.

As I stood at the door of the pool room looking back at the poker table, a moment of my life came back to me and I was a child watching a pageant of big boys dressed as sheepherders trying to be statues bent over something mystic in a shining light.

Turning to the barkeeper nursing his shot of moonshine, I said, "It looks like Sunday school at Christmas," and I walked rapidly toward the back room, nervous that I was making any noise at all and nervous also about that .38 I was leaving in my back.

Although Mr. Smith was standing at the door of the poker room where he should be, he wasn't happy. According to the plan, he was to be the palace guard and keep out all except our guys, but when the earth had tilted he obviously had been covered by a landslide. I told him, "The barkeeper has a .38." He didn't say a thing to me, but he shoved people aside until he got me to a spot right behind the cook. Before I really looked at the cook I looked at the pile in front of him. It was a pile all right, not big but forty dollars anyway. The other three at the table had big hat brims but small piles of money. Bill Bell was standing right behind Biggest Brim. The light shade over the table almost cut Bill in half. In the semi-darkness above the light his shoulders and hat were gigantic; then suddenly beneath the light his hands glared on his hips, as if he had a gun. My attention stopped jumping while I studied him for a bulge around the waist or a shoulder strap, and I knew finally for sure it was going to be just a plain fight. As I was studying Bill, Biggest Brim moved his chair to the right and, when he moved a second time, I guessed that Biggest didn't like Bill directly behind him. Just as he took a look at Bill, Bill pushed a bystander to the right and got behind Biggest again. I thought, "If they go on doing this they'll be in front of me before long." Just then, the red-headed kid developed out of the shadows and became a form on one side of Biggest Brim. The red-headed kid was about my size, but he didn't budge an inch when Biggest tried to make another move to get another look at Bill. I didn't have to guess any longer about whether he would have shot on the fireline.

Then who appeared on the other side of Biggest Brim but the gassed Canadian. He coughed but he didn't move either.

In front of me, the cook looked just as cocky as ever. In fact, standing over him, I could look down on that bluejay tuft sticking up from the back of his head. Being the only player not hidden by a hat and being the only player with a fair-sized pile in front of him, he was the one we all watched most.

He stood out even more when it was his turn to deal, and it was clear to me after a couple of rounds that the strategy of the Faceless Three when it came to dealing cards had changed completely since early evening when they had tried to draw me into the game by looking clumsy. Now every player knew the other was a gambling man, so the psychology had changed to shaking the other guy's confidence in his game. The three Brims were pretty handy with cards, but no better than that. I was just beginning to find out that there were quite a few differences between my picture of a gambling man and a small-town shill who lies in wait for working stiffs with monthly checks. The cook, though, was a flash. The cards leaped out of the messy pile into his hands, and then darted out of his hands around the circle of the table. For my money he was too flashy and was showing off, but our crew was proud of him, and, standing right over him as if I owned him, I guess I was, too, although never completely losing the feeling that something was missing in him somewhere.

By what he had said earlier, he was playing percentage poker, although I wouldn't have called it that. It was a lot more daring than just sitting there counting the spots and playing the odds. For instance, twice in a short time he had a chance to open the betting on a pair of jacks (jacks were the lowest openers) and twice he passed and twice somebody else opened and then both times he raised the opening bet. But from there on he played each hand differently. To the first hand, he drew only one card, as if to suggest that he was holding two pairs and hadn't opened the betting on them because of the difficulties you can get into with two pairs if you have to bet on them before getting an idea of what anybody else has. The smallest of the Faceless Three, who was sitting to the cook's left, opened the betting, and he drew an honest three, which meant, since jacks were openers, that he could be holding any one of three pairs that would beat the cook—and, at worst, he couldn't be holding less than a pair of jacks, which was all the cook was holding after he drew his one card.

Bigger Brim and Biggest Brim dropped out after the raise. Since Big Brim had opened, it was his turn to bet first after the draw and, thinking a long time about the raise the cook had given him, he passed. The cook had done his thinking long before. He bet two dollars. Two dollars at that stage of the game was a pretty good-sized bet—not staggering as if you were betting big because you weren't holding much but big enough to look as if you had what you thought could win and you wanted to get the other guys to stay in the betting. This time Big Brim had done all his thinking. He showed a pair of queens for openers, and the cook lowered his elbows and embraced the pile of money. Biggest Brim grunted. If I had been playing against him I would have figured he didn't like to be bluffed.

The second time that the cook didn't open the pot on a pair of jacks but instead raised, he drew not one but two cards, as if to suggest he had three of a kind, and damned if one of the two cards he drew wasn't another jack, so he ended with three of a kind. Of course, when you're that lucky, you don't have to be Nick the Greek to play them. This time Big Brim and Biggest Brim both stayed in the game, and it cost Biggest Brim nearly five dollars to think he discovered that the cook didn't bluff because he ended up with three jacks.

As the cook's winnings increased, he became cockier and he began to talk and his game got even better. He was the only one who talked, and he talked all the time about his cards. One of the best poker players I ever saw was a punch-drunk prizefighter who, like the cook, talked all the time about what he was holding. You couldn't tell what to believe about anything he said, but you couldn't stop listening. The cook would say, "I'm going to raise you on a pair of jacks," and he'd have three kings, and then later he'd say, "I'm going to try to raise you again on a pair of jacks," and this time that's just what he had. Always he talked about his hand, and generally he lied but every now and then what he said was what he held, and only I who was behind him could tell the difference. I was glad I wasn't playing against him. Obviously, it was also the flashiest poker the three Brims from Hamilton had seen in some time. Biggest Brim twisted around in his chair until he could pull out his purse from his hip pocket. It was a little black purse that snapped shut and he unsnapped it and un- folded several bills. Then he untwisted, traded bills for silver dollars, started a new pile with the dollars and went on losing.

Although only the cook talked, there was an audible re- laxation of muscles between deals except for Bill who never moved unless to keep Biggest Brim in front of him. Otherwise, Bill was a giant hat and pair of shoulders in shadows, and in light a pair of hands resting on hips that by now everyone besides me had studied. Mr. Smith was a full-time giant beside the door, occasionally looking back in the direction of the .38 Smith & Wesson.

My left arm was slightly brushed, and looking down on me but pretending to look at the card game was Mr. McBride. He was standing so much over me that if it had been raining he would have dripped off the corners of his moustache on to my head. I was glad to have that feeling over me, and I reached inside my shirt and touched the sugar sack. Still, I didn't like it that nearly all our crew were standing in the rim of light around the table, except Mr. Smith and the two lookouts, whose names and locations I can't remember. I wasn't much worried about the three Faceless Wonders at the table. After all, we had them outnumbered, and, if they were fighty, they'd been sitting soft all summer around a green table while we'd been getting case-hardened climbing the high hills. I was worried about the extra help that might come out of nowhere. I'd seen at least two housemen working the poolroom earlier in the evening. Then, some of those clumsy pool players had to be housemen who were only faking and would take you to the cleaners if you dropped in from another town and thought you were good. There was also that .38 behind the bar. Still another question: How many of the customers would stick with the house in a fight? There was no way of answering that now. It could depend on who was winning or on how the Oxford treated its customers or on how many friends Bill had in the house. At present, they were standing back in the shadows, but probably were all for war up in front. As for me personally, I knew I'd take a beating. It was getting so that every few minutes I'd feel the sugar sack.

Evidently, the barkeeper hadn't yet dared come as far as the door to look.

The cook kept on winning—not big but steadily—and I began to think he would go on playing his so-called percentage game for the rest of the night as it would have been percentage to do, but I kept forgetting that one thing you can be sure about a show-off is that he will show off.

When it happened, there was a good-sized pot, not big enough to risk your shirt on and certainly not big enough to risk getting shot over, but still a fair-sized pot. Three or four deals in a row had been passed without an opening bet and of course each time everybody had to ante so the pot got to be a pretty good one. Actually, the cook had made the last deal and, when nobody had an opening bet, I knew he was still dealing honest. Everybody chipped into the pot again and the cook passed the cards to Big Brim, who was sitting to his left. Big Brim handled cards better than anyone in the game except the cook, and was even slightly ahead, but by now I was sure that none of the Brims was a great card player. I asked myself, "Anyway, what the hell ever made you think a great card player would be staying in Hamilton?" Now I had them cased as pretty good card players who probably had a few two-bit tricks up their sleeves to fool the ranch hands and us Forest Service stiffs from the high brush.

Big Brim dealt out the hands and the cook picked his up and had just started to sort it when he put his cards face down on the table, leaned over and slightly raised Big Brim's hat.

"I beg your pardon," he said with a little stately speech, "I always like to see a man's face when I play cards with him."

I saw something flash and disappear as the cook withdrew his hand from the hat, like the tail of a rabbit into the brush, but even though I stretched my neck I couldn't get sight of it again. I knew, though, that something had happened to Big Brim from the sudden stir among people across the table who could get a front view of him. Biggest Brim closed his cards in one fist and half pushed himself up from the table. Bill stepped from behind him for a better view and perhaps a better shot. Bigger Brim, who had done littte more in the game than lose, raked in his little pile of money, whereupon I reached in my shirt and got a fist on the sugar sack.

Big Brim himself, though, didn't seem to notice that a rabbit had ducked into his hat or something like that. With his hat now tilted away from me, he leaned back and started to sort his cards. He had his move timed perfectly, just when the cook had finished sorting his hand and had definitely assumed possession of it.

"Sorry, pardner," he said to the cook, "but you'll have to throw in your hand. You've an extra card."

"Who? Me?" asked the cook.

"Yes, you," said Big Brim. "You have six cards in your hand. You must have had that extra card up your sleeve just for a big pot like this one."

"Count 'em," said the cook, and he spread them face down in a small fan in front of Big Brim.

Big Brim spread them even further apart and counted. "How many?" asked the cook. Big Brim went back over the cards, spread them even further apart, felt each one, and gave them another count.

From across the table, Bill asked, "How many?"

Big Brim looked at the cook and not at Bill. "Five," he said, still feeling the cards.

The cook said, blown wide open with pride, "If you're looking for that extra card you dealt me to get my hand thrown out of the game, you'll find it in your hatband."

Big Brim took off his hat and rested it on the table while he tried to believe it. There in his hatband was the deuce of clubs, the lowest card in the deck, but if it had still been in the cook's hand it would have put him out of the game.

The aces the cook had palmed into my shirt pocket at Elk Summit jumped out of my mind like rabbits and arranged themselves around the band of Big Brim's hat. Nobody needed to tell me how the deuce of clubs got there or where the rabbit had gone.

I went for the money.

First for the pot on the table, figuring that the cook should be able to protect his pile until I got there. I don't know who started the fight. I heard a chair crash. Either somebody got hit with a chair or was knocked off one.

Somebody slugged me as I reached for the pot, and it happened just as I had imagined it would—somebody from the side slugged me high on the jaw, and I never saw him. I guess it was Big Brim, and it must have been Mr. McBride who flattened him. Anyway, while I was still reaching for the pot Big Brim lit on top of me and didn't move until I heaved up straight and let him slide off. There was still some money left in the pot that hadn't spilled or been taken but, when I reached over to pick up the remains, somebody grabbed my arm and somebody else stretched out and helped him twist it. I could also feel things hurt in my ear where I was hit on the side of my head.

When I finally got my arm loose it was so weak I couldn't pick up the rest of the pot, but I didn't miss much, maybe a couple of dollars of change that were hard to pick up with numb fingers. Instead, I went for the pile of money in front of the cook, who, so help me, was just sitting there. You would think that somebody would have flattened him right off, but there he sat with the tuft on his head and nobody had laid a hand on him, probably because, as I said earlier, among men the cardshark is a sorcerer in everyone's eyes, and this one had just performed magic. Maybe they were afraid they'd go up in smoke if they touched him. So there he sat, untouched and maybe untouchable. The son of a bitch didn't even help me stuff his money into the sack, although I think I got it all.

Then somebody hit me between the eyes harder than I was ever able to remember. I just stood there and my clothes felt like a potato sack and my body felt like potatoes, and the sack sank to the floor with me inside it. I tried to remain conscious. I tried to think, knowing I was nodding at the fringe of reality. I tried to think big thoughts, as if I were having thoughts about life. I even started sentences that began, "Life is . . . ," but I never finished them, because I never had any thoughts to put in them.

At first, everything corresponded exactly with my foresight. I reached across the table for the money, and there was no way I could protect myself. Next, as in anticipation, I felt actual blood from inside my head slip down my throat.

But, as I folded on the floor, everything became unexpected. Suddenly, as if from nowhere, I got not one but two ideas of how I could have protected myself when I reached across the table, whereas for weeks before, when an idea would have done some good, I couldn't get a single one. I struggled to my elbows to see if it was too late to act, but, once on the tripod of my elbows, I could tell the ideas weren't worth a damn. And in another moment they disappeared, never to be remembered again.

While my body was still raised off the floor, though, I managed to shove the sugar sack into my shirt. In the process, I realized I recognized some of the feet under and around the table.

Lying again on the floor on the side of my face, I wondered, since I couldn't think believable thoughts, whether, by watching feet, I could figure out some of what was going on. I lifted my face again from the sawdust and stained Bull Durham butts, and again put it on the tripod of elbows. This was to be the biggest fight I ever viewed almost entirely from the prone position. And under a poker table.

Right off the bat I could tell us guys from those guys. They were the cowboy boots and we were the logging boots, and I remembered with a sickly feeling that later this night we were going to clean out all the ranch hands in town. It took me time to sort out this fight between men up to their knees. But things got clearer, and first there was the biggest pair of cowboy boots right across from me. The knees were spread wide apart and the boots were turned up at the toes. Bill, the redhead, and the Canadian must have nailed him to his chair before he ever moved. Then suddenly a pair of cowboy boots went straight up in the air and then just dangled there—one of our boys must have draped this body across the poker table and left his head and feet hanging over. To check, I looked on the opposite side and, sure enough, there was his head with saliva stringing out of his mouth. I looked back real quick to see who of our guys had stretched out the body, and, just as expected, there were Bill's big loggers spread out. Bill's loggers, you remember, had that fringed extra tongue, you couldn't miss them, and they were working slowly toward me.

Suddenly, a pair of city shoes jumped into the front ring, belonging, I guessed, to one of the housemen who racked up the pool balls. His legs danced once and disappeared rhythmically into the blue. I don't know what happened to him, but he left so suddenly that Bill must have taken him, too.

A faded pair of Levi's went bowlegged and kept on spreading until Mr. McBride sank down beside me. I didn't have strength to move out of his way, so he just leaned against me. The pair of loggers that skipped in and out across the table had to belong to his red-headed son. He could make those loggers move, and I could see that it helped him and our guys to be wearing loggers and not cowboy boots. Everybody in town yelled at us stiffs from the Forest Service when we walked indoors, because admittedly the sharp caulks in the soles of our loggers left little holes in the floors, but when that fast red-headed kid jumped back to duck and counterpunch, those loggers held on the wood floor and the slick high-heeled cowboy boots trying to sidestep his counterpunches slipped and then skidded.

It's hard to believe, but the Canadian puttees were standing most of the time, only once in a while bending at the knee and coughing.

All the time, sitting flat-footed next to me, was a pair of low canvas shoes with rubber soles, like a pair of girl's basketball shoes. They just sat there flat-footed. I started to climb to my feet even before I determined to. It took me a couple of pushes and I wobbled on the way up. It was funny, but right there I thought of my Presbyterian father, and I quit wobbling.

The cook picked up the cards and strained them through his hands. Just keeping his hands soft, I suppose.

I hit him on the side of the head about where I thought I'd been hit. He bounced to the floor, and I went down softly. I knew that I hadn't hit him hard. I didn't have the strength. Mr. McBride must have been coming to, because he rolled over slightly to make room for me. I was fairly sure that the cook, who was curled up, was playing possum. I saw one of his eyes open and study me. Then, when he became sure that I was pretty much beyond recall, he jumped up and started kicking me. Among lumberjacks, this is known as "giving the guy the leather" and you not only put the boots to him when he's down but you also rake him with the sharp caulks bristling from your soles and what you leave behind is full of dirt and takes a long time to heal. Only I wasn't being kicked by loggers but by girl's basketball shoes. Even so, the bastard managed to kick me once on the side of the head just about where I'd been hit and I could feel blood start down my throat again. I tried to catch one of his feet and trip him and I caught one but I couldn't hold it.

Then suddenly both canvas shoes went straight up in the air and I heard something crash and later I was to have it confirmed that the cook hit the wall and that Bill threw him there. Anyway, spread in front of me was a pair of loggers with a fringed double tongue. Then Bill reached over and picked me up with one arm, and before he had fully straightened he reached down again and picked up Mr. McBride with his other arm.

He shook both arms and said, "How are you?" and we both said, as if we'd talked it over together, "Oh, we're all right." We both started sliding out of his arms, and he took a fast new hold on us and said, "Now, wait a minute." Then, with his arms around us, he made us walk a few steps, and just a few steps helped to clear things up, and both of us, feeling embarrassed by being held, muttered, "Thanks, Bill," and tried to push free, and he grinned to see us better, but he still held us tight. This time he walked us five or six steps and back again, and this time we pushed free from him and regained our manhood and tried to appear as if we were looking for more fight.

But the fight was nearly over. Off to one side the redhead was fighting with some town guy in a buttoned shirt. Mr. McBride wobbled over and broke it up just as his son absorbed a roundhouse punch to his belly, but the old man wouldn't let him go on, and the town guy was glad to quit on the strength of getting in the last punch. His son walked off with bowed head thinking deep thoughts, and then he whirled and ran after the town guy to start the fight over again but now the crowd came out of the shadows and held him back. The crowd that was all for war when I disappeared under the table and they disappeared into the shadows was now all for peace.

As my brain cleared, I began to feel like the redhead, and was surprised and disappointed to see that the fight was over. This was the first fight I was ever in where there were a lot of other guys, and I hadn't learned yet that when there are a lot of guys in a fight it usually doesn't last long, for the simple reason that a lot of guys don't like to fight. Only a few like to fight and know how. Most guys take a couple of punches on the nose and swallow blood and suddenly grow weak with sisterly feelings about brotherly love. All that was left of the war now that the redhead had retired was old Mr. Smith standing by the door with a bear hug on the barkeeper. This was probably the first and last time in his life that the barkeeper would walk into the arms of a man who swung a jackhammer for a living. The head of the barkeeper, which was the only part of him that could move, moved wildly. Finally his arms must have run short of blood, because the revolver dropped from his hand. Bill picked up the .38, flipped open the chamber, shook out the shells, and the war was officially over.

My head hurt and so did my feelings. I was still trying to figure how the war could have been won without me. Mr. McBride had been out of business most of the time, too, and Mr. Smith had been standing at the door with a bear hug on the barkeeper. As in a lot of big fights, most of the fighting had been done by one fine fighter and a kid who might grow up to be one. Together they got at least two of the Hat Brims and all the housemen who racked up the pool balls and whatever customers were overcome by loyalty to the Oxford. The Canadian was sitting bent over in one of the poker chairs. He was doubled up as if he had to cough but couldn't. Whatever he'd done was done nobly but it couldn't have counted for much.

The three Brims sat by themselves, with their brims pulled lower than ever, but they didn't look badly hurt. They were showing each other their fingers. Then they went around the spectators trying to explain that they didn't get into the fight much because they were card players and were afraid to break the bones in their hands. Probably all three of the tin-horn gamblers pimped on the side for a living. I even suspected one of them was my next-door neighbor last night, but I never got a good enough look to be sure. Mostly, I was trying to get used to the fact that no one seemed really hurt except me—and probably Mr. McBride. Even the place, which looked torn apart when Bill had pulled me from under the table, was being quickly straightened out by the barkeeper and the housemen. Customers helped set up the chairs. The rest of the regular customers started talking, and then one pair started playing pool with a loud bang of the balls. Others followed. Everyone was acting as if nothing had happened, and nothing looked as if it had.

I spit out a clot of blood and went over and sat down by the

Canadian to find out how he was. He put an arm around me and I put an arm around him, and that had to be the answer.

It seemed suddenly like everybody in the house was Bill's friend and they all came over to shake his hand or feel how hard his arm was. The cook got up from the floor where he had been leaning against the wall and tried to be near Bill while Bill was accepting congratulations, and clearly Bill was pleased with everything. The redhead held on to his father, but his eyes still smoldered.

Otherwise, all was peace. I couldn't get over it. For at least two weeks we had been building up steam, and each of us was going to win a summer's wages by some sweep of a black cape and then we were going to clean out the town. Well, the black cape had swept and I reached inside my shirt to feel my ten-pound sugar sack, and all the money that was in it could have been put in a Bull Durham sack. We had cleaned out the town and I already knew that I'd always talk about it, but everything already was running normally again at the Oxford. Even the three tin-horn gamblers had moved back to the poker table and had started an innocent-looking game among themselves, hoping all over that some sheepherder with his summer check would saunter by and they could deal him a sixth card. All the tables were being played on but the billiard table, but it was the time of night that barbers and vice-presidents of banks spend with their women before going home to their wives.

It's lucky for towns that good fighters first have to be fighters and that there aren't many of those to start with. Otherwise, towns would be destroyed overnight, because in late summer every town is going to be cleaned out every night by some crew and usually is, and then the town straightens up the chairs and goes on taking the crew's money as before.

Bill rounded up his bunch, and herded us out like sheep. The barkeeper raised his head and said good-bye to us directly. He was selling chits to two married men who were going to get into the pinochle game.

Mr. McBride and I were holding each other by the arm,

and we felt better when we got outside. But I was hurt and everyone in the bunch knew it. They also knew I had the money. They helped me around the block and we stopped at a street corner under an arc light. I sat down on the curbing near the light and rested a few minutes before taking the sack out of my shirt. Everybody gathered close. They gathered so close Bill finally said, "Get back a bit. We can't get enough light to see." Then he and Mr. Smith went back to counting. I didn't try to help them count. I didn't think I could.

First, they gave each of us the money he had bet. Then Bill asked, "Any objection if we split our winnings even nine ways, no matter what each of the nine bet? We are one crew, aren't we?" Heads nodded, and he started to sit down again. Then he got up and made what was a speech for him. "And a pretty damn good crew. We always did what we had to." Besides, none of us could do the arithmetic to figure out exactly each one's share.

Bill sat down to finish counting our winnings, and we stood around and didn't know what to do but to admire ourselves. I suppose factually we were probably not much to brag about. We were fairly representative of early Forest Service crews as I came to know them—maybe not even that good, because the war had ended less than a year before and many of the best men had not yet returned to the woods, and the earth was still pretty much in the care of the old with corrugated skin and tiny steps and young punks looking for a fight and gassed Canadians and anonymous lookouts who had to be there but can't be remembered. Not one had ever seen the inside or the outside of a school of forestry. But, as Bill said, we were a pretty good crew and we did what we had to do and loved the woods without thinking we owned them, and each of us liked to do at least one thing especially well—liked to swing a jackhammer and feel the earth overpowered by dynamite, liked to fight, liked to heal the injuries of horses, liked to handle groceries and tools and tie knots. And nearly all of us liked to work. When you think about it, that's a lot to say about a bunch of men.

At the moment, in our hearts we felt indissoluble, although

in our heads we knew that after tonight we might never see one another again. We were summer workers. We belonged to no union, no lodge, and most of us had no families and no church. In late spring, we had landed jobs in a new outfit called the United States Forest Service which we vaguely knew Teddy Roosevelt had helped to get going and which somehow made us feel proud and tough and always looking for trouble of some sort, like fires, dynamite, and rattlesnakes on mountains too high to have any. Besides doing what we had to, we did a few other things, like playing practical jokes and distilling dried apricots and having some troubles among ourselves. And at the end we banded together to clean out the town—probably something also that had to be done for us to become a crew. For most of us, this momentary social unit the crew was the only association we had ever belonged to, although somehow it must have been for more time than a moment. Here I am over half a century later trying to tell you about it.

While the ranger and Mr. Smith finished counting, the moths fried on the arc light over us and the blood again slid inside my head.

Bill said to Mr. Smith, "You announce it." Mr. Smith stood up and announced, "The total is $64.80. Split nine ways, that's $7.20 apiece." Everybody said "Wow" and forgot all about $7.20 being several hundred dollars short of summer expectations.

Bill divided the money and Mr. Smith said, "Now for the ranch hands and the whores." Some wanted to reverse the order, and then, since we were a crew, they suddenly got solicitous about me, but in succession. "How you feeling, kid?" "You sure took a beating but you got the dough." "Good going, kid." And then Bill said, "We'll walk you back to your hotel."

"Hell, no," I said, "The night is but a pup."

Bill said, "You've had a big night. Now take it easy. But I want you to come to the corral before noon tomorrow and help me saddle up."

Then everybody said, again not together but one after

another, "We'll walk you back to your hotel."

So they walked me back, and when we got in front of my twenty-five-cent lodging for the night, we all put our arms around each other but none of us tried to sing because none of us could carry a tune. Instead, we stood in a circle with heads bowed like a college glee club just before beginning to hum. Then I suddenly felt weak and turned away and started up an uncarpeted stair and was too tired and disappointed in myself to say, "So long."

I rolled over against the plaster wall for comfort. In the center of my brain the pain from the side of my head met the pain from the front of my head. Never before had I taken two beatings in two days. I felt especially sensitive to pain, being young and used to winning. Though it was dark in the room, I squeezed my eyes extra tight hoping to keep out the sight of my lying on the Chinaman's floor with toothpicks in my hair. And I tried to squeeze out the sight of my head leaning over the table ready to be punched. My head shook in revulsion and tried to back away from what it did not see coming. I thought, it was the biggest fight I was ever in, and I swung only one punch. Thoughts came slowly, so it was some time before I followed up with the next thought, "But if a man had only one punch to give for his country, I sure picked a good target." When I quit pulling my head back from my thoughts, I could feel the muscles in my neck relax and I fell asleep.

It was late in the morning when I woke, and I felt just a little better and, while I washed from the pitcher, I was glad there was no mirror. As I awoke, I wanted to take one step from the bed and be with Bill at the corral, but when I jumped into my clothes I looked again at my watch and asked myself, "What's your rush?" Also I realized that some of the sickness might go from my stomach if I had "a little something for breakfast," as my mother would say. It was ten when I got to the Greek restaurant, and the girl from Darby was on shift.

She seated me at a table in a dark corner, started to the front counter to get me a menu and then came back. "I knew you were in for big trouble last night," she said. "You'd better come and let me wash you off." Then she led me into the ladies' room and locked the door and made me sit down on the cover of the toilet, which to my surprise looked the same as the men's toilet. From there I could lean my head over the basin, and she washed all my head, including my hair. "Don't argue," she said. "You must have rolled in the dirt."

"Sawdust," I said.

"Oh," she said. I was becoming embarrassed by getting the motherly treatment and also by the prospect of being seen coming out of a ladies' toilet with my hair dripping, but she wouldn't let loose of me. She opened her purse and took out a little tube of something—cold cream, probably—and dabbed some of whatever it was on the cut in my forehead. Then she took a comb from her purse and parted my dripping hair, using her apron to dry my face. When she leaned over I could see that her freckles enlarged as they went down her neck and that her breasts were all brown. "There you are," she said, and let loose of my neck and I tried not to be seen with her as I came out of the ladies' toilet, but she didn't seem to give a damn.

She acted as if it was all business until I finished breakfast. Then she said, looking down at me the way waitresses do while pretending they are looking for dirty dishes, "There's a friend of yours sitting in the alley. I think you had better go out to see him."

"Who?" I asked. "I don't know," she said. "But he's one of your crew." Knowing she didn't have to say any more, she picked up the dishes and I paid the check and then she led me through the kitchen and opened the door to the alley.

He was sitting on a cardboard box full of old newspapers. Although his head was bowed, without doubt it was the cook's because in a world of men with black hats he was always bare-headed with a tuft at the top. One of the old newspapers was on the ground between his feet and he was bent over as if he were reading it except that blood dropped on it from his unseen face. I walked over slowly toward him to be sure about the blood.

"What happened?" I asked. "I'm broke," he said, never

raising his head. "But are you hurt?" I asked. "I'm broke," he repeated.

"How come?" I asked. "I'm broke. They rolled me," he replied. "Who?" I asked. He looked up at me and when his head was lifted the blood ran down his lip into his mouth.

Finally he said, "She was as crooked as a tub of guts."

Having scanned that line before, I didn't wait to ask, "Was she just a little whore?" He replied, "I don't feel hurt. I feel broke. I need money to get to Butte." I repeated, "Was it a little whore who rolled you?" He replied, "She had a big guy with her. They beat hell out of me and took my money." I asked, "Did he have a hairy ass?" He replied, "I didn't see his ass." "Well," I told him, "it is hairy."

Then I said to myself, "don't be such a wise guy," and a great shame swept over me for asking him a show-off question that he couldn't possibly answer. By this time blood had spread into the corners of his mouth. Then I think it was my father who spoke out of the whirlwind of my mind, and said unto me, as if he had just written the Bible, "Be ye compassionate." My father reserved the right to speak to me on any occasion and on any subject, even if he knew nothing about it. It was his voice that went on to talk to me about card playing, and in summary he said I should not rejoice because someone with great gifts in handling cards turned out not to be even a good card player on account of something little (so he said) inside him. Although my father knew absolutely nothing about cards, what he said sounded like him, including his not knowing anything about cards or the cook.

"How much do you want?" I asked. "Would you lend me ten bucks? I'll pay it back."

As I remembered, it was about 170 miles to Butte and the coach fare then was three cents a mile.

I told him, "No, I won't lend you anything. But I'll give you enough to get to Butte. I'll give you $7.20. It's all yours and I don't want it back."

He lowered his head and reached out his hand, and the blood began dripping on the newspaper again.

I went into the restaurant and, since it was still a long time before lunch, Miss Brown Breasts was alone. I said to her, "It is the cook." "Yes?" she said. I said, "It is the cook." She said, "Yes?" I knew I must say something else. I said, "He is hurt. Would you wash him and give him something to eat?" She asked, "Has he any money?" And I said, "Yes," and she said, "He didn't have any money before and the boss threw him out," and I said, "He has money now," and she looked at me and said, "Bring him in."

So I went outside and brought the cook in and gave him to the girl from Darby who took him into the ladies' room and locked the door.

Then I started for the road to the corral where I knew Bill would be saddling up.

Bill's Dog was there and saw me when I was still a long way off. He got up and started toward me. I heard Bill speak to him from the corral, and he quit growling, but he kept coming. He walked around me as if I were a pole, sniffed me once and then went back and lay in the trail watching the horses. He lay flat on his long belly. His neck, too, was outstretched and he looped his front paws over his nose. About all you could see of him from the front were his big eyes and bulldog ears. Along the side of one eye was an open cut, and where it was still draining was a fly that he kept trying to blink off. The dog lay there watching over us as if we were sheep.

Bill said, "A girl brought him this morning."

"Did she have freckles?" I asked. "Lots," he said.

"She's nice," I volunteered. "She's a hasher down at the Greek's joint. Here's a note she sent you when she thought maybe she couldn't get the dog here in time. She wanted me to be sure you got it."

"Thanks," he said, and stuck the letter in his shirt pocket beside the Bull Durham sack. The dog knew we were talking about him, so he got up and came over and stood by us, ready to be obedient.

Bill was taking only five horses back with him, counting his own saddle horse, Big Moose, and all but one of them, a pack horse, were saddled. I went into the warehouse and got the blanket and saddle and I spent an extra amount of time smoothing the blanket on the horse's back. Finally I said, "She is real nice," and pointed at his shirt pocket.

Bill looked over the saddle and down at me. "She's just a kid," he said. "Why don't you take her out?"

He evidently thought I was wasting time fussing around with the blanket. He picked up the saddle which I had dropped at my feet and he put it on the horse himself.

"How many horses are you packing on the way back?" I asked. He said, "They're all going empty but the 'original.'" I knew then he was going to go fast.

"The original" was a big iron-gray that was faster and tougher than any of the mules. And meaner. Everybody said the reason they called him an original was that one of his testicles had been missed when he was castrated so he wasn't either a gelding or a stallion. You would have thought, though, that he had two or three complete sets. He started chasing mares the moment you took the saddle off him at night, and it didn't seem to make much difference if you hobbled him. He was the only horse I ever saw that could catch and screw a mare with two front feet tied together and only one testicle. After he finished with the mares, he started chasing the geldings. If you were the one to wrangle the horses in the morning, you had to start long before daybreak, because by then you would be lucky to find even one of your string in the state of Idaho.

I went slowly to the warehouse to haul out his packs. I went slowly because I wished I were going back with Bill. Here on the valley floor it was late summer and hot noon. Tonight, they would camp on the divide at Big Sand where it would be deep in autumn. There the needles of the tamaracks had already turned yellow. A delicacy of ice would fringe the lake in the morning. I would be willing to get up and wrangle the horses myself, provided Bill had let me picket the original to a two-ton log the night before. If so, perhaps I might hear again the most beautiful sound that comes through darkness—the sound of a bell mare. Perhaps, too, at daybreak I might see my four-gaited moose steaming beside a lilypad. It is certain that for an hour or two in life I would again be higher than the mountain goats and above nearly all men. And it is certain that, if I weren't dehydrated, I would piss on the state line and wonder where in the world I had flowed.

I set a pack on each side of the original. I don't care what anybody says, it is a great advantage to be a big man if you are a packer. I admit I have seen some fine packers who were middle-sized and some even who were small, but a big man picks up a pack and just pushes it away from him and it's about where he wants it on the saddle and he can work with everything in plain view in front of him. At seventeen I was probably about five foot nine, and had to hoist the pack up on my shoulders and work from underneath, sometimes not seeing the hitches I was tying and also sometimes not finishing my sentences.

"The cook . . . ," I said, and the pack slipped as I tried to hoist it up on the saddle, and besides I didn't know how to go on.

"He didn't look good this morning," I said, even though I hadn't got a good hold on the pack yet.

"What was the matter?" Bill asked. Bill didn't look too good himself. When he leaned his head back to push the pack up, I could see dried blood in his nose, and his hands were swollen and we packed slowly.

"They rolled him and beat hell out of him," I said. "Did they get all his dough?" Bill asked. "I had to give him money to get to Butte," I told him.

The dog figured we weren't talking about him anymore, so he went back to watching the horses.

"Seven dollars and twenty cents," I said. You could almost hear Bill from the other side of the horse multiplying 170 miles by three cents. "That's enough," he said.

I wanted bad to say one more thing about the cook, but the

dog was uncomfortable and got up and circled stiffly and then lay down again. He looked a lot older than when I had seen him last spring. Besides the open cut near his eyes, he had several fresh scars that were also close to his eyes. I thought to myself, "What can you expect if you fight coyotes for a living?" so I didn't say this other thing about the cook for fear I might end up in the same trouble as the dog.

Although Bill was putting a light load on the original, we started to tie it tight together with a diamond hitch, because clearly he was going to travel fast. Bill threw the canvas manty over the load and each of us smoothed out his side of it. Bill asked, tossing the cinch to me under the horse, "What'r you going to do next summer?" Until I heard my answer tremble, I did not know how long I had been waiting for the question. "Nothing yet," I answered.

"Let's tie a double diamond on this last load," he suggested. "Fine," I said. "How would you like to work for me next summer?" he asked.

I went looking for words like "privilege" and "honor" and ended with, "It's a deal."

"It's a deal," he replied. "I'll write you early in the spring."

"When I get here next spring," I said, hidden by my side of the horse, "I'll date that girl with all the freckles."

"She's nice," he said, "real nice."

"I know," I said.

Suddenly I realized I had been scared for a long time, because suddenly I wasn't scared any more. I had been scared ever since I had started getting in trouble with Bill, but didn't dare admit it to myself. I don't believe I was ever afraid he would take a punch at me, because I don't believe I ever thought he would. I was scared because I had to lose something I wanted to be like and yet wanted to keep when the trouble was over.

On our last load of the summer, we threw the double diamond, and Bill was ready to go. He didn't tie his string together—he had picked his best horses, and they would trail each other.

We stood beside Big Moose, his giant saddle horse. We

stood close together and never said a word. Then he turned
slightly, twisted his stirrup, and with his back to me started a
180-degree swing into the saddle. When he completed his
semicircle, he was looking down at me from the sky. From my
angle below I could see right up the barrel of his .45 and up
his nostrils rimmed with dry blood.

"I'll be seein' you," he said.

"Me, too," I answered, but didn't quite know what I meant.

I let down the bars of the corral, and the moment the outfit
was on the road each assumed his own character and
collectively all became Bill's string. Big Moose immediately hit
his five-mile-an-hour stride; dark brown and mooselike, with
head thrown back, he coasted on slipperlike feet. You
wouldn't realize he was covering five miles an hour until you
noticed that the other horses, except the original, would drop
behind when they walked and every now and then had to trot
to catch up. The original kicked a horse that got too close.
The dog trotted to one side, stopping now and then with
raised paw and in his mind clearly protecting the string from
all possible attack and any combination of coyotes.

Bill sat twisted in his saddle like the Egyptian bas-relief.

Collectively, Bill's outfit—Bill himself, his favorite saddle
horse, his favorite pack horse, and his dog—were about the
finest the early Forest Service had to offer.

For a while the road went mostly down the valley and only
slightly toward the mountains, and then it took a sudden turn

to the left and headed nearly straight for Blodgett Canyon. Bill studied his horses almost to the turn. Then he must have stood up in his stirrups, for suddenly he took off his hat and gave me a big wave, and I stood on the middle rail of the corral and gave him a big wave back. He must have been feeling great. Why not? Maybe for the first time in years the Ranger had got out of a card game while he was still ahead—by $7.20. Although I still was not well, I felt great, too.

I had the promise that I could work for him again. I was only seventeen, and I hoped more than ever that someday I would become a packer.

Then the string swung to the left and trotted in a line toward Blodgett Canyon, with a speck of a dog to the side faithfully keeping always the same distance from the horses. Gradually, the trotting dog and horses became generalized into creeping animals and the one to the side became a speck and those in a line became just a line. Slowly the line disintegrated into pieces and everything floated up and away in dust and all that settled out was one dot, like Morse code. The dot must have been Morse code for a broad back and a black hat. After a while, the sunlight itself became disembodied. There was just nothing at all to sunlight, and the mouth of Blodgett Canyon was just nothing but a gigantic hole in the sky.

"The Big Sky," as we say in Montana.

Although I had no way of knowing it at the time, I was never to cross the Bitterroot Mountains again. When early spring came, I was offered a job for the summer with the engineering department of the Forest Service on a mapping crew that was going to work in the Kootenai Forest. For a long time I wondered why by the spring of 1920 it seemed to me that having a different and more professional job in a different part of the woods was better than working again for Bill Bell, and I think the answer has something to do about my becoming eighteen. I was very conscious of becoming eighteen.

So I was never to see Bill Bell or any of the other men again. Or the girl my age from Darby. When the dot of Morse code disappeared into the sky, another Summer Crew of the United States Forest Service had come and gone forever.

Everything that was to happen had happened and everything that was to be seen had gone. It was now one of those moments when nothing remains but an opening in the sky and a story—and maybe something of a poem. Anyway, as you possibly remember, there are these lines in front of the story:

> And then he thinks he knows
> The hills where his life rose ...

These words are now part of the story.